A STORY OF PILEAUS

THE BLACK YONNIX
A BITTER END

Scott Colby

THE BLACK YONNIX: A BITTER END
A STORY OF PILEAUS
Copyright © 2020 Scott Colby & Jeremy D. Mohler. All rights reserved.

Published by Outland Entertainment LLC
3119 Gillham Road
Kansas City, MO 64109

Founder/Creative Director: Jeremy D. Mohler
Editor-in-Chief: Alana Joli Abbott
Senior Editor: Gwendolyn N. Nix

ISBN: 978-1-947659-77-3
Worldwide Rights
Created in the United States of America

Editor: Gwendolyn N. Nix
Cover Illustration: Chris Yarbrough
Cover Design: Jeremy D. Mohler
Interior Layout: Mikael Brodu

Printed and bound in the United States of America.

Visit outlandentertainment.com to see more, or follow us on our Facebook Page facebook.com/outlandentertainment/

— PROLOGUE —

Strong hands shoved Kensey Vardallian forward. He tripped over his own bare feet but managed to catch himself even with his wrists shackled behind his back. The unmistakable weight and shape of a blade pressed itself to his jugular through the burlap sack covering his head.

"This is the man you asked for, Your Highness," a crisp voice announced proudly. That tone belonged to a man used to making such proclamations. And royalty? That was interesting. The jailers hadn't told him where he was being taken or for what reason. At the time, he'd assumed they'd tired of beating him and asking the same questions over and over and were delivering him to the gallows—but then they'd roughly bathed him, clothed him in a cheap but clean tunic and pants, and thrown him on a boat.

"Take that silly thing off his head," a female voice ordered. That tone belonged to a busy ruler tired of wasting time on unnecessary etiquette.

"Yes, Your Highness."

The pressure against Vardallian's neck relaxed. He closed his eyes and winced against the sudden burst of light as the sack was yanked back over his face and away from his head. A rough patch chafed his chin on its way past. When he opened his eyes a few moments later, he found himself in a throne room—or what was left of one, at least. What had once been a grand, soaring space trimmed with gold leaf and gargantuan columns had been reduced to a ruin. The rubble had been pushed to the sides, leaving a path from the main entrance to a raised dais and a throne. The wall beyond the royal seat had been blasted out entirely, leaving a jagged scar that overlooked the capitol city of Deos below and the harbor beyond. Shards of shattered glass twinkled in the bright sunshine that streamed in through that gap and washed out the prisoner's view of the figure upon the throne. He suspected that was intentional.

"My name is Losa ruo Deos," the woman said. "I am the Empress of Pileaus, and this is my palace. And you are?"

He didn't know much about the Imperial government, but last he'd heard, ownership of the Imperial throne hadn't been settled following the last Emperor's demise. Was this his daughter? From what he could see, she certainly looked the part. Clad in black plate armor, her long form filled the throne as if she'd been born in and always occupied that very spot. Her black hair, streaked with white, was pulled up tight underneath a dark, slender crown. His vision hadn't quite cleared enough to make out her facial features, but he could feel her hard gaze dissecting him from afar.

A familiar sliver of metal brushed against his bare shoulder. "You will answer the Empress's queries promptly," the guard to his right demanded.

That sounded like wise advice. "Vardallian," he croaked through parched lips. "My name is Kensey Vardallian."

"Get this man water and something to eat," the empress commanded. Behind Kensey, the clack of boot heels on the polished marble floor confirmed acceptance of her order. The thought of a meal set his dry mouth struggling to water. The thin gruel he'd lived on in prison had left him weak and emaciated. Kensey knew for a fact that he was young and dumb, but he wasn't stupid enough to think he wasn't being manipulated.

"Do you know how many pretend Vardallians my father executed?" Losa asked. "A few dozen, I think. The emperor was not a man of idle hobbies, but your family's history was one of them."

Stories about Kensey's seafaring ancestors—and their huge stash of treasure—had spread far and wide, but he'd never expected to hear of people faking a Vardallian lineage or that a person as powerful as Emperor Pileaus would take an interest. His upbringing in the distant south, far from the family's ancestral home, had insulated him from the name's infamy. He wished he'd managed to hold onto even a small shred of evidence proving that all the myths were true.

"I'm told you claim to have served aboard the *Black Yonnix*, and that you accurately described both the vessel's special capabilities and its captain—and I began to wonder just how a southern peasant boy would have such knowledge of former Imperial property and personnel if his story were not at least partially true."

Kensey's brain knew it was best to remain quiet, but his mouth had never had much patience for one-sided conversations. "It's true," he said. "All of it."

Losa stood, unfurling herself from the throne like a sail from a mast. The empress was easily the tallest woman Kensey had ever encountered. In that dense black armor, framed by the afternoon sun, she descended the dais like an avenging angel sent to smite the unworthy—which, if her father's claims of godhood had any validity, may have been the case exactly. Her hard, stern face did little to dispel that impression.

"You sailed on a ship that sank eight of my own. Every syllable you utter had better be the absolute truth. You will tell me *everything*, and if it doesn't lead me to the recovery of both the *Black Yonnix—and* your family's treasure—you will wish Lagash had gutted you before he tossed you overboard.

"And you will start by telling me about Lucifus Vardallian's journal."

— CHAPTER ONE —

Written by the dread pirate Lucifus Vardallian, scourge of the Steps—and my great-great-great uncle twice removed on my father's side—that journal is the only remaining vestige of my family's former wealth. Legend has it that the only thing Lucifus hated more than his own children was the idea of bequeathing his riches unto them. Grandfather, for what it's worth, suspected our ancestor's mind had been warped by alcohol or disease. Whatever his reasons, Lucifus secreted his treasure hoard away in an unknown location and left his cryptic journal behind so that, as the very first line reads, "any greedy rutter what has eyes on me gold and jewels don't find it without a lifetime o' work!" Supposedly it was bound in the skin of a Fae lord, but it always smelled like regular old leather to me. Family tradition was that only one child of each generation would learn how to read the journal. Grandfather taught me after my parents died. The journal seemed like nothing more than the ramblings of a crazy old man, but reading it was a special thing only

Grandfather and I could do, and so I enjoyed traipsing off into the jungle around our little home to do just that.

Which was exactly what I had been doing the day the journal was taken from me.

Emerging from the jungle, I instantly recognized the tall brown mare with the crimson saddlebags as the local tax collector's mount. Normally, Rocher made his yearly rounds alone, protected only by the dagger in his belt and the threat of his lord's sovereignty. He was about a month early by my reckoning, and the pair of black stallions tethered beside the mare meant he'd brought back up this time. Grandfather and the other poor villagers of Brennik's Reach typically sent him back to his master with little to show for himself. Evidently the Nefazo had decided to do something about that.

I ducked back behind the green foliage to consider the situation. Grandfather had always sent me away whenever one of the local children arrived to spread word that the tax collector was on his way. I know now that it was so he could deal with the slimy Nefazo without distraction or the possibility of threat to my welfare. Back then, three years younger and about three decades dumber than I am now, I thought it just another interesting situation an adult was keeping from me. The smart thing to do would've been to heed the little voice in the back of my mind that sounded suspiciously like Grandfather and retreat into the thick jungle from which I'd just emerged. Instead, I set my sights on the nearest window. Its shutters were closed as usual to keep the bugs out, despite the heat of the day. As the sole window on that side of the building, no one would be able to see me approaching through its slats. I kept my lean frame low to the ground as I skulked around the small herb garden between the jungle and my home. My soft sandals moved silently through the thick, flaccid grass. Halfway to my destination, I noticed the familiar weight tapping my thigh inside the satchel at my side. Yes, Your Highness, the journal was in my satchel. No, I didn't really consider stashing it in the jungle or the herb garden. That was not a day of sound decision making.

When I finally reached the house, my heart was pounding so hard that I feared Count L'Vaillee's men would hear it. I pressed my back to the wall and shuffled along to the window, impressed with how thoroughly sneaky I was being. There was no way I was going to get caught. In all eighteen of my years, I'd never done anything so exhilarating.

I settled in beneath the window to listen. The sounds of the argument taking place within the building echoed out into the otherwise serene landscape, setting my nerves even closer to the edge. The tax collector's thick, city-slicked voice demanded that my grandfather produce more coin; Grandfather's soft, creaky alto insisted that he'd already given up all he had, that there wasn't any more to be found. That was a bold-faced lie. My grandfather was the only doctor within two days of Brennik's Reach, and as such, he made an above-average living for a relocated Yuinite. I augmented our income by selling the rare flora I collected during my jaunts through the jungle. Between the two of us, we made enough to live in relative comfort while also stashing away what we hoped would one day become a big enough savings to send me to school in Mana'Olai. Grandfather had taught me everything he knew about being a healer, but he and I both knew I was going to need formal training if I would ever have any hope of leaving Brennik's Reach behind and making a better life for myself.

"We know there's more, old man," Rocher drawled impatiently. "You've been holding out on us for years. Where is it?"

"You know as well as I do there's no money to be made in this backwater," Grandfather snapped. He'd never shied away from the fact that he'd only fled the Empire because his parents had insisted he join them.

"Oh really? The Vendergott boys told us how much you charged for setting their mother's arm."

"Mrs. Vendergott died five years ago. You tried that same line last time you were here. I've given you all we have. Now, scoot!"

My chest swelled with pride. Grandfather was my hero, the one person in my life I could look up to. Our neighbors who'd known him here in the Empire loved telling me stories about his rugged upbringing. In his youth he'd been a huge, hulking brute of a man, sturdy as a fire oak and strong as a thul bear. He'd been a ferocious fighter, but he was also extremely intelligent and possessed an innate understanding of anatomy that served him well as a medic. At age fifty, he'd been the only refugee older than forty years of age to survive the harsh trek down from the north. Even my much younger parents hadn't made it. Now at sixty-eight years young, my grandfather may have been a bent, arthritic shell of his former self, but he wasn't about to let the count's goons intimidate him.

"Thuroth, just give us the money," the tax collector pressed. "It will serve you better in Count L'Vaillee's coffers than on Captain Lagash's ship."

Pirates! I thought happily to myself. *Here!* News traveled slowly to Brennik's Reach, but even we had heard the tales of the merciless Captain Lagash and his *Black Yonnix*, the former flagship of the Imperial navy and supposedly the fastest ship in the south. Piracy in the area was rare, but Lagash and his crew had carved out quite a little niche for themselves. Even the shuen, the supposed guardians of the sea, were at a loss as to how to stop him. My ancestors had been some of the north's most nefarious privateers, the scourges of Braillee's Steps and Ururo Bay. But that was before the rise of Pileaus, before his empire and his blasphemy—uhh, sorry, Your Highness—drove my family and their people south.

My grandfather chuckled softly to himself, and I couldn't help but smile. "So the *Black Yonnix* and her fine crew have finally gotten sick of plundering the Mana'Olai and the shuen and have turned their attention to the Nefazo, eh? Old Count L'Vaillee must be shaking in his diamond studded britches!"

Antoine L'Vaillee was the local Nefazo lord, a man infamous throughout his holdings as a vicious, money-grubbing cheat who hid behind the vicious mercenaries that did all his dirty work. L'Vaillee's father, however, was then and probably still is revered in Brennik's Reach. He'd welcomed our band of Yuinite refugees to Nefazo with a smile and a helping hand, providing most of the raw materials used to construct the new settlement. The elder L'Vaillee had seen our arrival as an opportunity to develop a previously uninhabited area while also welcoming a whole new group of grateful taxpayers to his domain. Antoine, however, raised our tax rates every year and took advantage of our remote location to sell us goods and services at prices often twice what they would cost elsewhere.

"Bah!" Rocher boomed. "Count L'Vaillee has nothing to fear from that dog. He's merely looking out for the wealth of his people, who may encounter great difficulty defending themselves against such criminals. Lagash would have no problem raiding a Yuinite stink hole like Brennik's Reach, but he would never be able to breach our fortress at Mont Lichaud. Your gold and valuables will be safe in the count's coffers."

I leaned tightly to the wall, awaiting Grandfather's next verbal riposte with bated breath. Surely it would send Rocher and his goons packing, empty-handed as always. I couldn't wait.

My heart leapt into my throat when a heavy hand took firm hold of my left shoulder. I tried to bolt, but the vice-like grip of those gloved fingers jerked me back off my feet and slammed me backwards down to the grass.

"Stupid," the mercenary said as he bent down and grabbed me by my hair. It was a lot longer back then, almost halfway down my back. I've kept it short and tight like this ever since.

I'll never forget the satisfied sneer on the mercenary's face as he yanked me up to my feet. Up to that point in my life, I'd mostly only interacted with the pacifist Yuinites of Brennik's Reach. Coming face-to-face with someone who simply enjoyed hurting people was a shock to my system. That man could've torn my hair right out of my scalp and then laughed about it. I had no choice but to follow him around the corner and through the front door. His blocky, scar-pocked face sometimes still haunts my nightmares. A short chain of tiny emeralds dangled from the lobe of his left ear, marking him as an inexperienced trader at best and thus fairly low on the Nefazo social ladder, which was probably the reason for his position as one of L'Vaillee's hired blades.

I didn't dare struggle as he dragged me around the corner. "In the house, whelp," he growled as he threw me forward. I stumbled through the open door, tripped on the threshold, and tumbled onto the floor. My satchel cushioned the impact to my torso, but the uneven wooden planks scraped my palms and the side of my face unlucky enough to break my fall. See this scar on my jaw? If I ever managed to forget that day's unforgivable stupidity, my next look at this would bring those memories right back.

As I stood, I noticed our usually tidy little home had been reduced to a tangle of overturned furniture and equipment. Provisions spilled out of our ransacked cabinets. The table at which we took all our meals had been shattered into dozens of pieces and scattered across the room. The greedy bastards had even flipped the beds and torn the straw out of our mattresses. Count L'Vaillee's men came to collect his tribute once a year, and though they generally took any piece of gold their slimy fingers came across, I'd never seen them leave that sort of destruction in their wake. I tried not to look too hard at the loose floorboard under which we'd hidden our savings.

Grandfather sat in the center of the house, naked, in the wooden tub we used for bathing. The big old ox barely fit in the thing. His knees were pulled up tight to his broad chest and every motion sent a dollop of soapy water splattering to the floor. I'm sure the tax collectors thought they were putting him in an awkward situation by barging in on him in a compromising position, but he'd obviously turned things in his favor by making it clear he didn't care. He scrubbed his armpit with a brush, feigning disinterest in my arrival. His dark eyes, though, told an entirely different story—one I'd only encountered a few times prior while watching him reassure terminal patients that everything was going to be ok.

"Found this one listening by the window, Lord Rocher" the merc said. "Thought you'd like to meet him."

Forgive my vulgarity, but if Your Highness has ever encountered a pregnant sow wrapped in and sweating through a set of red satin sheets, well—then Your Highness already has an excellent picture of the rutting Lord rutting Rocher. He loomed in the corner, strategically beyond soaping distance, his beady little eyes twinkling with malice. Jewels and charms of all shapes and colors speckled his short, dirty blond hair, marking him as a successful merchant and thus a man of high status in Nefazo society. He was flanked by a second soldier almost identical to the one that had caught me. Perhaps the two were identical twins; perhaps the hardships of mercenary life had simply twisted them into similar shapes.

"What's the boy's name, Thuroth?"

Grandfather sighed. "His name is Kensey, after his father."

"There's a definite family resemblance. Boy's got your square jaw and brutish shoulders." The pig paused for dramatic effect. I could practically smell the grease dripping from his vile grin. "It'd be a shame if something happened to him."

Grandfather used his brush to flick a soapy gob across the room and mark the access to our secret stash. "Lift that floorboard."

My heart sank as the mercenary beside Rocher lumbered toward our savings. If I hadn't been such an idiot, Grandfather never would have been forced to give up that secret. They could've threatened to hurt him, or to burn down the house, or to turn our fields fallow—he would've stonewalled them through it all. I was the only leverage they could've successfully used against him.

The Nefazo dropped to his knees and drew a short knife from his boot. He used it to slowly pry the board up out of the floor, wary of the traps that existed only in his imagination. He reached one hand down into the hole, fished around, and retrieved the little brown bag of gold that contained our entire life savings. Rocher snatched the bag away and peered inside. "That's it?" the pig asked. "Check again, Remy."

The merc shrugged and did as commanded. As he rooted around underneath our house, I wished we'd filled that hole with scorpions or a hoosa snake or at least a few brend nettles— anything to reflect some of the pain I felt back upon our tormentors. Grandfather used to laugh whenever I'd suggested we boobytrap that hole. I wondered then if he regretted it.

Rocher pocketed our savings and turned his attention back to Grandfather. "How old is the boy?"

"Eighteen."

The pig sauntered a few steps closer to the tub. The mercenary that'd caught me matched his master's movement.

"Old enough to have started a family of his own," Rocher said. "You know the rules, Thuroth: unwed adult males are to report to the nearest garrison for conscription. We've a pirate problem on our hands, after all."

"I do know the rules, and the rules say that exceptions are made for those responsible for the welfare of their elders. In case you haven't noticed, I'm rutting old. I couldn't get by without my grandson."

That sent a flash of pride radiating through my chest. Grandfather didn't distribute praise lightly. That warm feeling didn't last, however, as the three Nefazo closed in on the old man like the pincers of some vicious trap.

"So, to clarify," Rocher hissed, "your grandson is not contributing to the glory of his honorable benefactor, Count L'Vaillee, because he has to stay here and take care of your decrepit old ass?"

Grandfather's face twisted in anger and his knuckles went white around the handle of his brush. He burst upward out of the bath, only to be pushed right back down into it by the nearest merc. Grandfather's bare feet and legs shot up toward the ceiling as Remy shoved his torso and head underneath the water. Suds splashed everywhere as his hands groped wildly for purchase on the sides of the tub.

"Don't let go until he stops kicking," Rocher instructed calmly, like he was telling a servant how best to mop the floor or scrub a counter.

For a moment, I couldn't move. It was like I simply couldn't process the horrific scene before me as part of the real world. Ours was a peaceful, cooperative village populated with good Yuinites doing their best to live in the image of the Oprin. No one fought. No one tried to hurt each other. That someone could walk into my home and attempt to murder my grandfather—and do it so casually—was a thing I'd never imagined possible.

Then the anger and adrenaline kicked in. I launched myself toward Remy, thinking to knock him away from Grandfather. I might've succeeded if I hadn't screamed. The other mercenary—the one who'd caught me outside—lashed out with his left arm. It was like getting hit with a tree. The impact broke my nose and rattled my skull. The landing knocked the wind right out of me. As Grandfather's thrashing grew weaker, all I could do was lie on the floor as blood streamed down my face, gasping for breath and praying to the Oprin that the room would stop spinning.

The thrashing stopped. I closed my eyes and started to cry, sure that I was next.

"Check his bag," Rocher ordered. My satchel was ripped from my torso.

Not the journal, I thought desperately. *Leave me something!*

"Just some jungle herbs and an old book," the merc said. He didn't know what he was looking at. There was a chance.

"I had absolutely no idea you Yuinite worms knew how to read!" Rocher exclaimed. He opened the front of his robe and tucked Lucifus's journal into an inside pocket. "The count's son has developed quite an interest in obscure texts. I'm sure he will enjoy this."

The pig knelt down beside me and grabbed my cheeks with his fat fingers. "I could squash you like an insect if I wanted to, boy," he growled. "But I think instead I will leave you alive, so you can continue to work for the glory of the good Count L'Vaillee. Don't forget: marriage and taxes, or service in the count's military! We'll be back in a few months to find out how it went!"

He released me and they departed. I rolled onto my stomach and watched the count's men meander triumphantly through the front door of the house, taking with them my grandfather's life and the dingy old pages that concealed my one chance to reclaim my family's lost glory. Shame and anger burned through my veins, turning my vision red. Rocher's last words of warning echoed through my skull.

Come back in a few months, pig, I thought. *I'll be ready for you.*

— CHAPTER TWO —

Thuroth Vardallian was put to rest in the old Yuinite way. The night after his murder, a procession of those he held dear carried the corpse, draped in a simple black shroud, to the top of a small hill outside the village. His body was propped in a sitting position against the tallest tree atop that hill, facing east so that he might see the sunrise trickle through the jungle canopy. The priest read a passage from the Maunin and then quickly departed. One by one the mourners did the same, pausing by Thuroth to whisper a thing they'd never told him in life so that he might carry the truth of the world with him to meet the Oprin in the afterlife.

As his only family, I was the last to depart. I'd heard that people in other parts of the world bury or burn their dead, and that the shuen consign theirs to the sea. Leaving Grandfather in a place of life and beauty seemed somehow better to me—even though I understood intellectually that the animals, insects, and some of the plants in the surrounding jungle, would soon be sampling him for lunch. Guess that's more constructive than just tossing the dead into a hole.

Alone, I leaned down beside Grandfather and took a deep breath. The lingering aroma of the minty soap the priests had used barely masked the sickly odor of looming decay. "I love you, Grandfather, and the pig's as good as dead."

I burned the bathtub.

My neighbors—bless them—did what they could. I spent the first few days aimlessly wandering the jungle. There was always a hot meal waiting for me when I returned home at night. Someone repaired the torn strap on my satchel. Fresh sheets wrapped my bed, topped with a pile of new clothing. Blessings and charms made of local wood, vines, and flowers spread across the exterior of my home like a fungus. Riar Onculus even left a bottle of his infamous homemade taperfly hooch for me one day. On some level, yes, the efforts of Brennik's Reach and the obvious love they showed for me and my grandfather made me feel better, but that part of me was buried so deep below layers of rage and shame that it didn't seem to matter.

I obsessed over my promise to be ready for the tax collectors when next they returned. Wild plans burned through my mind. I could hide on the roof and ambush Rocher and his goons as they tried to enter my home. I could brew a pot of tea, spike it with dreadwort, and serve it to them with a smile on my face. Maybe I could hide in the jungle, trusting them to once again check our secret stash hole, where an angry gatten snake would be waiting for them, venom dripping from its inch-long fangs. I envisioned Rocher on fire, impaled on a stake, tied to a pair of habback ready to sprint in opposite directions—and through it all, the pig begged for his life. In every fantasy, he'd eventually offer up the return of my family's journal.

That all probably makes me sound like a bad Yuinite. To be honest, Your Highness, my faith died with my grandfather.

My plans were all dumb and I knew it. Still, I had no intention of signing up to fight the Count's battles for him. The other option—starting a family—well...there was a girl. Mahlin. Mahlly for short. She and I had been best friends for as long as I could remember. Turns out she was responsible for repairing my satchel. Most of Brennik's Reach, Grandfather included, always assumed she and I would end up together. We hadn't simply because I wasn't quite ready to give up on my dream of traveling to Mana'Olai to study medicine.

Mahlly's father, Tibius, was waiting for me when I returned home one night, four or five days after the funeral. He'd brought dinner: his daughter's famous mushroom stew. The savory aroma that filled the house almost wiped the thought of revenge from my mind right then and there.

"You'd have my blessing," Tibius explained.

"I know." Our eyes met, but my gaze quickly dropped to my feet.

He stroked his long beard and smiled warmly. The gap in his mouth reminded me that Grandfather and I hadn't been able to save his tooth. "It's not something to be embarrassed about."

I didn't have the heart to tell him that I couldn't look him in the eye because he seemed impossibly weak. Tibius was a hard worker, a talented farmer, and a man respected throughout Brennik's Reach. He also hadn't raised a finger against the Nefazo tax collectors, and I knew he never would.

"I can't. They'll use her against me." My tongue struggled with every word. I suspected Mahlly had put him up to this. She'd met me halfway down the hill after Grandfather's funeral and basically carried me the rest of the way back. The girl cared for me, and I for her. Under different circumstances, settling down to start a family with my best friend would've been a dream come true.

Tibius shook his head. "Fighting back will only make things worse. Keep your head down, marry my girl, and you can lead a nice long life as part of our family. That's the smart thing to do. Mahlin loves you, you know."

"I know."

He waited, obviously expecting more. I didn't give it to him. The knuckles of my balled-up fists turned white at my sides as my body refused to speak the truth in my mind. I couldn't marry Mahlly because I was going to die standing up to the Nefazo.

Outside, soft footsteps scampered away from the house. Tibius and I both turned toward the sound. It was like all the air was sucked out of the little room. I should've known she'd be listening by the window. The irony wasn't lost on me.

Tibius hooked his thumbs in his suspenders and looked at me thoughtfully. He almost seemed proud of me, in an odd way. The Nefazo were not popular in Brennik's Reach but none of the locals had the guts to stand up to them. "Kensey," Tibius proclaimed, "you are a Yuin-damned fool. If you're set on this path, do us all a favor and go see Ognar. Maybe the old Omman can teach you a thing or two."

I thought that was a brilliant idea.

After a night of the best rest I'd had since Grandfather's passing, I headed for Ognar's at first light. The old Omman lived at the edge of a swamp on the opposite side of Brennik's Reach. I stuck to the jungle and skirted the village proper until I bisected the narrow game trail leading to Ognar's home. Strips of white fabric turned brown with age dangled from low hanging branches every fifty paces or so, clearly marking the way. Swarms of gnats and flies greeted me as I neared the swamp. I stopped here and there to collect flowers and herbs to supplement my medical supplies.

Past a particularly large strip of whiter, cleaner cloth, the jungle gave way to a clearing of dark, hard-packed mud. The old woman looked at me from her knees as she tended a small fire beside her simple hut. Ognar's husband—like my parents—hadn't survived the journey south. She never told me how they'd met, but I'd heard enough local gossip to know that the pairing of an orthodox Yuinite and an Omman wasn't a common occurrence.

Then again, Ognar was certainly not common. I've never met a more fearsome woman. Yes, Your Highness, I can see where an entire nation of her kind would be a thorn in the Empire's side.

I pulled the bottle of Riar Onculus's homemade taperfly hooch from my freshly repaired satchel as I approached. A toothless smile warmed Ognar's wide, wrinkled face.

"Few who come to Ognar bearing gifts do so without expecting something in return," she said. Her crackling voice scraped down my spine like a blade across a whetstone.

"You heard what happened to my grandfather." There was no reason to make it a question rather than a statement. Ognar valued her privacy, but she always kept her finger on the pulse of Brennik's Reach.

The bones and shells woven into her wild gray mane clattered as she nodded her head. "Thuroth was a good man—too good to approve of what you're about to ask. Speak it anyway."

She had a point, but I wasn't about to concede it. "Teach me to fight so that I may avenge my grandfather."

Ognar poked at the fire with a blackened stick as if searching the coals for some sort of truth. "When the blood lung took my Reginalt, I did not seek to behead the disease. I did not raise my blade against the land where the sickness lives or toward the journey that brought us there. I moved on. I lived as best I could. You would be wise to do the same."

"I can't." There was no other way to explain it. My need for vengeance burned that deep.

She shrugged. "Hasn't even been a week."

"Why wait? I've only got a few turns of the moons before the tax men come back around."

"Hmm. Most young men of the Reach come to me to learn the ways of war. I send them all back to their families. Some with broken bones for you and Thuroth to set." She raised herself to her full height and took a step forward. As usual, she was completely naked. Wiry muscles rippled underneath her leathery skin. I kept my eyes on hers. "Knock me down before I can do the same to you, and I will teach you. Leave the bottle somewhere safe. You don't get to keep that."

I took my time shirking my satchel and placing it on the ground beside the alcohol so I could consider my options. I'd seen her drop men twice her size without blinking. Ognar occasionally acted as the town's enforcer, scaring off would-be bandits or cowing angry drunks. I was taller, heavier, and younger, but in a straight up fight I didn't stand a chance.

I needed an angle—perhaps a distraction, or a weapon, or some sort of surprise. There was little to work with in the muddy clearing.

So I darted into Ognar's hut.

The Omman cursed in her native tongue and hurried to follow. I beat her inside. There wasn't much to work with.

None of the small tools and foodstuffs carefully arranged on the room's only shelf would pack any sort of punch and trying to hit her with her own sleeping pallet seemed silly. I almost didn't notice the stone ax lying on the ground beside the straw mattress. Clods of dark mud camouflaged its crooked wooden handle. The roughly carved rock set as its blade looked deadly, but I thought I could maybe trip Ognar with the hilt.

I tried to lift the ax with one hand. That rock turned out to be a lot heavier than it looked.

As I reached down with my free hand, I caught what I later learned was a right cross to the jaw. At the moment it felt like I'd been hit in the face by the flank of a stampeding horse. I didn't fall so much as I crumpled. No one's hit me that hard since, not even Your Highness's interrogators.

"You have the jaw of a boulder," Ognar grumbled. "Get up."

I made it to one knee before a wave of vertigo threatened to knock me right back down, so I decided to stay there. The inside of my skull rang like a bell. I spit out a bloody tooth but nothing else felt damaged.

"That was almost clever," Ognar said. I took some small pride in the way she shook the pain out of her right hand. "Moreso than the other dumb bulls who've come seeking my knowledge. Tell me...why did you fail?"

"I'm not a fast runner. When I got in here, I wasn't strong enough to lift that ax quickly."

She nodded. "We will fix these failings. Follow me."

My scrambled equilibrium fought me all the way up as I stood. The first few steps were crooked and sudden like those of a newborn foal. My balance gradually returned as I followed Ognar back outside and around the hut. She waited for me beside a tower of flat, heavy chunks of granite stacked one on top of the other. I knew the woman was strong, but I couldn't fathom how she'd managed to build a tower three thick stones taller than she herself stood.

"I will teach you what my people know of battle so that you might triumph over your enemies," she said ominously, "on two conditions."

My heart leapt. I'm still not sure exactly what she saw in my mad dash into her hut, but apparently she'd seen enough. "Name your terms."

"You will complete the tasks I set before you to the best of your skills and you shall do so without complaint."

"Fine. And your second condition?"

"You will serve Brennik's Reach as healer like Thuroth before you."

"I can do that."

"Good." She set her gnarled hand against the stone tower. "You are weak, Vardallian. I could teach you the most powerful blow and your opponent would feel it as a gentle spring breeze. The ondelheim here will correct that. This makes Omman youth strong and keeps our elders fit."

She pointed to another flat stone set in the mud twenty paces away. "Today you will rebuild the ondelheim upon that base. Tomorrow you shall move it back to this spot. You shall bring the ondelheim back and forth until you are useful. Only then will I teach you."

I didn't think I could move even one of those stones, let alone an entire tower. Still, I couldn't let that stop me. The tax collectors needed to die. "I'll do my best."

"Good," Ognar said with a crooked smile. "Bring me that bottle and then get to work."

— CHAPTER THREE —

Thus my path was set. I visited Ognar every morning. I moved as much of her damn ondelheim as I could before my new mentor grew tired of watching me struggle. That first day I managed to knock two stones from the tower and drag them through the mud to the other base. Within a week I was suddenly carrying three. Say what you will about the simplicity of Ognar's methods, but there's no denying they worked.

Then she'd assign me other tasks. I took the fish and small animals she caught in the swamp into town to barter for other necessities. I patched the roof of her hut twice. I swept the mud surrounding her home. I ascended a nearby tree and sat there for an hour so that I might contemplate my insignificant life against the scale of the jungle. I hunted the seaside tide pools for a blue starfish Ognar claimed tasted like the milk of the gods themselves. She made me stand still as she shoved a red toad down the back of my pants and bade me to remain that way until the annoyed little creature found its out through the bottom of my pants leg.

Sometimes I thought she was messing with me to amuse herself. Other times I thought she was trying to break me so I'd give up on my dreams of vengeance and run off to Mahlly. I suspect the truth was a combination. Once I could move five stones we began to spar. She taught me how to throw a punch, how to set my feet, and how to anticipate an opponent's movement. I was terrible at all of it. I tripped, I fell, and I got hit—a lot.

"Good thing you are Thuroth's grandson," she said after knocking me into the mud for what must've been the dozenth time that day. "Perhaps being tough and persistent as a mule will be enough. For now, if you find yourself in a fight, run. If you can't run, fight dirty. There's no honor to be found at the bottom of an early grave."

When we were done, I conducted business as the village healer. I mended wounds, set broken bones, and delivered tonics and poultices to the ill. In between I scoured the jungle for the herbs, roots, flowers, and other ingredients I needed to keep my supplies stocked. I made a solid living that way, but all that work left me with little time or energy for socializing. Most nights I'd collapse in bed as soon as I returned home. Sometimes I'd find a hot dinner waiting for me, although the gracious chef was always long gone.

For a while, things settled into a comfortable routine. I enjoyed my work with Ognar despite my utter lack of skill. Caring for the denizens of Brennik's Reach turned out to be immensely rewarding. Perhaps that could've been a good life, but my need for vengeance was a constant itch at the base of my skull that wouldn't go away no matter how hard I threw myself into my daily tasks. Best of all, I had complete confidence that Ognar's lessons would prepare me to face down my nemesis, the Lord Rocher, and extract the righteous vengeance that was my due. Because Fate hates me, however, all that changed during one of my assignments.

While foraging in the jungle east of Brennik's Reach one day I heard the unmistakable sound of someone calling for help. It came from my right, about thirty or forty yards beyond a section of thick, overgrown valuta vines. The area through which I traveled was a particularly dangerous one. Straying from the game trails was not recommended. Others in Brennik's Reach may have simply continued on their way, condemning the wayward traveler to his fate and dismissing him as a fool for wandering off the beaten path. But if Grandfather had taught me anything, it was that one never disregards a call for help.

I parted the stand of purple valutas and took a few cautious steps into the dense jungle. The air seemed thicker and more humid, as if the wall of flora I'd just penetrated was a barrier between two distinct climates. Trees of all shapes and sizes reached up toward the sky, some barely the width of my arm, some thicker than my home. A mélange of green plant life coated the ground, mirroring a similar growth that stretched from tree to tree dozens of yards above my head. For the most part it was dark, but here and there a sharp sunbeam sliced through the canopy to bathe a small area in an eerie glow. Everything was leaves, a spattering of deep crimsons and soft violets and vivid blues against a backdrop several million different shades of green. Such landscapes were magical to me, and during my treks through the jungle I often wondered if this was what the Dreaming Lands looked like. Looking back, it amazes me I ever had such wistful thoughts regarding anything having to do with those horrible Fae.

The cries for help became more desperate by the moment. I kept my wits about me and progressed slowly, paying close attention to every stride I took. There were millions of things in that jungle that could kill, and most of them chose tactics that didn't involve barreling through the brush while snarling and baring a set of sharp teeth. I wouldn't be any good to whomever was in trouble if I couldn't make it to him in one piece.

Deeper into the jungle I went, always conscious of the direction from which I'd come. The voice was very close, but I still saw no sign of its source. I stopped and scanned the immediate vicinity, worried that I'd missed something. I couldn't find the person I was supposed to rescue, but I did notice several trees that were missing large chunks of bark. I'd walked right into the middle of the territory of a thul bear, one of the stealthiest and most dangerous creatures in that jungle. If it decided to take offense to my trespassing, well—let's just say it's a good thing Ognar's training had taught me how to run faster.

Through a stand of wispy trees to my left I glimpsed the ruddy brown head of a rather large fox trapped up to his neck in a pit of dark brown quickmoss. A thin line of white fur slashed diagonally across its distressed face. I regretted the fact that I didn't have time to save the poor creature, but I had to find whomever was in trouble before the bear found me. I continued on my way.

"And just where in the Dying Lands do you think you're going?"

It took a moment, but I recognized that angry voice as the same one that had just been crying for help. I stopped and glanced back in the direction of the fox in the quickmoss. He looked a bit annoyed.

"Don't just stare at me," he barked, "get me out of this infernal muck!"

I took a few cautious steps toward it, worried that my last round of failed sparring had resulted in a head injury. "Did you just say something?" I asked.

"I've been saying a lot of things, like 'Help!' and 'I think it's starting to eat the fur on my leg!' That *is* the reason you came moseying over here, isn't it?"

The fox really was talking to me! And then it dawned on me: he wasn't a fox.

"You're a marii!"

His eyes were the color of polished copper. They shimmered mysteriously as he rolled them. "And you...you're hairless, you're too tall, you smell like the wrong end of a habback, and you have horrible taste in clothing...you're a lij!"

Missing his sarcasm, I nodded dumbly to indicate that his conclusion was correct. "Great," the marii muttered. "I spend an hour and a half wallowing in this slime, screaming my lungs out, and do I get a valiant hero scouring the countryside for wrongs to right? Do I get a master woodsman? Do I get anyone who's even *remotely* useful? Of course I don't! The only person that comes to rescue me is the village idiot!"

This was not at all what I'd expected, and I told the marii so. "Those in need of assistance are usually grateful when help arrives. I could just leave you there."

"Ah, but you won't. You won't! I can tell by the look in your beady little eyes and the way your overcooked sense of honor weighs upon your shoulders that you're far too compassionate to do such a thing."

"Sure about that?" I growled. "This honor is awfully heavy—so heavy, perhaps, that I've little strength remaining for valiant rescues."

"Yes," he said so matter-of-factly it was as if he'd just read it from a book. A clump of muck dangling from the end of his long snout plummeted into the bog as if adding to his statement. "Now if you don't mind, I have moss in places where I never thought moss would want to go, and I would very much enjoy removing said moss from said locations."

"Fine," I said. "Hold on."

"I don't think I'm going anywhere." His perky ears twitched in annoyance.

I quickly scanned the area for something I could use to pull him out. The downed tree limb to my left would do. I took it in both hands and bent it against my knee to test its strength (and, to an extent, my own). Satisfied that it would hold, I returned to the edge of the quickmoss pit and extended it toward the marii. He dug his claws into the wood and clung tightly as I yanked him toward solid ground. His short, slender torso jerked up out of the bog, but the quickmoss wasn't willing to give up its meal so easily. The brown mire clung tightly to his fur and yanked him back down.

"Rut, can't you pull harder?" he asked. "I weigh less than your thigh!"

"Your scrawny ass isn't the problem," I replied, gasping in between breaths, "it's the hundred pounds of quickmoss that doesn't want to let you go."

His copper eyes flashed. "Pull!"

I shrugged and put all my weight into it. He yelped in pain as the moss threatened to tear away his skin in response. I eased up, deciding that a slow, steady approach would work better, despite his complaints. He thanked me with a steady stream of insults and profanities with which I will not soil Your Highness's ears.

When he let loose a sudden burst of profanities the likes of which I'd never heard before, I knew something was definitely wrong. "What is it?"

"Umm—don't worry about it!" he said a bit too quickly. "Keep pulling, and don't turn around!"

Of course, I glanced over my shoulder—and standing not thirty feet behind me was the thul bear I'd been worried about earlier. More a cross between a giant sloth and a predatory cat than an actual bear, the hulking beast was about twice my size and three times my weight. Patches of short, spiky hair sprouted in black tufts from its oily brown skin, a poor impersonation of the thick coats enjoyed by its cousins that lived farther north. A sharply curved tusk hooked upward from either side of its mouth. Feared by even the most accomplished outdoorsmen, the thul bear was a creature no one wanted to encounter.

And its coal black eyes were locked squarely upon my back.

"The pulling should not have stopped," the marii growled from the quickmoss.

The bear unleashed a howl that would've woken the dead. Then it sprang forward, a roiling mass of pumping muscles and gnashing teeth. Against the marii's protests, I dropped the limb and spun to face the charging beast. What choice did I have?

Ognar's voice echoed in my mind. *Run, you rutting fool!*

My only chance would be to avoid its initial assault and make for the game trail. It wouldn't follow me out of its territory, and I was pretty sure it wasn't dumb enough to dive into the quickmoss after the marii.

In theory, my plan was a good one. In execution—I was a rutting fool. I'd hoped that by waiting as long as I dared before making my move it wouldn't have an opportunity to adjust before I was well on my way toward the game trail. Fear overcame my judgment and I didn't wait long enough. As I dove to my right to avoid the bear's charge, it adjusted its course and rammed its huge head into my ribs. The momentum of the crash sent me flying until the small of my back collided unceremoniously with a rather sturdy tree. I hit my head hard on the way down, and my spinning perception split the single thul bear into two. The blurry twin beasts turned to finish the job, snarling and pawing the forest floor in anger. Waves of pain echoed through my throbbing skull as it loped toward me to finish the job. The beast was coming for me, and there was nothing I could do to stop it.

I closed my eyes, unwilling to watch. Visions of Grandfather shaking his head in disapproval danced across the inside of my eyelids—only to be replaced by the pig himself, the Lord Rocher, laughing villainously at the poor peasant who'd failed so miserably to exact revenge upon him.

The bear's sudden roar snapped me back to reality. A clump of quickmoss with a ruddy brown head clung to its back. A sharp flash of metal slashed across its jugular, releasing a geyser of blood. Its legs went limp beneath it and the whole of its mass crashed to the jungle floor, skidding to a halt just a few feet from my face.

The marii cleaned his dagger on the dead beast's fur and struck a rather heroic pose on its back.

"All hail Tehenessey Blue!" he shouted. "Slayer of savage beasts and savior of silly peasants!"

— PARLEY —

Y our Highness," Vardallian said timidly, "am I going into too much detail? I don't want to waste—"

The guard to his right slapped him in the side with the back of his gauntleted hand. Vardallian buckled in on himself, gasping for breath. "You do not get to ask the Empress questions!"

"And you do not get to speak for me," Losa said coolly from her perch upon the throne. "Leave us, Adrius."

"Yes, Your Highness." The man bowed, turned on his heel, and stomped away, leaving the prisoner alone with the most powerful woman in the known world. Vardallian knew better than to see that as a sign of trust or of opportunity. It merely meant that Losa didn't view him as a threat. He didn't doubt she could tear his heart out with one hand if she so chose.

"Continue," she ordered. "I find your tale...illuminating. Is Tehennessey Blue still but a humble minstrel in search of unique tales to tell and new audiences to entertain?"

Every fiber in Vardallian's body went rigid. The left side of Losa's tight lipped mouth curved upward in satisfaction.

"If you truly know Tehenessy Blue, Your Highness, then you know better than that."

— CHAPTER FOUR —

The marii was somewhat less than forthcoming when I inquired about his reason for straying so far from the game trail. He wasn't interested in talking about much of anything, though occasionally he would fling an insult in my direction. I'd always heard that Blue's kind were supposed to be happy and playful and full of rambunctious energy. This one was downright nasty.

"We're going to get this shit off me," he explained, "and then you're taking me into Brennik's Reach. What's your name?"

"Kensey Vardallian."

"Good. Let's go."

Etiquette dictated that I tolerate his orneriness. We had, after all, saved each other's lives. I didn't have to like him, but I did feel obligated to help him clean all the pesky quickmoss that still clung to his fur and clothing. The outlines of a vest, trousers, and boots were barely visible under all that muck. If he wandered into Brennik's Reach looking the way he did, a few of the more superstitious locals might've mistaken him for a demon come to steal their children and subsequently stoned him to death. Though they hadn't lived in the north for two decades, some of my neighbors still clung to far too many of the old ways.

I escorted Tehenessey Blue back to my home, mirroring his stony silence and ignoring his intermittent insults. There were a thousand and one questions I wanted to ask him about being a marii. As far as I knew, I was the only person in Brennik's Reach to ever have made the acquaintance of someone of his race. On top of that, he had the look of a person who'd spent a fair amount of time traveling, and I longed to learn of the places he'd seen and the people he'd met. Despite my curiosity, his sour disposition stayed my tongue. I assumed his mood was merely a consequence of spending almost two hours in a quickmoss pit, and I hoped a thorough cleaning and a warm meal would open him up to my questioning.

Unfortunately, his attitude got even worse the moment he set eyes upon my home. He stopped at the edge of the jungle, set his hands on his hips, and examined the area with a look of such disgust that I thought he was about to throw up. He sniffed the air suspiciously and made a weird smacking sound with his lips.

"What's wrong?" I asked.

He pointed to the short, squat, wooden building in the center of the clearing. "Is that the place?"

"That's it."

"It's so—" He paused for a moment, his muzzle twisting with disdain as he searched his memory for the proper adjective. "—rustic."

"Well, what did you expect?" I asked defensively. "Brennik's Reach isn't exactly Deos."

"No...it most definitely isn't," he said. "Sometimes I forget that people actually live like this."

Now I was really confused. "I thought you marii lived in trees, in the woods."

He glared at me as if I'd just struck him. "Do not equate yours truly with those filthy barbarians."

We continued onward toward the house. His step was light and cautious, as if he were picking his way through a field of dung, which was probably exactly what he imagined he was doing. I almost mentioned that I didn't own any animals, but I decided it would be more fun to make his life just as difficult as he was making mine.

Inside, he adopted a pose similar to the one he'd struck when we'd first emerged from the jungle. "You *live* in here?" he asked as his strange coppery eyes dissected the interior of my home.

"All my life," I replied. "It's everything Grandfather and I needed. Beds to sleep on, a table to sit at, a hearth for cooking, shelves for storage—"

"I've seen jail cells with more warmth and personality," he interjected. "Does Yuinism include strict rules against the ownership of carpets or throw pillows?"

"No."

"Get some, then." His eyes widened when he noticed the charms left by my neighbors after Grandfather's passing. "Hello! What manner of quaint local bullshit are you?"

"That quickmoss is hardening by the second," I growled.

"So cram the chit-chat and draw me a bath!" he shouted.

I'd traded a bushel of pain-relieving herbs to one of the neighbors for an old wash basin to replace the one I'd burned. Blue didn't like that either. "Looks like something a farmer would use to feed his cows," he said. I ignored his comments, grabbed a bucket, and went outside to get water from the well pump. Experience had taught me that I would have to make about sixteen trips back and forth to fill the basin completely, but I hoped half that much would suffice for my small guest.

While I worked, the marii stood beside the basin like some royal inspecting the work of the help. No offense, Your Highness. I could feel his sanctimonious copper eyes judging every step I took. Why wasn't I moving faster? Why was the pump so far from the house? Why not build a larger fire in the hearth so each bucket would warm faster? What sort of uncivilized backwater made a man wait so long for a bath? Although he didn't voice any of those questions, they bounced around the inside of my skull as if he'd screamed them in my ear over and over again.

"The water's yellow," he said as I poured the fourth bucket.

"Only a little," I said, "and only because I haven't used the pump yet today. It'll be gone in another trip or two."

He glared at me as if I'd just asked him to bathe in another quickmoss bog. "Empty it and start over."

I glared, doing my best to channel Grandfather. "No."

Blue's black nostrils flared in annoyance, then he turned his head toward my neighbor's charms again. "Remind me what those protect you from. Some vengeful peasant god? A local elemental with a taste for the flesh of obstinate hosts? It'd be a shame if they somehow end up in the fire while you're on your way to the well."

I somehow resisted the urge to clock him with the bucket. "They're supposed to inflict terrible luck upon rude visitors," I lied, though his ensuing sigh told me he didn't buy it. "I'm not emptying this basin."

"Fine," he said. His hand disappeared into the mass of quickmoss covering his torso and rooted around for something under his vest. I set my feet in a poor impersonation of what Ognar had taught me and gripped the bucket's handle tighter, preparing to strike first if he drew a weapon.

The object he produced was far more curious. "Is that a rock?" I asked.

Blue shook his head. "Rub the quickmoss off of it. You'll see."

I held the thing out at arm's length and scraped the quickmoss away with my thumbnail. I expected something angry and full of teeth to burst forth from it at any moment. What emerged instead was a hard, smooth surface with a deep green shine.

"A gemstone?" I asked, shocked.

"Not quite," he replied matter-of-factly. "That is an anxei ri, a sort of pearl the local shuen harvest on their taishu. It's reasonably popular among Nefazo looking for something exotic to add to their silly jewelry collections. They're not rare by any means. What you're holding won't make you rich, but it'll feed you for a week or two. I have two more. Draw me a proper bath and escort me into Brennik's Reach and they're all yours."

I cleaned the thing up a little more. The little green egg certainly had an organic feel to it. Food for a month or more was nothing to scoff at. I pocketed the anxei ri and emptied the basin.

When the bath was finally to his liking, he puffed out his chest and declared, "You will wait outside while I disrobe."

The idea of a giant fox asking for privacy brought a smile to my face. "You're covered in fur and quickmoss," I said.

"Nonetheless, I will have my dignity!"

I passed the time seated on the grass beside the door, daydreaming about the weapons I could buy with my new anxei ri. Sustenance would've been smarter, sure, but what about a dagger I could hide in my vest and plunge into Rocher's heart when he got close? Or perhaps a bow with which I could take him down from afar? Eventually I settled on a cutlass, a trusty weapon apropos of my ancestry. Maybe, I thought, I would have enough to get one with a fancy blade guard, like the pirates aboard the famous *Black Yonnix* all carried.

Yes, Your Highness, of course I was suspicious. Three shuen pearls seemed like a hefty payment in return for a bath and a trip into town. Either my guest was more grateful for my help with the quickmoss than he was letting on, or the marii was up to something. I worried about the consequences, but the reward was far too great to turn him down.

"Oh Kensey!" Blue's musical voice cut through my thoughts. "My clothing has been thoroughly scrubbed of that vile vegetation! Please deposit it by the hearth so that it may dry!"

"Yes, sir," I said as I stood and entered my home. He'd draped his wet clothing over the side of the basin. "Is everything to sir's liking?" I said drily as I collected it.

"It'll do," Blue replied. The sight of his little head barely peeking out through the soapy bubbles is still one of the stranger things I've seen. He'd managed to scrub most of the moss off his face, revealing a streak of white fur running between his eyes and nose between his usual reddish brown. "You may now return to your whimsical visions of your impending wealth. Perhaps there's a special woman who'd enjoy a small expenditure on her behalf?"

There was, but I wasn't about to admit that. "I'm buying a sword," I growled.

The marii sighed. "Young men are so predictable."

Blue appeared in the doorway almost an hour later. The quickmoss was gone, replaced by brown slacks, a sharply cut green vest with shiny silver clasps, and freshly brushed fur. The small dagger he'd felled the thul bear with was tucked into his leather belt. He looked more like a banker than a whimsical woodland creature.

"I will be taking a nap," he said haughtily. "I will awake at the rise of Diun, and you will escort me to Brennik's Reach." Before I could protest, he handed me my hairbrush. Thick tufts of his hair clogged the wire bristles. "No need to wake me," he continued. "My internal clock is impeccable."

"Grandfather made this brush," I said before I could catch myself, "and now it's ruined."

Blue shrugged. "Ask him for another."

"He's dead."

"Oh." The marii scratched his nose. "I owe you a fourth anxei ri. Tax collectors?"

My blood turned cold. "How did you know that?"

"I didn't, not for sure. I met three of them on the road a while back. Horrible people, but their campfire was warm. They... gloated, about killing some old Yuinite from a famous pirate family and making his grandson an orphan. That's you, right?"

Hearing the worst day of my life summarized so succinctly was jarring. I wouldn't have been able to speak, even if I'd known what to say.

Blue read my silence as affirmation. "The chords of the World Song are always in tune."

"Did they have the journal?" I blurted out.

His copper eyes twinkled. "There was a book, yes. What's so important about it?"

I hesitated. Did Blue really need to know about the journal's connection to Lucifus's treasure? Would it be just one more thing he could use to rile me up? I decided I'd had enough of this line of questioning. "It's just a book." I could tell by the tilt of his head that he knew I was lying. "Not worth dwelling on, then." He pointed at Grandfather's brush. "I might need that again after my nap. I'll want to look my best when we head into town." He winked, spun on his heel, and disappeared back into my home.

I stared at my ruined brush as he went back into the house, anger bubbling up in my chest. Ognar had tried to teach me how to break someone's nose, shatter an opponent's ankle, and gut a man with a slightly sharpened stick. I wanted to practice all three. Instead, I tossed the brush into the jungle and descended upon the weeds in the herb garden.

"This is for Grandfather," I snarled under my breath as I plucked a tiny yellow sprig from underneath the basil, pretending it was a tuft of Blue's freshly coiffed fur. "This is for my neighbors' charms. This is for the thul bear that should've eaten you." I forget the rest, but I know I lost track of the time and didn't come to until that garden was pristine. Weed holocaust complete, my regrets got the better of me and I fished around in the jungle until I found Grandfather's brush.

My new acquaintance hadn't lied about his ability to sense time. He appeared in the doorway again just as the sun set and left great silver Diun alone above the blue-black horizon. "A truly marvelous Diuntyne," he mused as he straightened his vest.

He was right. The clear sky was a deep blue-black, speckled with the few stars that shone bright enough to reveal themselves at that early hour. The huge moon loomed over it all, attempting to save the day and simultaneously fight off the night. A soft breeze spun pleasantly warm air bearing the sweet smells of the jungle around my head. A whole host of birds and animals that lay dormant during the day and the night were suddenly abuzz with activity, their calls mixing together into a peaceful, soothing melody. Sparkling silver caretta flowers bloomed in the canopy around my home, coerced to open by the change in light. They'd close again when Diun set, extinguishing the sort of intermediate starry sky they created in the trees. Diuntyne has always been my favorite part of the day.

"Best that we not delay," Blue said as he sauntered to my side. "Lead the way into town, please."

I did just that. The sooner I could pawn off the offensive little creature on some other poor fool, the better. Back then I was still a good enough Yuinite that I couldn't entertain the wish that I'd left him to rot in that quickmoss. These days...well, I still like the fellow well enough, but I can't help but dream of a simpler life where I'd never met him.

"You know," Blue ventured as we embarked upon the jungle path to Brennik's Reach, "your home is very well kept and too... decorated...for a young bachelor such as yourself. There's a girl, isn't there?"

That line of inquiry was the last thing I had patience for. I decided to try changing the subject. "Remind me again what you're doing in Brennik's Reach?"

"As I mentioned when we met, I am but a humble minstrel in search of unique tales to tell and new audiences to entertain. Your evasion of my previous inquiry suggests there may be a bit of trouble in paradise, eh?"

I ducked under a low-hanging bough draped with gennel moss glittering blue in Diun's light. "What makes you think you'll learn any worthwhile stories in a place this remote?"

"Your village was settled by a group of displaced pilgrims fleeing their motherland for religious persecution. Your forebears spent years traversing the continent's untamed interior before finally settling here, thanks to the patronage of a benevolent noble. There are epic tales to be found in Brennik's Reach, my friend." He paused. "Perhaps, at least, a single tragic yarn of unrequited love?"

In the distance, a giant toad I can't recall the name of unleashed a thunderous *gigga-dumm*. Perhaps the wise decision would've been to let the local wildlife fill in the silence, but the little marii had finally wriggled his way under my skin. "Fine. I'm the scion of a family of famous pirates. The local tax collector—who happens to be a rutting pig—murdered my grandfather and stole the journal that supposedly leads to my ancestor's long-lost treasure. I'm to marry or enlist before his return, but instead I've sworn vengeance upon his fat rutting head. An Omman who traveled south with my people is teaching me how to fight. The girl I probably should marry is not happy about any of this and wishes I'd come to my senses but refuses to abandon me completely because she knows I still can't quite manage on my own. How's that?"

"Hmm," Blue said critically. "I suppose it's a start. Tell me, does the Omman lie with beasts? An Imperial I met in Ouillaine claimed they do that, mostly on holidays."

I walked faster. Yes, Your Highness, I suppose I do find that exchange funny *now*.

The trail wound up a small rise and then back down its opposite side. The dim light and the dense foliage hid the village from view, but a familiar shift in the air told me we were close. The salty smell of the ocean lingered just underneath the rich earthy air of the jungle.

I'd always felt like Brennik's Reach came upon travelers just as much as travelers came upon it. One moment, we were trudging along a narrow trail surrounded by thick trees, draping vines, and Yuin knows how many beasts hiding in the near dark—and then suddenly it all disappeared and there was a little town, ringed in a simple fence and glowing warmly in the light of outdoor cookfires. It smelled lived in, not like the jungle but like a place where lij came together to live and trade and entertain themselves. There couldn't have been more than two, maybe three dozen buildings, all of them squat and wide and built for function over form. My neighbors were neither architects nor engineers, and their mastery of the local materials had never progressed in a particularly aesthetic direction. Their thatched roofs kept them dry and their wood and mud walls kept the bugs and the wind out, though, and for that they were grateful.

"Here be stories," Blue said dramatically, his eyes beady glittering. "It's ugly and it stinks."

I decided I'd had enough. "Here we are, then. Brennik's Reach. Ocean's on the far side if you want to wash off the smell. I'm heading back home."

"Kensey! You can't abandon me quite yet. Lead me to whatever passes for a town square, please."

"It's in the middle, under the big tree. You can't miss it."

His eyes narrowed. "Lead me to whatever passes for a town square, *please*, or I shall track down your beloved and inform the young maiden that you despise her cooking and think her additions to your home inelegant and distasteful! Perhaps I will even romance her myself!"

I rolled my eyes. Yuin, I hoped we wouldn't run into Mahlly.

"Fine. Follow me, *sir*."

"Just Blue will do."

Although we could've easily hopped the fence, certain neighbors would've judged such an entrance harshly—doubly so given the stranger at my side. I led my charge a quarter turn around the village to the main guardhouse instead. Unluckily for us, one of Brennik's Reach's most judgmental experts on the ways of the world was on duty that evening.

"Halt and state your business," Vont Gannek said humorlessly when we were twenty paces from his position inside the tiny lean-to. A thin vest of cheap Nefazo chainmail clung tightly to his torso, showing off his muscular chest just as it did his bulging gut. His thick mane that started at the very top of his head tumbled halfway down his back in a cascade of tight gold ringlets. A few lines of verse from the Maunin were tattooed on the right side of his face in flowery script:

> *Strength of arms,*
> *Clarity of mind,*
> *Purity of faith.*

The holy book itself sat open upon a small stool at his side, beside a rusty broadsword propped up just so. To the uninitiated, Vont Gannek must've appeared as a perfect specimen of the Yuinite faith. He claimed to all who'd listen that he'd never cursed, never blasphemed, and never allowed a single drop of liquor to touch his lips—but I'll never forget the horrible things he screamed the evening Grandfather had to extract a whiskey leech from the roof of his mouth.

Village scuttlebutt—which was known to be accurate, as far as such things go—claimed Gannek had been given a job on the watch primarily to keep him away and to keep him quiet. His father had once served some minor function in Your Highness's Imperial military before joining the group of unhappy Yuinites headed south in search of a safe place to practice their faith. In a tale told throughout the Reach, the elder Gannek had fallen somewhere in the Shoro, bravely defending the meager caravan from a pack of giant wolves. Young Vont had a lot to live up to and was failing every second of it.

To make matters worse, he'd always hated my family. Angry that the journey had taken my parents from me, Grandfather had denounced his faith entirely upon arriving in Brennik's Reach. Most of the village understood and didn't hold it against him, at least in public. Some—notably Vont Gannek—weren't so accommodating.

Normally he would've let me pass without more than a dirty look and maybe a muttered comment or gob of spit headed for the dirt, but that night I had brought company of an oddly short and furry variety. I wasn't sure how much the night watchman knew about the rest of the world, but I suspected it wasn't much. If Gannek decided that Tehenessey Blue was a demon I'd summoned to lay waste to Brennik's Reach, I was in big, big trouble.

I stopped at the big man's command, but Blue did not. "Good evening, noble sentinel!" he exclaimed cheerily, much to my horror. "Would you be so kind as to grant two travelers access to your fine city?"

Gannek's eyes narrowed and he stroked his knobby chin with a thumb and a finger that were both as wide around as sausages. His gaze flicked quickly from Tehenessey Blue to me, then back to my companion. "What business does a marii have in Brennik's Reach?"

"I am but a humble minstrel in search of unique tales to tell and new audiences to entertain," he said, predictably. "Master Vardallian here has politely agreed to be my guide for the evening."

Gannek grunted. "A minstrel? Nothing humble about that vocation. A soulless purveyor of blasphemies and vulgarities, more likely."

Tehenessey Blue cocked his head slightly to the side and smiled, revealing an impressive mouthful of sharp white teeth. "When the occasion dictates it, yes. I've laced the air in many a dirty pub with strings of obscenities the likes of which would make even the most repugnant demon blush like a virtuous young maiden—but I've also filled cathedrals and seminaries with the melodies and verses of the righteous. Like any good performer, I merely conform to the will of my audience."

Gannek raised one bushy blond eyebrow. "Prove it."

Tehenessey Blue bowed deeply. "My pleasure."

He executed a perfect backwards cartwheel, giving himself a little more room in which to operate. With a flourish he produced a tiny black flute from within the folds of his vest and twirled it in his fingers as his wet black nose suspiciously sniffed the cool night breeze. Finally satisfied with the air, he licked his teeth and pressed the end of the flute to his lips.

The soft notes Blue produced as his fingers twitched across the instrument were slow and solemn, haunting in a way I'd never heard before and have heard only seldom since. He played a sad song of sacrifice and persecution, a song of cold nights and lonesome days and cloudy skies that refused to clear, a song that began with desperation and finished with a piercing ray of hope. I'd never heard the piece before, and yet I felt like I'd known it all my life.

Vont Gannek's eyes had glazed over. He swayed slowly back and forth to the beat. Tehenessey Blue's melody had him under its power, and not a muscle in his body dared to fight that spell. The song ended on a long lonesome note, and as that last beat faded, it seemed to take something good and warm along with it. Gannek blinked twice and shuffled his feet to steady himself. There was a soft twinkle to his eyes I'd never seen in him before. A single tear trickled slowly down the right side of his chiseled face.

"The Hymn of the Oprin," he murmured, his rough voice barely more than a whisper. "I've never heard it performed so beautifully."

Tehenessey Blue smiled smugly and twirled the little flute between his fingers. "I thank you for your praise, kind sir. Now, may my companion and I proceed?"

The sides of Gannek's mouth curled upward in a rarely seen smile. "Of course. Allow me to open the gate."

That gate, as always, was already open, and Gannek's face flushed red when he realized his mistake. Blue's music, as I'm sure Your Highness knows, has that effect on people.

The marii politely ignored the watchman's gaffe and bowed deeply at the waist. "I thank you again, noble sentinel. May you be blessed with an uneventful evening."

Blue headed for the entrance. It took me a moment to recover before I realized I needed to follow. Gannek also found himself, grabbing my shoulder roughly as I attempted to hurry past. "If your friend does anything unseemly, you're the one I'm going to hold responsible," he growled. I swallowed against my dry throat and nodded weakly. He gave my shoulder a sharp squeeze to emphasize his point, then he let go. I sprinted after Tehenessey Blue.

"Before I get down to the business at hand, I'd like you to show me the sights," the marii said when I'd caught up.

I scratched my head as I caught my breath. "There really aren't any."

He cocked his head sideways again, which was quickly becoming a familiar gesture. "No sights? Every place has something worth seeing! For instance—what are those over there?" he asked, pointing over my shoulder.

I turned. A pair of round buildings reached up toward the stars, their peaks tipped sharply. They stood a few heads higher than the surrounding homes and were built of local stone rather than the rough lumber used in the rest of town. "Those are just Durgan's silos. It's where he ferments the oil he refines from the felta mushrooms that grow in the jungle. The Nefazo use it in perfumes and colognes, but they give him a horrible price for it."

Tehenessey Blue rubbed the tip of his muzzle. "Felta oil. Well, if that's it for sights, that's it for sights! To the town square, if you'd please!"

"Right this way, *my lord*," I said angrily.

"I believe you're finally getting a hold of my kind of banter, Vardallian," he said happily.

The little flute reappeared in his hands as we approached the outer ring of homes. A jaunty tune of sunshine, cool breezes, and young love ensued. Blue bounced and twirled from one side of the dirt street to the other, the way a fisherman dances a fly across the surface of a pond to attract a fish. Several of the settlement's residents poked their heads out or looked up from their labor to see what all the noise was about. Some decided to follow, like sailors trailing after a nobleman's beautiful daughter. My face flushed with embarrassment; there'd be no avoiding association with the strange marii after half the town had seen the two of us parading through. When I noticed Mahlly looking on curiously from within the trailing throng I almost bolted for the jungle.

The town square of Brennik's Reach was nothing more than a circular patch of dirt a few shades redder than that which that lined the streets. Upon establishment of the town, the old count had gifted his newest citizens with a charming wooden gazebo within which they could relax or conduct municipal business. The new count had sent his men to tear it down and install a cheap statue of himself in its place. Locals who didn't want to disparage their lord in public described the pinched look on its face as one of deep thought and introspection. I always thought he appeared rather constipated.

Tehenessey Blue ceased his playing and vaulted up onto slightly raised dais supporting Count L'Vaillee. I stopped a few paces short and the crowd filled in around me. "Friends!" Blue shouted with a flourish of his hand. "I see that my song has piqued your curiosity—hopefully more so than my appearance! Correct me if I'm mistaken, but it's not everyday someone as cute and furry as myself wanders into your fair city unannounced!" Several of the children giggled at this, and he favored them with a quick smile before continuing. "What whim of fate led a marii to the remote seaside village of Brennik's Reach?"

Mahlly had wound her way through the crowd to find a place at my side. We traded a glance, and then I crossed my arms and rolled my eyes in anticipation of the marii's usual line.

"The music!" Blue shouted. He played a quick scale on the little flute. "It's everywhere, you know: the breeze, the ocean, the stars, even the dirt at your feet. Most people can't hear it, but it's there, nonetheless, interweaving itself inseparably with the very fabric of existence. Despite its importance to the universe, the music is often restless. It is not content to sit silently in the background! It yearns to be heard! It seeks out those with the gift to hear it, and it guides our journeys across the world, urging us to spread the music far and wide. Dear friends, that is why I'm here tonight! The music wants to be heard, and it needs you to do the listening!"

With one hand on the statue's hip, he deftly swung himself around to the other side of the dais. "All the World Song asks for is one night—just one night—of your precious time. In return for your time and attention, it will grant you your freedom. Freedom from the everyday grind of life! Freedom from the chains of your wants, your needs, and your desires!" He tapped the statue's crotch with his flute. "Even freedom from the good Count."

At this there was a cheer. No matter what else he may have been—or may be—no one could deny Tehenessey Blue's skill as a showman. I certainly found my guard dropping. Even Mahlly, usually reserved and stoic, cheered along.

Blue released his grip on the statue and stepped to the front of the dais. He twirled the little flute in his fingers again, raised it to his lips as if to play, then stopped. "One more thing, folks: the life of a wandering minstrel is a hard one, and although donations are not required, they are genuinely appreciated. May Yuin bless you all."

He quickly swung back into the tune he'd been playing on the way to the town square, squashing the laughter that was about to spring from my lips. The imagery returned, washing away my suspicions, and suddenly, I was completely content with life. People all around me were dancing, and I was soon swept away by the festivities.

The ensuing hours were a blur. Tagred dragged a few kegs out from the basement of his tavern and tapped them right there in the town square. Small fires were lit around the perimeter, bathing the area in sharp, flickering light. The music and the dancing and the drinking and the laughing all blended into a thick mélange of excitement, a subliminal force that ensnared the entire settlement and refused to let go. I quickly lost track of the number of people who clapped me on the shoulder or toasted me in thanks for bringing Blue to Brennik's Reach.

Mahlly and I collided as if fired at each other from opposing cannons. "What the rut?" she asked, her eyes darting toward Blue just as his own locked onto her.

"He paid me," I squeaked as she took my hand in hers and wrapped her arm across my shoulders. I gripped her hip as if it were the only thing keeping me from blowing away in a storm.

She raised an eyebrow, just as she had when we were both five years old and I'd told her I was going to be a dragon when I grew up. "You're sure it's worth it?"

"No," I replied as we whirled into motion. "I'm only making four anxei ri."

Her eyebrow crept even higher. "Not bad. The music's pretty good, too."

We danced for what felt like forever, spiraling around the square in a mass of humanity propelled by Blue's song. The night became a blur—especially after Tagred foisted a pair of frothy steins upon us—but there are bits and pieces of it I still cling to. The electricity zipping between our clenched hands. The fire in Mahlly's dark brown eyes as her long braid whipped out behind her. The weight of her hips against mine as the passage of time spent blissfully together closed the distance between us.

Whenever I looked in Blue's direction, he appeared to already have been watching us. I wondered at the time—and still do—if the raucous part of his performance had mostly been for our benefit. Mahlly and I had both desperately needed it. I think he knew, and I think he wanted to give me one last joyous night before dragging me fully into his schemes.

Eventually Blue's music began to slow. The marii took a seat on the edge of the dais beside the pile of gold and trinkets offered in payment and examined his haul as he continued to play. A mellow hint of relaxation crept into his tune, slowly melting away the atmosphere of excitement he'd wrapped us all in. A few people fell asleep right away, right there in the middle of the town square. Others sat for a while, absorbing as much of Tehenessey Blue's music as they could before sleep claimed them. Mahlly went limp against my chest but I held her up and continued rocking us both slowly to Blue's tune. I was one of the last still conscious, sustained by my curiosity, but the power of his song eventually overwhelmed me.

And the people of Brennik's Reach slept beneath the stars, oblivious to the danger that lurked in the waters just beyond the town's edge.

— CHAPTER FIVE —

The gentle scrape of claws on the back of my neck roused me from my musically-induced slumber.

"Come on now, up with you," Blue hissed in my ear. "We've much to do."

I rolled onto my side, grunted, and scratched the clump of dirt and saliva crusted to the side of my mouth. My body felt heavy, as if my muscles had somehow turned to stone. Someone snored behind me—Mahlly, I realized. Blue's furry hand clamped down over my mouth just as my eyes fluttered open.

"Here's the deal," he whispered as he lowered his canine face close to mine. "Follow me quietly and your beloved stays safe, we get your family's journal back, and maybe you get a taste of that sweet revenge you seek so desperately. Do something stupid—like raise the alarm—and my friends will do what they have to. Got it?"

I could tell from the steel in his eyes that he was deadly serious. Seeing no other option, I nodded slowly. Although I sincerely doubted he'd follow through on his promises, I had no choice but to play along. At the very least I had to get him away from Mahlly.

"Let's go," he hissed as he helped me to my feet. "I'll explain when we're clear."

All around us, Brennik's Reach slept. Blue deftly led the way between sleepers, guiding us around the square and toward the seaward side of town. The small fires built during the celebration had safely burned down to coals. I was surprised to find that Blue had left his little pile of tribute behind at the foot of L'Vaillee's statue. Diun hung low on the horizon but hadn't quite set yet. Something flickered down on the beach—a signal fire, I realized, summoning someone out at sea. It seemed I'd been right to worry about Tehenessey Blue's intentions.

We veered to the right, toward Durgan's silos. The felta oil inside was the only thing in town worth stealing. Like the majority of the merchants under L'Vaillee's rule, Durgan was forced to sell his goods to the count at whatever price was forced upon him, and then L'Vaillee would turn around and resell them for a huge profit. I had heard rumor that the shuen willingly paid the Nefazo a pretty penny for felta oil, though no one knew exactly why. It made perfect sense for a discerning bandit to seize Durgan's stock—especially given Blue's sudden disinterest in learning more about the town when I'd point out the silos.

Guilt settled heavily on my shoulders. This was all my fault. I'd helped Tehenessey Blue gain entrance to Brennik's Reach, pointed him at the most valuable target in town, and danced merrily as he suckered in all my neighbors and played them to sleep. I'd suspected he was up to no good but I'd gone along with him out of sheer boredom. I'd found excitement, for sure, but not of the kind upon which we all look back fondly. If his promises to take me away proved empty and he left me with the locals, my life was as good as over.

We rounded the corner and started down the street toward the entrance of Durgan's property. Ahead, a trio of figures exited Durgan's wide open gates, each laboring to carry a barrel of felta oil on his shoulder. Two others remained on guard, one on each side of the entrance. One was built like a tree trunk, short and thick, with broad shoulders and arms twice the size of my legs. The other was long and lean with darker skin and even darker eyes. Both wore a vest and long pants, though I couldn't tell exactly what color, and each carried a cutlass on his hip and a small torch in his hand. They reminded me a bit of Rocher's mercenaries: hard men who'd survived difficult lives and weren't above getting their hands dirty if it meant they'd see another day.

We reached the pair just as the harsh bong of the town bell battered the otherwise silent night. The two guards stood a little straighter, and the shadows darting in and out of the silo quickened their pace. A chorus of shouts and screams rose from the town square as the villagers woke. They'd all be rushing toward the armory that housed the only weapons in Brennik's Reach. The armaments were crude, but the mass of villagers wielding them would easily be able to run off the outnumbered bandits. Although my neighbors interpreted Yuinism as a religion of peace and love, they were also a hardened group of people who wouldn't hesitate to defend themselves when pressed. They'd lost far too many loved ones during their journey south to operate otherwise.

"Rutting night watchman," Blue growled. "Did we get enough?"

"Aye, a good haul," the short guard said. In the flickering torchlight his rough, jowly face looked almost demonic. "We've a card left to play, though."

An explosion rocked the settlement, and a bright red and yellow fireball leapt up toward the sky behind me. "That was the armory!" someone shouted. The town bell rang again, its rhythm stuttered to signal the evacuation of Brennik's Reach. With no weapons left to fight off the bandits, the safest thing for the townspeople to do was hide in the jungle until the attackers departed. I sighed with relief, hoping no one had been injured in the blast.

"This the kid you mentioned?" the tall guard asked. "Thought he'd be bigger."

"He's the one," Blue replied. "I'm sure of it this time."

An ear-piercing shriek cut me off before I had a chance to ask what *this time,* meant. "Yuin everlasting!"

Vont Gannek's broadsword cleaved into the neck of a man stepping out of Durgan's silo. The barrel of felta oil on his shoulder tumbled to the dirt and stuck there, joined a heartbeat later by his corpse. The night watchman's sword hadn't been sharp enough to cut clean through its target. Gannek pulled his weapon out with a sharp jerk and turned to face us. He must've crept around behind the silos, hoping an ambush would give him the advantage.

The tall guard charged first, followed a split second later by his shorter companion. Gannek calmly parried the tall one's thrust, then spun and swept the short one's feet out from under him with a surprisingly deft kick. He brought his sword back up and around with an uppercut stroke that gutted the tall one from thigh to shoulder, snarling wildly as he felled the man. The other stabbed out for an ankle, but Gannek sidestepped the attack and booted the cutlass away. The short man tried vainly to scrabble across the dirt on his hands and knees, but Gannek was on him instantly, snapping the man's neck with a quick yank.

I wondered if maybe the bandits should've left the armory alone and blown up Vont Gannek instead.

The night watchman flicked a gob of blood from his blade and pointed it my way. "You're next, traitor."

I raised my hands defensively. "Hold on, sir! Whatever's going on, I'm not part of it!"

"You brought the rat here," he said as he tightened his grip on his weapon. Ognar's lessons on disarming an opponent may as well have been lectures on Nefazo history. Gannek spat at my feet. "How much are they paying you?"

Just then a shadow appeared to Gannek's left, between the big man and Durgan's silo. It stood a good five inches shorter than the night watchman, and it was maybe half as wide, despite the big coat that hung from its frame. A long feather sprouted from the side of the gaudy tri-corner hat that sat slightly askew atop its head.

"Not too shabby," the newcomer said. His voice was deep and rough, but it twinkled with a slight hint of underlying mischief. "Ever dreamt of life on the sea? We pay good coin for skilled swordsmen, and it appears we're newly in need of...well, one. Two of these fools were worthless with a blade."

Gannek turned to face the man and spat angrily at his feet. "I fight for a power higher than gold."

"That's a mistake," the figure said mockingly, drawing a cutlass identical to the ones carried by the two fallen bandits. "May your honor serve you as well in the afterlife as my wallet serves me at the pub."

Gannek howled and charged, his broadsword raised high over his right shoulder. The other man stood his ground firmly, waiting for the absolute last second possible before sidestepping the night watchman's wild chop. Gannek spun back around with a kick, which the man hopped back from, then with a wild slice, which the man ducked. Gannek pushed the assault, grunting and growling as the man dodged blow after blow. Gannek was big, but by no means was he slow. The other was just too fast—faster than any man had a right to be. I'd never seen anyone move that smoothly, not even Ogrid.

And then the man tired of his little game, and the next time he dodged one of Gannek's attacks he flicked out his cutlass and sliced the big man's right cheek. Then he dodged a wild thrust and slashed Gannek's face two more times, striking lines through the remaining lines of his tattoo. Enraged, the night watchman howled as he swung back at his attacker, who ducked the assault and countered with one of his own. The man's razor-sharp cutlass sliced easily through Gannek's weak mail and up into his heart. The massive broadsword clattered uselessly to the street, and for a long moment the two figures just stared at each other.

"'Strength of arms' my *ass*," the bandit snarled.

Then he yanked his weapon back out the way it came, and Gannek joined his broadsword on the ground.

"Sorry about that," Blue said sarcastically at my side. "You two weren't friends, I hope?"

"Far from it," I replied, relieved I'd managed not to vomit. Working with Grandfather had exposed me to a fair amount of blood and gore, but I'd never seen men inflict such violence upon each other.

"And who might you be?" the man said as he approached, the tip of his cutlass pointed at my face. He was about my height and my weight, and maybe four or five years older. His face was square and handsome, with dark eyes and a mischievous smile. His brown hair was pulled into a tight ponytail that just reached the top of his shoulders. A bright red coat with gold trim and huge gold buckles hung loosely from his spare frame but was cinched tightly to his waist. The coat ended just below his knees, revealing tight black slacks and scuffed black boots. A long black feather sprouted from the left side of the tri-corner hat that perfectly matched his coat. He was dressed far too well to be just another thug, but nothing about his appearance betrayed his employer.

Then I got a good look at the cutlass, and I knew exactly what he was. The blade itself was nothing remarkable—the special part wasn't the dangerous end. A deep crimson blood ruby adorned the end of the gold hilt. The wrist guard had been formed in the shape of a predatory bird, its long black wings wrapped protectively around the bottom of the blade. A shock of feathers reached back sharply from the top of its head. Its short beak curved down toward its chest, below a pair of evil crimson eyes.

I'd seen that bird in countless childhood nightmares. To make me adhere to my curfew, my grandfather used to tell me stories of an Ainghid Fas that took the form of a huge black bird with terrible red eyes that roamed the night searching for stray children to snatch up and take away.

It was a black yonnix.

"You're one of Lagash's crew!" I blurted before I could stop myself.

Before its life as an infamous pirate vessel, the *Black Yonnix* had served as the flagship of Pileaus's enormous navy. As I'm sure Your Highness knows, all those who served aboard the *Yonnix* were issued specially crafted cutlasses with wrist guards shaped like her namesake. Captain Lagash had been the scourge of the southern coast for years. Everyone in the region knew to run at the sight of one of those blades.

The pirate smiled mischievously. "Guilty as charged, although I'm much more than just one of the crew: I'm Lagash's first mate. I suppose you'll have to run and get the magistrate so you can collect the bounty. By now it must be large enough to buy a discerning peasant such as yourself a whole herd of sheep."

"Nah," came Tehenessey Blue interjected. "This one would be better off investing in a new outfit or two, and perhaps some dancing lessons." He elbowed me in the side. "I truly do not understand what that bonny lass sees in you."

The cutlass disappeared into a sheath dangling from the pirate's belt. "Well met, friend Blue! Well met!" The two shook hands vigorously, though both kept a careful watch on me out of the corner of their eyes. "Any shiny pretties worth liberating from this shithole?"

"Not a one, Ulysses," Blue said sadly, "unless we count my new friend here."

I didn't like the sound of that. Despite my dashing good looks and first aid skills, only one thing made me even remotely valuable, especially to a group of marauding pirates: my last name. Grandfather had told me stories of northern sailors trying to enlist my parents in their get rich quick schemes. Some of them had ended in bloodshed.

Ulysses frowned and took a step back, his dark eyes scanning me up and down. "This scrawny little goat herder? He is neither shiny nor pretty. Are you sure, or are we going to have to fill his pockets with cannonballs and toss him over the side like the last three?"

Blue glared at him. "This time I'm positive."

Ulysses took a step closer to me. My breath caught in my throat. "Well, if Blue here says you're the one, we'll have to take you with us. Although for your sake, you'd better hope he's right. The cap'n's getting a bit sick of false alarms."

He punctuated that last frightening bit with a wide smile and the offer of a handshake. I saw my opening: Ognar had taught me how to twist an offered hand into a position where I'd be capable of snapping a man's arm. I needed answers, and I needed leverage. After a moment's hesitation I took Ulysses's hand. His grip was warm and strong, and he pumped my arm vehemently three times in quick succession.

That was when I felt a pair of sharp fangs sink into the skin above my thumb.

I jerked back reflexively. Ulysses released me and raised his hand to his face, stroking the chin of the little yellow snake poking its head out of his sleeve. "Roderick wanted to meet you too," he said as the snake's tongue flicked happily toward its master's nose.

Inertia washed over me, and I fell to one knee. I couldn't make my tongue work to ask for help or to curse the pirate's trickery. Blue caught me by the shoulder and gently lowered me toward the ground, but I was unconscious before I got there.

— PARLEY —

L osa cocked her head and frowned. "Tell me the serpent's name again. I'm not sure I heard you correctly."

Vardallian shuffled his feet and took a moment to study the marble floor. "The snake's name is Roderick, Your Highness."

The empress leaned back in her throne and stroked her chin thoughtfully. "The child Lagash fled the north to protect named his pet serpent after my father?"

"It...uh...would seem so, Your Highness." Vardallian prepared himself for the worst. Surely Losa wouldn't stand such an insult to her family. He should've skipped that part all together, or renamed the snake, or...

Losa's eyes lit up and she unleashed a sharp cackle. Vardallian flinched as if struck. "Of course he did," she mused. "Continue."

— CHAPTER SIX —

He sure don't look like anything special," grumbled a deep voice to my left.

"You think Ulysses is losin' his mohu?" responded a slow, smooth voice to my right.

"His what?"

"His...touch."

"Oh. I think he never knew exactly what he was lookin' for in the first place."

"Sure is startin' to look like it. I just wish the chu'ono wouldn't leave all the failures stranded on whichever island seems most convenient."

"Agh, cap'n usually leaves 'em along a trade route. Most of 'em get picked up."

"Most of 'em?"

"At least some of 'em, I'd expect."

I was wide awake, but I kept my eyes closed, hoping one or both would be foolish enough to divulge further information regarding my predicament. I couldn't feel any bonds or ties that might be used to restrain a prisoner such as myself, which I found a bit odd. Then again, the type of men I'd seen raiding Brennik's Reach probably would have no difficulty dealing with an unarmed peasant.

Somewhere to my right, a soft bell chimed three times.

"Breakfast is ready," said the slow voice. "Chu'ono don't like to be kept waitin'."

"Aye. So you going to do the honors, Apo, or should I?"

"The pleasure is yours, friend Tarik."

A wave of cold water splashed across my face and my nerves jerked me up into a sitting position. I wiped my eyes with my knuckles and spat against the water trying to trickle down my throat.

"On your feet, boy," said Apo, his voice smooth and sweet like molasses. He was Mana'Olai, a lean, dark-skinned man with a wizened face and short, curly white hair almost like lamb's wool. Despite the advanced age his face and hair betrayed, the taut muscles in his bare upper body belonged to a man much younger. His only clothing was a pair of bright blue pants that billowed out from his legs like sails in the wind, a red sash tied through the loops at his waist to keep them from plummeting off his spare hips. "My friend here has been known to amputate an ear or two from hu'alas who don't cooperate."

"Aye," growled Tarik. The man was a little shorter than me, but he was muscular and built like a barrel. He had a big, blocky face to match, with a wide mouth, a large nose, and a pair of furry brown eyebrows above dark brown eyes. He'd shaved his head bald, but the beginnings of brown stubble were just starting to show. A brown vest and matching pants strained against his girth. "Ears make great bait. The sliver fish just love 'em."

I did as ordered, despite the protests of the cramped muscles in my legs. We were in a jungle, but not my jungle. None of the plants in the area looked the least bit familiar. The calls and hoots of strange animals echoed through the foliage. A hint of nearby saltwater wafted upon the cool breeze.

I wasn't in Brennik's Reach anymore.

"Follow me, if you please," Apo commanded.

"You've got an appointment with the cap'n," Tarik added.

My heart leapt. An appointment with the captain! Judging from the wrist guard on the cutlass each of my captors carried, that could only be one man.

A man who used to be one of the highest-ranking officers in the Imperial Navy. Former adviser to the emperor himself. Infamous scourge of the seas off Nefazo and Mana'Olai. The captain of the *Black Yonnix*.

Bron Lagash.

"Stop gaping and get moving," Tarik growled.

Apo led me down a narrow game trail. Tarik brought up the rear. This jungle was warmer and buggier than the one I was used to, but neither discomfort bothered me. My mind was elsewhere, my gaze locked to the exquisite blade jouncing against Apo's hip. Two pirates from the *Black Yonnix* were escorting me to an audience with Captain Bron Lagash!

I couldn't decide whether to be awestruck or petrified. Perhaps Blue's promises hadn't been empty after all!

The trek through the jungle was short, maybe only a few minutes. The dense vegetation ended abruptly at the top of a small rise, giving way to a beautiful beach of fine white sand that had been transformed into a dining room. A long, ornate table of the finest fireoak, polished to a glistening sheen, stood about halfway between the jungle and the gently rolling surf.

Places had been set for three people, with porcelain dishes and sterling silver utensils and mugs. A ring of slender torches sprouted from the sand in a protective circle around the table, spewing bluish smoke that dissipated quickly but seemed to keep the hordes of insects at bay. To the table's left, a young woman in a sleeveless blouse and long skirt tended to a small pig roasting on a spit and a pot of coffee hanging from a wooden jig above a second, smaller fire. To her right, the pirate named Ulysses conversed softly with a massive bear of a man in full military regalia, all in black save for the frocked tunic that puffed out from the neck of his jacket. A thick gray beard framed his chiseled face, and a mane of the same color spilled out from under the back of his tri-corner hat, pulled into a tight ponytail that just kissed the collar of his jacket. The man stood like a statue as Ulysses spoke, his thick arms crossed tightly in front of his broad chest, his face cold and stern.

No, Your Highness, I've never met another man as intimidating as Bron Lagash, and I don't think I ever will.

My escorts stopped me beside the table. "Captain," Tarik called. "May I present Kensey Vardallian of Brennik's Reach."

Ulysses instantly went silent, and he cocked his head in my direction. The only part of Lagash that moved were his steely blue eyes. For several moments the man just stared at me, dissecting me with his icy gaze. My stomach twisted into a knot, and my enthusiasm for the situation was washed away by a feeling of intense dread. The man was wanted by every lawman between Mana'Olai and the Empire. His crew were killers and criminals. I suspected the young woman tending to breakfast probably wouldn't hesitate to cut a man's throat, either. My mind flashed back to the earlier conversation between Tarik and Apo.

Most of 'em get picked up.

Most of 'em?

At least some of 'em, I'd expect.

The captain kept his arms crossed and his gaze locked on me as he traversed the beach, his strides long and confident. Ulysses trailed, sporting a bright, cocky smile.

Lagash finally stopped at the head of the table. "Vardallian," he growled. I don't think he knew how to speak without growling. "Your father's name?"

I was speechless until Apo elbowed me in the ribs. "My mother's."

The captain raised an eyebrow, evidently waiting for an explanation. The young woman scooted in front of him and grabbed his plate.

"I was raised by my grandfather," I stuttered. "It was his name, so he passed it on to me."

"And his name?"

"Thuroth. Thuroth Vardallian."

The captain shifted his feet. Ulysses' smile widened. The young woman returned with Lagash's plate, now loaded with slices of juicy pork and a side of potatoes I hadn't noticed roasting beside the coffee. She snagged the other two plates and zipped away again.

"Don't lie to me, boy!" Lagash thundered. "You would not enjoy the consequences."

The pure force of the man's voice rattled my bones. "I'm telling the truth," I squeaked.

The woman darted back to the table, returning the plates, each with a heaping pile of food. She then moved to the fire and took a seat on a nearby log, sipping softly from a steaming silver mug.

Lagash chuckled deeply. "The old goat did it, then. He actually survived the trip south, to build his little Yuinite utopia."

"You...you knew my grandfather?"

He nodded. "Only priest I'd ever met who didn't cower at Pileaus's name. Tough as nails, that one."

His mention of my grandfather surprised me. Stories of the *Black Yonnix* circulated through the countryside like wildfire, and rarely would I make the trip into Brennik's Reach without hearing a new one. Tales of the infamous pirates always excited me, and as such, I always repeated them to my grandfather. But not once had he mentioned that he'd actually met Lagash. He'd never told me much of anything about life before the trip south, save for an occasional curse aimed at Pileaus when he was angry but couldn't find anything more convenient to swear at.

"How is Thuroth? The old bastard must have a thousand converts by now, especially with your parents by his side."

My face flushed and my throat tightened. I directed my gaze toward the sand at my feet and spoke softly. "My father died of a fever about halfway through the journey south. My mother went into labor in the clearing where my grandfather built our house. S—she was weak from the trip, and she didn't survive. My grandfather disavowed his faith, abandoning the other settlers to build and manage Brennik's Reach without him. And...about a month and a half ago...L'Vaillee's goons came..."

I couldn't finish the thought. Lagash was unmoved. "The world is a lesser place without Thuroth Vardallian," Lagash said thoughtfully. "It seems that as the last of your family, you and I have much to discuss. Breakfast first."

Lagash and Ulysses sat, and Apo elbowed me to do the same. The woman returned with the pot of coffee, pouring a cup for each of us. She joined Apo and Tarik at the fire, where they ate their own meals and conversed in hushed tones.

Lagash, Ulysses, and I ate in silence. Roderick darted out of Ulysses's sleeve at one point to snag a bite of bacon from his plate. The captain continued to examine me, and his first mate just kept smiling. I tried to focus on my food, which was extremely good, but my mind was overwhelmed with worry. There was only one thing a pirate captain would want to speak with me about. I feared what would happen when Lagash discovered I couldn't readily produce it.

The captain devoured his meal quickly, then pushed his plate aside and leaned across the table. "Did your grandfather teach you any of the family history?" His fingers fidgeted with each other, a gesture I later learned meant the man could barely conceal his excitement. At the time I read it as impatience.

I almost choked on the coffee I was trying to swallow. This was it. "I am."

"Then you know of your great-great-great-great grandfather's adventures." His fingers worked even faster.

I shifted uncomfortably. "I do."

"And of the journal."

"Yes."

"And the unimaginable treasure it leads to."

"Yes."

"Can you read it?"

I nodded. Lucifus Vardallian had been an extremely paranoid man, distrustful of his own crew, his own wife, and his own shadow—but he'd also possessed an extraordinary intelligence. He'd developed his own language for use in the journal, which he taught only to his eldest son, who in turn taught his eldest son…and thus Grandfather had taught me, since my own father wasn't around to do the job.

Lagash licked his lips before he spoke. "You can decipher the journal. I have a crew and the former flagship of Pileaus's navy. I think we might be able to help each other out."

And there it was. Lagash was after my great-great-great-great grandfather's treasure, and there was only one way to reach it.

"L'Vaillee's men took the journal," I grumbled.

The old sailor's eyes went hard. He leaned back in his seat and crossed his burly arms. Then his mouth shifted into a crooked grin. "I know that already, my boy."

Beside him, Ulysses burst out laughing. The crew gathered around the fire followed suit. I tried my best to melt down through my chair but couldn't quite manage it. Of course Lagash would know everything I'd told Tehenessey Blue. I still don't understand why I ever would've thought otherwise.

The captain leaned forward again. "Forgive an old salt his poor sense of humor. Even after years of pillagin' and plunderin', few things brighten the day like watching a man squirm."

Yes, Your Highness, Lagash and his crew had most certainly spent far too much time at sea.

"It's all right," I muttered, not sure where to look.

The old pirate nodded. "If you'll help us read it, we'll get your journal back."

"After all, what's one penny-pinching Nefazo lord against the crew of the *Black Yonnix*?" Ulysses added.

"Can we also kill a tax collector named Rocher?" I asked meekly.

That triggered a raucous round of laughter. Ulysses slapped his thigh and the woman at the fire spilled coffee all over her skirt.

"Aye, my lad!" Lagash replied, wiping a tear from his eye. "Wouldn't Thuroth be proud of you!"

I wasn't so sure of that, but I kept my mouth shut. Had Grandfather risen from the dead to find me in the company of nefarious pirates, plotting theft and murder...there would have been a disapproving scowl, at the very least.

"But first, we have cargo to unload," Lagash growled. "The shuen aren't known for their patience."

— CHAPTER SEVEN —

After breakfast, the pirates led me back through the jungle toward the opposite side of the island. The brooding Lagash took point, walking well in front of the others, who'd clustered into a tight knot of rowdy discussion. Tehenessey Blue melted out of the forest and fell into step beside Tarik. I didn't know it at the time, but the captain preferred the little marii keep his distance. None of them seemed to be paying particular attention to me, but none of them really had to. Even if I did sneak off, where was I going to go? Nothing looked familiar, and certainly my chances of reaching Brennik's Reach alone would not have been great. I fell in behind Apo and Tarik and listened intently as Tehenessey Blue and Ulysses regaled Loridgid—the woman who'd served breakfast—with tales of their exploits in Brennik's Reach.

"...and then a Yuinite as tall as the main mast descended upon us, dripping in the blood of that morning's virgin sacrifices," Ulysses declared with a sweep of his arms. "The eldritch gods heeding the horrible barbarian's summons unleashed a thunderbolt from the heavens, which he deftly captured in his horrible knobby hands. Thus armed, the dark priest murdered Rewen and Lag with deft strokes and then turned his fury upon yours truly. I drew my humble blade and faced the towering behemoth—"

"If I'm not mistaken, what you're trying to say is that the village's lone defender got the jump on those two fools but lacked the skill to handle himself in a fair fight?" Lori asked.

Apo and Tarik guffawed. In spite of my nerves, I chuckled under my breath. "In a manner of speaking," Ulysses replied, feigning defeat, "although the battle itself was much more dramatic."

"There was sacrilege," Blue added.

"Indeed! I wiped several Yuinite verses off the face of…well, the man's face."

Lori patted his arm. "Extra bacon for you tomorrow, then."

Again the jungle ended abruptly, transforming into a small area of flat white sand. A pair of black longboats waited where the shore met the surf. Beyond that, the ocean crashed and roiled, crystal blue with just a hint of green. And beyond that…

Well, if there's ever existed a ship more beautiful than the *Black Yonnix*, I don't know of it. Even back then, having seen only a few ships from the shore outside Brennik's Reach, I knew she was something special. There was a glow about her; she shone as if she'd never been touched by the ravages of the sea. She was long and tall, her main deck a valley between the higher forecastle at the bow and the even higher quarterdeck at the stern. Gleaming white sails fluttered softly from tall, thick masts. Black trim traced the edges of her glistening mahogany hull. The bow was pointed toward the beach at a slight angle, just revealing the massive figurehead of a black yonnix, wings stretched and talons extended, its ruby eyes glittering mena-cingly in the sun.

Without realizing it, I'd stopped to gawk. The *Black Yonnix* was the most magnificent thing I'd ever seen. I couldn't tear my gaze away from it. The two longboats were about thirty feet offshore before Captain Lagash called out to me.

"If you prefer to be marooned, that can be arranged!"

That snapped me back to reality. I rushed down the beach, stopping at the edge of the water. "Come back!" I shouted. "I can't swim!"

Ulysses stood at the stern of his particular longboat, looking back at me with his hands on his hips. "You want to sail with a bunch of pirates to find the pirate treasure hidden by your pirate ancestor, yet you can't *swim*?" He shook his head. "Then it's time you learned!"

It may not seem like much, but to someone who'd never swam before, thirty feet of crashing surf seemed an impassable obstacle. And then there were the shuen, who guarded their holy ocean with fanatical violence. The waters near Brennik's Reach were supposedly full of them, and swimming was outlawed so as to avoid their wrath. Though there were a few rivers and ponds in the surrounding jungle, Grandfather had taught me to steer clear. Leeches, I'd learned while ministering to the other villagers who enjoyed an occasional dip, were not fun things to remove.

The longboats halted and the pirates looked on expectantly. They were testing me. If I didn't have the courage to at least attempt a short swim, dragging me along in search of Lucifus Vardallian's journal and his long-lost treasure would be a waste of their time. Besides, I had no doubt they were ready to dive in to save me—and their own chance at fame and fortune—if my attempt went sideways. I had to try.

I waded out toward the boats. The water was warm, like bathwater, and the bottom was soft and muddy. I walked out past where the waves crested, until the water was all the way up to my neck. Then I stopped, took a deep breath, and dove forward.

I'd never seen anyone swim before, but I'd read about it and Grandfather had described the process to me a few times. I paddled my arms and kicked my feet as rhythmically as I could. This kept me afloat for about five seconds, then I swallowed a mouthful of saltwater and went under. I thrashed wildly, panicking in a vain attempt to get myself back above the surface. I must've made my initial leap forward from a coastal shelf, because I sank much farther than I figured I should have.

Just as I was about to resign myself to a watery grave, something took firm hold of my collar and yanked me upward. I burst through the surface so quickly it stung my head and shoulders and left my ears ringing. I coughed up a lungful of bitter seawater and greedily sucked in the sweet, sweet air. The brine in my eyes clouded my vision, but I could clearly see that I was headed for a black mass of some sort, which I assumed to be one of the two longboats. The pirates, unfortunately, had been forced to rescue me.

I landed butt first on the black mass, the surface hard and unforgiving. Three figures towered over me, tall and lean and blurry and slightly green. I waited for one of the pirates to chastise me or make a snide remark, but none came. The words I heard were all hard consonants and sharp, quick syllables. I thought there might still be water in my ears, garbling their speech—but then my vision cleared, and my saviors came into focus.

They were shuen.

I glanced over my shoulder just in time to see my rescuer—a long black tentacle—dart back under the water. It hadn't deposited me on a boat, at least not the kind I was used to. I sat on a floating platform of craggy coral with no sails, no helm, no oars—nothing that looked like it would provide any sort of steering or propulsion.

All the horrible stories I'd heard about shuen from the wise folk of Brennik's Reach rushed to the forefront of my mind. "I'm sorry!" I shouted wildly. "I didn't mean to trespass in your ocean! Please don't eat me!"

The three shuen looked at each other quizzically. Each stood over seven feet tall. Powerful muscles rippled beneath their greenish skin. Their heads were small and round, hairless and earless, with heavy brows over dark, beady eyes. Dark spots speckled their joints and the backs of their heads. Each wore a sleeveless black garment made of the scaly skin of some denizen of the deep, a combination of vest and pants with a large white collar open to about half the length of their torsos. Each carried a zykel in a loop cut into the garment just above the right hip, a long knife built of a hilt carved from whalebone and a long, jagged blade made of a tooth that once belonged to a terrifyingly huge shark. They looked truly alien to me, even more so than Tehenessey Blue. Yuin, I still think the shuen are more frightening than even the Fae I've since encountered.

They didn't seem convinced by my pleas, so I tried again. "Please!" I squealed. "I promise I'll never swim again!"

Two of them exchanged a confused look. The third stamped his foot on the coral platform, and it began to move—straight toward the *Black Yonnix*. The platform traveled swiftly, with no concern for the currents below the surface nor the winds above. Most of the shuen craft, I would later learn, were propelled by a living organism that carried said craft upon its back. This one, luckily for me, happened to have tentacles. The shuen all waved at the stunned pirates as Lagash and his crew grabbed their oars and spurred their longboats back into motion.

"Fear not, Kensey!" Ulysses called out. "This is how the shuen say hello when they meet new people! We'll be right with you!"

Dozens of similar craft zipped across the surface, swarming around the much larger *Black Yonnix* like angry bees defending a hive. Each carried three or four shuen clad in the same black garment. They all stood like statues, their glistening eyes glued to the *Black Yonnix* and the two longboats being winched up to her deck. Despite their composure, I could sense a barely contained ferociousness waiting impatiently for a reason to burst forth.

My little craft pulled up beside the mahogany hull of the *Black Yonnix* and stopped. One of the shuen cupped his hands around his mouth and shouted up to someone on the ship's deck. His voice was deep and raspy, the language hard and guttural. There came a reply, and the shuen stomped on the coral three times. A tentacle shot up out of the water and wrapped itself around my leg. One of the shuen waved sarcastically.

Then the tentacle jerked me up into the air and deposited me roughly on the deck of the *Black Yonnix*. A pair of strong shuen hands grabbed my shoulders and pulled me to my feet. I was surrounded by shuen, all tall and muscular, all wearing the same black garment.

This was it. I'd trespassed in their seas, and now I would have to pay the price.

"I'm sorry," I gasped pathetically. "I didn't mean to." A round of guttural laughter brought an embarrassed flush to my face.

"One of yours, Lagash?" came an unmistakably shuen voice from somewhere in the crowd.

The shuen that held my shoulders pushed me forward, goading me through the crowd toward the voice.

Lagash grunted as he hoisted himself onto the deck. "My crew is none of your concern. I believe we have a bit of business to discuss." The others clambered up behind him.

"That we do. But for the moment, I'm curious about the boy."

"We took him on as a favor to an old friend," said Ulysses. "He'll be lucky if he lasts a week, but it's what the old man wanted."

The shuen clicked his tongue. "As always, the first mate speaks out of turn. Sleep lightly, Captain, or you may find his blade in your throat."

Then I was shoved through the front row of shuen, stumbling to keep my balance. To my immediate right stood a shuen in a long black cape that hid his entire body. A jagged pink scar ran diagonally across his face, starting just above his left eye and running down to the right side of his chin. This one, I sensed, was different. I could see it in his eyes, deeper and darker than those of his companions. They were empty eyes, yet at the same time they were full of something dark and forbidding. When the other shuen warriors had looked at me, they'd seen a prisoner. When this one looked at me, he saw a victim.

He took a step toward me and hooked an arm through mine. "Ulysses thinks he's got me fooled. But I know better. The crew of the *Black Yonnix* doesn't have any friends."

The lump in my throat stifled any reply I could've mustered. This shuen was terrifying.

"Let him go, Thranax," Ulysses snarled from the opposite side of the deck. The ship's crew had gathered there, behind the captain and the first mate. Tarik and Apo stood at the front of the pack, each with a hand on the hilt of his blade. Tehenessey Blue sat on the rail at the edge of the quarterdeck, clipping his nails and looking extremely disinterested in the proceedings. The rest of the crew, a little less than two dozen strong, were a ragged, motley collection of hardened men and a few women. About half were lighter-skinned northerners; the rest were a mix of olive-skinned Nefazo and darker Mana'Olai.

"I believe you owe me compensation for services rendered," Thranax said steadily. "Or I could throw him back."

"How much?" Lagash growled.

Thranax's alien smile sent a chill down my spine. "How many barrels of felta oil did you acquire from Brennik's Reach?"

"Captain!" shouted a deep voice from the back of the crowd. "That haul's worth a few thousand, easy!"

Lagash didn't respond. He crossed his arms across his huge chest and glared at me. I averted my eyes and stared uneasily at the deck. I didn't believe for a moment he'd trade that kind of plunder for a penniless orphan whose only claim to fame had been stolen out from under him.

"Think his second swim will turn out better than his first?" Thranax goaded.

The captain waved his hand dismissively. "Ulysses, have Davanon prepare the cargo for release to the shuen. You've got a deal."

"Of course I do." The towering shuen turned to me, licking his finger. "Your captain has paid for the return of his crewman—now you must pay for your life."

Before I could protest, my shirt was torn away and Thranax's finger was sketching a complex rune on my chest. The area tingled, then the rune itself appeared, a shimmering green symbol that marked me with shuen magic.

"One day, the shuen will ask for your assistance. Think of that mark as a guarantee of your compliance. Now, go to your captain!"

Thranax shoved me forward, and I stumbled across the deck until I collapsed at Lagash's feet. I was too ashamed to look up.

"Think he's worth it, Cap'n?" Tarik muttered.

I could hear Lagash shift his feet uncertainly. "He'd better be."

— PARLEY —

Losa leaned forward on her throne and studied her prisoner. "You still bare the shuen's mark?"

Kensey nodded meekly. "I haven't found a way to remove it, Your Highness."

"Show me."

Vardallian's fingers slipped over and over as he unbuttoned his tunic. He'd dared to hope that maybe he'd won the Empress's trust, but if she found Thranax's rune offensive or threatening...

She examined the rune thoughtfully for several moments. "That is very old, and not a design I can decipher. The shuen of the southern seas are a mystery to us here in the empire. You are aware that one of their taishu has been spotted just beyond my harbor?"

Vardallian's eyes went wide. "No, Your Highness, I had no idea. I thought Thranax lost beneath the waves."

"Under the circumstances, you'll forgive me if I keep my distance," Losa said wryly.

"Yes. Yes, Your Highness, certainly." Vardallian punctuated that with a deep bow and a sigh of relief.

"Good. Continue."

— CHAPTER EIGHT —

Ulysses broke the silence. "All right boys, let's get a move on! The quicker we get these chowderheads off our boat, the better she'll smell later!"

No one griped, no one grumbled, no one moped. In seconds much of the crew had disappeared down a hatch in the deck to my right.

Thranax issued what I assumed to be a similar command to his men in his guttural native language, then he turned to consider Ulysses. "This ocean is mine. You defile it with your presence because it pleases me for you to do so. The day it ceases to please me is the day I carve out your heart and serve it to my children."

The shuen made a sharp clicking sound with his tongue. A tentacle shot up over the deck, gently wrapped itself around him, and carried him away.

I remained on the deck at Lagash's feet, too embarrassed to move. I didn't think I could've made a worse first impression on the crew if I'd tried.

The captain grabbed my shoulder with one massive hand and hauled me to my feet. "Loridgid!" he bellowed.

Lori appeared at his side. "Yes, Captain?"

"Take this mess below and clean him up."

"Aye, sir." Lori took my hand and led me away. She patted the green rune on my chest reassuringly. "Nothin' a good scrubbin' won't fix."

She led me over the lip of the hatch and down the twelve narrow stairs into the main hold of the *Black Yonnix*. It was an expansive space, longer from bow to stern than it was from aft to port, which kept it from feeling claustrophobic despite the low ceiling. Every surface was made of dark brown planks attached to the ship's skeleton with heavy nails. Timbers thicker than Vont Gannek sprang from the floor as support columns every eight feet or so. To my left, toward the back of the ship, the crew worked quickly to untie the netting that bound the barrels of felta oil to the *Yonnix*'s hull. There was another compartment three columns farther aft, secured by a pair of heavy iron doors.

"That leads to the crew quarters," Lori explained. "Not very spacious, but it's home. We installed the thick doors because sometimes the cargo we haul tries to cause trouble."

I looked around nervously. "What kind of trouble?"

"Oh...rampagin', murderin', mutilatin'...that kinda thing."

I stopped at the bottom of the stairs. Lori looked back at me and giggled at my pale, horrified expression. "Just kiddin'. We don't carry anythin' that can fight back. Usually it just smells." She pulled me to the right, toward an immediate set of similar doors. "C'mon, we're goin' to the galley, where we'll be outta everybody's way."

She shouldered her way through the entrance and dragged me along behind her. The galley looked much like the hold, save for the additions one would expect to find in a galley. Three long tables ran lengthwise across most of the room. Two brick fireplaces were built into the center of the back wall, surrounded by a vast array of cabinets.

"You just sit down right here," Lori said, directing me to a bench at the center table. "I'll fetch the soap and water."

As she headed toward the kitchen area, I took in the scope of the room with wide-eyed wonder. I was in the galley of the one and only *Black Yonnix*! Here was a room in which Captain Lagash himself had eaten, plotted strategy, and relaxed with his crew. My previous trepidations melted away; I was somewhere few people had been, somewhere I'd only dreamed of being, and no mark on my chest could change that. Perhaps Grandfather wouldn't exactly have been proud of me, but he'd be impressed that I'd made it this far.

A sound like a trickling stream called my attention to Lori. She held a metal bucket below a spigot in the wall between the fireplaces.

"You've got running water?"

"Aye," she said with a smile. "Here in the galley, in the crew's quarters, and in the captain's cabin. Distilled seawater, forced through a series of pipes as the ship travels. Just one of Davanon's many tricks. Ship's full of 'em."

"Who's Davanon?"

"That would be me," came a soft, deep voice from my left.

The speaker bent to close a square hatch that blended perfectly into the floor, through which he'd entered the room. He was taller than Lagash, but it would've taken three of him to match the captain's girth. Though his straight, shoulder length hair was white and wispy, his perfectly sculpted face didn't betray a single hint of age. His bright eyes were a sharp contrast to his olive skin, one green, the other a sharp blue. A heavy set of brown robes hung loosely from his spare frame, tied at the waist with a white sash.

"What's down there?" I asked.

"The interesting bits," Davanon replied. He made his way to my side quickly yet apparently effortlessly, seeming to float more than walk. "Though nothing nearly as interesting as that mark you bear."

He reached inside the folds of his robe and retrieved what looked like a miniature telescope. I could hear lenses flipping into place as he gently turned a dial on the device's side and then leaned in for a closer look at my chest.

"What did that monster do to me?" I asked, fearing the answer.

"You've been marked, though for what purpose I cannot say," Davanon replied with a wave of his free hand. The lenses in his device flipped again as he made another adjustment. "Could be some horrible magic soon to blow up in all our faces. Could be as simple as a brand meant to communicate Thranax's ownership of you to the other shuen."

"No one owns me," I growled angrily, though honestly, I was more worried about the first possibility. I hadn't encountered much magic in my life, but I knew it was a thing to be wary of.

"Damn chowderheads," Lori added as she turned off the spigot.

"Do not judge an entire raced based on the actions of a few individuals." His voice was like molasses, sweet and relaxing. "The shuen themselves are an admirable people. Thranax himself is something altogether…different."

Lagash entered the room with Ulysses at his side. "Any idea what that Thranax's little scribble might be?" the first mate asked.

Davanon closed the telescope and stood. "Not a one. But I suggest we remove it posthaste."

Lori ducked between Davanon and myself with the bucket of soapy water and a large sponge. "Might tickle a bit," she said as she went to work.

She scrubbed roughly at my chest for almost a minute, to the point where it began to sting. I won't lie—that was awkward. I'd never been bathed by a woman before, and having an audience for my first time sent a flush into my cheeks. I couldn't help noticing the way Lori's eyes narrowed and the tip of her tongue stuck out between her lips as she concentrated. I braced myself against her efforts, surprised by her strength.

The mark remained. Defeated, Lori slumped away. "One tough stain," she muttered.

Davanon tapped his chin thoughtfully with the telescope. "Toss him over the side."

My jaw dropped. I was about to protest, but Ulysses got there first. "Toss him over the side? *Toss him over the side*? Davanon, he's a Vardallian. No—he's *the* Vardallian. He's Thuroth's rutting grandson, the last scion of Lucifus's line—the one we've spent the last decade looking for."

Davanon cocked one thin eyebrow. "He has the journal?"

Ulysses hesitated. "He knows where we can get it."

"Toss him over the side."

Ulysses just shook his head. "You're sure you don't know what that mark is?"

"I have no idea what that mark is. That's reason enough for you to be wary of it."

The flustered first mate turned to the captain, who stood calmly taking it all in. "You're not going to listen to him, are you? This is it! This is our shot!"

Lagash stroked his beard. "If Davanon wants him off the boat, I say we get him off the boat."

My heart stopped. "Sir, please, I—"

The captain silenced me with one look. For about the tenth time that day, I felt as if the world had pulled the rug out from under me. I got the impression that no matter how much Ulysses or I campaigned, the captain wasn't going to change his mind.

"We sail for Fromaille," Lagash declared. "L'Vaillee's keep is three days north. Vardallian goes with you. Whatever Thranax did will likely manifest itself soon, and when it does, it'll be your problem—not mine."

Ulysses nodded. "Thank you, sir. We won't let you down."

"Now get this boat to the mainland," Lagash snarled. "And do it *quickly.*"

"Aye, Captain, chowderheads won't be able to keep up!" Ulysses said with a smile. Then he turned to me. "C'mon, lad, this is the fun part of the job!"

I followed Ulysses out into the hold and back up the stairs onto the deck, still shirtless and soapy. The scattered crew lounged against the rails or passed around pipes spewing tendrils of viscous yellow smoke. Off the port side of the ship, Thranax's fleet was headed back toward a large, dark shape on the horizon: their taishu, their floating city.

"Cargo's away, sir!" Tarik shouted from his seat on the aft rail. "An' so are the chowderheads."

"And good riddance to 'em!" Ulysses replied. The crew responded with a cheer. "Now let's get this boat ready for departure, shall we?"

"Aye sir!" Tarik answered. He pushed himself upright from the rail and scanned the rest of the crew. "You heard the man!"

Ulysses spun and headed toward the stern, bounding quickly up the stairs to the quarterdeck. I took a moment to watch as the crew split into three teams: one raising the anchor, one checking the rigging, and another going below to secure all the hatches. Then I followed the first mate.

He was waiting for me behind the ship's massive wheel, flanked on either side by a trio of levers sprouting a good three and a half feet up from the deck. "Ever sailed before?"

"No."

He winked at me conspiratorially. "Then what you're about to see is completely normal. Nothing special here."

"She's all yours, sir!" Tarik called from the main deck.

"Excellent! Now if you would be kind enough to assemble the men along the port rail, we'll give the chowderheads a little something to remember us by."

Tarik laughed heartily. "Aye, sir."

Ulysses reached into his shirt and retrieved a tiny golden key attached to a long silver chain that hung around his neck. He inserted the key into a hole at the wheel's center and gave it a turn to the right. The ship shuddered, and I could feel the vibrations of machinery whirring to life somewhere in the *Black Yonnix*'s interior.

"Pontoons," the first mate explained. "One on either side. Fold right out of the hull. Don't want to tip the old girl over."

Something below us clicked, and then the ship shuddered one final time. Ulysses licked his index finger and extended it to test the air. "Just right. Hold on to your hat."

He turned the key to the right and suddenly, the *Black Yonnix* lurched forward. I grabbed Ulysses's elbow to steady myself, then, embarrassed, I let go. Granted, I didn't know much about sailing back then, but the ship seemed to be moving a lot faster than it should have—and in fact it was, a good three times faster, by my estimation. The feeling of the wind whipping through my hair as we cut across the sea was absolutely exhilarating.

But oddly enough, the sails hung limply from the masts. I had no idea what was propelling the ship, but it definitely wasn't the wind.

I'm sorry, Your Highness, what worked? Yes, my apologies, I'll continue.

Ulysses spun the wheel and the ship made a hard turn to port. We were coming up on the right side of Thranax's fleet of platforms, and we were doing it quickly. Tarik, Apo, and the rest of the crew were lined up single file along the port rail, their backs to the sea.

Tehenessey Blue appeared at the top of the stairs, shaking his head softly. "Is this vulgarity really necessary?"

"Not particularly," Ulysses said with a smile.

Blue shook his head again and sat down against the rail.

Moments later we were beyond the shuen vessels. After another sharp turn the *Black Yonnix* crossed right in front of them. Tarik gave the signal, and the crew gathered along the rail bent over and dropped their pants in unison.

Ulysses howled with delight and waved sarcastically at Thranax's ships. I couldn't help but laugh. I felt better about myself and my standing on the ship, like the crew had stepped up behind me to help get a little revenge on my tormentor.

Tehenessey Blue sighed. "Animals."

— CHAPTER NINE —

The shuen were mere specks on the horizon when the ship began to slow. Ulysses tested the air again, shrugged, and then turned the key. The *Black Yonnix* groaned as the pontoons retracted and whatever mysterious device had propelled us wound itself down. The sails billowed out in the wind and we continued along at much more realistic pace, looping back north around the island where I'd met the Captain and his first mate for breakfast.

With the ship steadily underway, the pirates threw themselves headlong into an activity I've never seen anyone perform with more enthusiasm: drinking copious amounts of alcohol. Bottles and flasks seemed to spontaneously pop into their hands from some secret pockets hidden deep in the magic of the world. Several lit pipes for themselves and their companions. Lori popped up from below to hand me a fresh tunic. Not one of them seemed disappointed with the loss of their haul from Brennik's Reach.

Life at sea is hard and unfair, Your Highness. Dwell too long or too hard on the setbacks and you'll soon find yourself staring a little too longingly into the depths of the briny deep—or so Tarik told me once.

Captain Lagash surveyed it all from the main deck. Satisfied with the direction of his vessel, he turned, nodded to Ulysses, and disappeared below.

"We're being summoned," he said to me with a friendly nod. "Apo! You have the helm!"

The cheerful Mana'Olai bounded up onto the quarterdeck and accepted his assignment with a slight bow. I followed Ulysses down onto the main deck and into the bowels of the ship once more. Tehenessey Blue trailed along like our shadow.

The *Black Yonnix*'s leadership awaited us in the galley: Lagash, Davanon, and a terrifying black clad man named Rindge. After much hemming, hawing, swearing, and arguing over maps, tides, winds, and other nautical concerns I still can only barely make sense of—and Lori's sudden strategic delivery of a bottle of rum right at the discussion's loudest moment—it was agreed that Ulysses, Tehenessey Blue, and I would be deposited ashore three knots east of our original destination of Fromaille the following morning, and that we'd then make our way to Vastille either on foot or via whatever transportation we could arrange.

Yes, Your Highness, it is odd that a military man such as Lagash would allow his council to descend into such anarchy. I suspect that when one lacks the might of an empire behind one's commands, one adopts a more flexible approach to leadership.

Decisions made, Lagash dismissed the other pirates—but not me. The big man motioned me to take a seat across from him, then pushed the bottle of rum across the table. I'd never drunk before, and I'd always been wary of alcohol because of stories my Grandfather told about my mother's misuse of it, but I knew this was an invitation I couldn't refuse. Somehow, I managed not to gag as the spicy liquor burned its way down my throat.

"That's enough," Lagash said with surprising warmth. "You'll need your wits about you tomorrow."

We studied each other for a moment. "Thank you for not throwing me over the side," I said when I couldn't bare the silence any longer.

"That thing on your chest is our fault," he admitted. "Leaving you on the beach so we could have a few laughs was stupid. Yuin, sending you into Vastille might be just as dumb—but you're the only one who will recognize Lucifus's journal."

That was the closest I've ever heard Lagash get to apologizing to anyone. "I'd rather be here than stuck in Brennik's Reach, waiting for the tax collectors to return."

Lagash nodded. "Can't say I blame you. Welcome aboard, Vardallian. We've only got one rule here on the *Black Yonnix*: my commands, or those issued by any officers acting in my stead, are to be followed quickly and completely. Can you do that?"

I'll never forget the warmth welling up in my chest. "Aye, Captain."

"All right, then," he said, his old bones obviously creaking a bit as he stood up. "Wait here for Loridgid. She'll appreciate a few extra hands with the potatoes."

His words didn't immediately register. I won't say I wasn't disappointed, but I did my best not to show it. I supposed I did need to earn my keep somehow, famous pirate ancestor or not. "Happy to help."

The glow on Lori's face as she bounded into the galley proved she did indeed appreciate the aid. "You would not believe how much these rutters can eat," she said as she walked past, headed astern toward the pantry.

She wasn't kidding. The sack of twilight potatoes she dragged over to the table had to have been bigger than Lagash. "You know how to use a knife?" she asked, producing a razor-sharp little blade.

"The metal end goes through the potato, right?"

She shook her head, flipped the knife in her hand, and offered me the wooden handle. "I suppose you learned that in yer fancy pirate journal. Peel 'em, then quarter 'em. We'll need about sixty."

Part of me was surprised Lagash's crew would leave me alone in the galley with a weapon and a Lori, but the smarter part of me suspected she wouldn't have much trouble putting me down if she had to. I took the blade and got to work. The potatoes were strangely cool to the touch and smelled fresh.

"It's one of Davanon's improvements," Lori explained. "Calls it an 'ice pantry.' He creates the cooling effect with the same steam lines that power everything else in the ship, but how is beyond me."

As I cut vegetables, Loridgid busied herself at the hearth. And talked. And talked. And talked. She told me of her parents' journey south with Lagash, how her pregnant mother, Elisabeth, agreed to the journey simply because she knew her husband, Richart, would've left without her had she refused. She talked of her father's death at the hands of shuen raiders a year later, and her mother's fatal fall from the quarterdeck during a storm when she was seven. She spoke wistfully of being raised by the crew and their families beside Ulysses, and she did so with a glistening sheen in her eyes that made me suspect she thought of him as something more than a friend and shipmate.

She spoke most reverently of a place called Haershore, which I quickly gathered to be the *Black Yonnix*'s home port. I'd never heard of the place. Lori claimed that in Haershore, it never rained but sometimes it snowed warmly, talking fish told each other jokes under the light of the stars, and that I would not believe the sweetness of fruits grown from the strange green soil. A woman named Merragh watched over the settlement in Lagash's absence, to which several of the older pirates who'd sailed south from the Empire had permanently retired and started families of their own.

She stopped suddenly. "Oh, I should change the subject. New crewmembers don't get to visit Haershore 'til the Cap'n gives the ok. I've probably said too much already." Then she launched into a story about the time Tehennessey Blue stole Ulysses's hat and the first mate couldn't find it for an entire week.

The monotony of my task and the constant drone of Lori's voice put me in a bit of a fog. Honestly, I enjoyed it. Grandfather used to tell me stories the same way when we'd work around the house or in the jungle. For the first time I felt at ease aboard the *Black Yonnix*.

I was taken completely by surprise when a huge fish flopped through the door and collided with my table, sending the potatoes scattering across the floor and dumping me unceremoniously on my rear end. It was a monstrous thing, easily twice my size, with a long, hooked snout and a huge dorsal fin rippling with specks of silver and gold. Its angry eye swiveled in my direction, and I raised Lori's knife in preparation to defend myself.

Loridgid was on it in a flash, driving her heavy carving knife into the side of its head. It spasmed a few more times before finally laying still. A heavy laugh echoed from out in the cargo hold.

"Don't do that!" Lori scolded whoever had tossed the fish into the galley. "It ruins the pigment in the scales!"

A tall northerner dressed in all black strode arrogantly through the door—Rindge, the man who'd been mostly quiet during the earlier planning session. His heavy build was evident through the thick furs and worn leathers wrapping his body. Black curls tumbled from his head in tight ringlets, and brown eyes burned brightly above his scarred cheeks. The man was a walking armory; in addition to the cutlass at his hip, he carried a variety of knives and dirks tucked into various sheaths across his body and a heavy battleax strapped to his back.

"Ah, but it reduces the time it takes to tenderize the meat," he said in a deep baritone with an accent I couldn't place. He glanced in my direction and cocked one bushy eyebrow. "Seems it also tenderizes scrawny whelps."

"Show some respect, Rindge," Lori said with a click of her tongue. "This scrawny whelp is going to make you very, very rich."

"That remains to be seen," Rindge replied, "but for now, he gets the benefit of the doubt."

"Nice to officially meet you," I stuttered as he pulled me to my feet. "What do you do here?"

"I fight," he said, "and I fish." With that he turned and stomped out of the galley.

"Don't mind him," Lori purred reassuringly as she helped me pick up the scattered potatoes. "He's always a bit suspicious of people until they've proven themselves to him—doubly so, I think, because it was a long time before the Cap'n trusted *him*."

"Sounds like an interesting story."

"Oh, it is," she replied with a smile. "Maybe he'll tell you some day, if he decides he likes you."

A little while later, Loridgid and I carried heavy wooden platters of the steaming kashima fish dressed with tropical fruit and twilight potatoes up to the deck and into a crisp, clear Diuntyne. Glass globes filled with sap from the local shimmer palms hung from all the rigging, glistening a soft blue in waning Diun's silver light. Most of the crew congregated around the kegs of ale that lined the port side of the main deck. Tehennessey Blue and a trio of Mana'Olai had set themselves up along the starboard rail, and a set of stringed instruments accompanied the marii's flute in a jaunty tune. An altar of some sort had been constructed at the bow and decorated with tall candles and a variety of seashells. A hearty cheer shook the ship as Loridgid and I emerged from below.

I hesitated, awestruck—not by the pirates' gathering, but by the view beyond. We were truly in the middle of nowhere. Inky darkness stretched out around us seemingly to infinity, gently lit by the moon's glow and the speckle of stars that were beginning to peek through night's curtain. The wooden ship on which I stood was the only island in that blue-black void.

Ulysses clapped a friendly hand on my back. "Men stronger than you or I have lost themselves staring too long at that horizon." He snagged a chunk of potato from my platter and popped it in his mouth. "We've much better things to focus on this evening anyway."

The revelry lasted long into the night. The meal Loridgid and I—yes, mostly Lori—had prepared was delicious. The crew reminisced with stories of days gone by, of good deeds and bad, of friends and family lost to the rigors of life at sea. I was toasted more times than I can remember, though none of the pirates offered me anything stronger than a mug of water—likely at Lagash's command. We danced and sang dirty songs and played a loud game of dice I didn't quite understand. It was all good fun, and it's an evening I will never forget.

Through it all, Captain Lagash observed from the pilot box like some benevolent deity watching over his children. Lori delivered him a plate of fish and a mug of ale. No one else dared approach him, and he kept to himself. I thought I saw him smile a time or two, but it was too dark to tell for sure.

The very last thing I remember of that night was being dragged to the altar at the bow by one of the Mana'Olai, a short young woman named Elenwe who turned out to be Apo's baby sister. Her older brother stood behind it, dressed in all black, holding a ceremonial blade to the throat of a bound seabird. Apo chanted softly in a language I didn't recognize, though I heard my name mentioned a few times, and then he cleaved the bird's neck with one mighty blow. One of the other Mana'Olai caught the bird's blood in a small white bowl, which was then passed around to all of his fellows for a quick sip. The northerners kept a respectful distance at the other end of the ship.

"For your good fortune," Elenwe explained, licking a drop of crimson from her lower lip. "Works better with a goat, but one makes do with what one has."

I looked down at what remained of the blood with trepidation. "Do I have to drink that?"

"No," Apo replied. He snatched the bowl away and drained what was left of it. Slender streams of blood trickled out of the sides of his mouth and down his face. "That would turn your luck bad, and we can't have that!"

Most of the pirates passed out on deck. Tarik slept with his arm wrapped protectively around one of the empty kegs. Lori led me below and helped me get settled in an empty bunk. I fell asleep immediately, warm and content under that rough blanket and looking forward to what I was sure would be a string of grand adventures to come.

— CHAPTER TEN —

I was among the first to rise the next morning, which I suppose was not surprising. Rather than linger in bed surrounded by the snores and occasional sleep talking of the crew, I quickly tiptoed out and headed for the galley. I assumed I'd be expected to help Lori with breakfast. I was not mistaken; a bushel of onions awaited my attention.

Ulysses and Tehenessey Blue arrived together within moments of the cook declaring breakfast ready. She insisted I join them at the table even though I'd only gotten through a quarter of the onions. "You three are casting off early today," she explained. "We reached the coast just as the sun rose."

Breakfast was our leftovers from the night before, chopped up and mixed with eggs and cream to form a dense, delicious meal. Lori also left us a basket of toasted bread and a small block of yellow cheese.

"Either of you been to Fromaille?" Ulysses asked. I shook my head.

"Horrible place," Blue replied in between mouthfuls. "Nefazo have no manners to begin with, but the Fromaillan take the cake. Their taste in topiary is similarly ghastly."

The first mate smiled. Roderick snuck out of his sleeve to snag a bit from his plate. "With any luck we won't linger long enough for the locals to offend your delicate sensibilities."

A Mana'Olai man named Klee rowed us ashore in one of the longboats. I tried not to stare at the left side of his face. He'd lost the eye, the ear, and all the hair on that side of skull in a fire a decade before, but despite his disfigurement he remained one of the hardest working sailors aboard the *Black Yonnix*.

"Even prettier than yer ma, ain't I?" he asked when he inevitably caught me sneaking a look.

"Don't know," I replied. "She died before I met her."

Ulysses laughed so hard I worried he'd fall out of the boat. Blue punched him in the ribs.

"Sorry about that," Klee said warmly. "Didn't know. Always sticking my foot in what's left of my mouth, I am."

I nodded and forced a smile, unsure how else to respond. That made Ulysses laugh even harder.

We made landfall several agonizing minutes later. Being on solid ground again felt strange; my body instinctively tried to balance itself atop rhythmic waves that simply weren't there. Blue caught me and held my elbow until I could steady myself.

"Best of luck!" Klee called as he rowed away. "Hope you get both your book and your revenge, Vardallian!"

We waved goodbye to the departing mariner and then headed for the jungle. I glanced up at the angry clouds marring the sky, hoping we'd find cover before the heavens opened up. This, I gathered, was the storm Lagash and Rindge had been hoping to keep the ship away from by dropping us outside

Fromaille. A warm wind whipped up the rough sand at our feet and sent it whirling down the beach.

We'd spent most of the morning camped out in a thick stand of jungle vegetation just off a sharp corner on the main road to the walled city of Vastille, Count L'Vaillee's capital, alternately swatting insects or huddling tight to a large tree that mostly blocked the quick bursts of rain sporadically unleashed by the clouds above. The plan, as Ulysses had explained it, was to "borrow" transportation and a bit of currency from whatever suitable traveler passed our ambush point first. He and I watched the dirt road from the prickly bushes at the edge of the forest while Blue did his best to do nothing at all. I'm not sure which of the three of us found this task most miserable, but I know none of us particularly enjoyed it.

"You're sure this is the right road?" the marii hissed softly from his perch on a stump behind the first mate and me. "It's about time we got moving."

"Patience, friend Blue," Ulysses cooed. "I hear the clip-clop-clip-clop of opportunity approaching."

"Well, tell opportunity to hurry up," the marii growled. "It's delaying lunch."

A rickety black carriage with tinted windows came creaking slowly around the bend, pulled by a pair of large brown horses. The driver was an extremely elderly Nefazo in a rumpled gray uniform. His face was a mask of thick wrinkles and heavy lines, his eyes pale and sunken. There were no other obvious guards, and no one trailing on horseback. This was exactly the type of situation we'd been waiting for, despite the fact that we wouldn't be traveling in anything even remotely resembling luxury.

"Blue, a little musical interlude, if you please," Ulysses whispered. The two of us crept a few paces back from the road as Blue stepped up into the bushes to take our place. A soft, somber melody wove its way through the air, seeming to come from everywhere and yet from nowhere in particular, and definitely not from right in front of me—and yet the deft movement of the marii's fingers across his flute confirmed the song's source.

I directed my attention back to the road. The horses had stopped right in front of us. The ancient driver shook the reins, cracked the whip, and shouted obscenities, but the horses refused to start moving again. He climbed down from the carriage to take a closer look at his misbehaving animals.

"Now, the driver."

The music stopped abruptly. A streak of green and brown clothing and reddish fur flashed through the bushes and suddenly the tip of Blue's blade was pressed to the driver's throat.

"Let's consider your tongue for a moment," the marii hissed. "Use it and lose it."

Ulysses turned to me. "Our turn," he whispered. "I've got the far door, you take the near."

And then Ulysses was in motion, scrambling quickly to the other side of the carriage. I tripped through the bushes in my excitement; I'd never done anything like this before, and the fact that I was doing it with the crew of the *Black Yonnix* made it all the more thrilling. I told myself that hijacking a carriage was far different from robbing and murdering your lord's subjects while collecting taxes, and for the most part I believed that. The idea that someone within the carriage might respond violently never crossed my mind. Surely any passengers would be so shocked by our daring assault that they'd have no choice but to surrender immediately. All would go well, and we'd be on our way to Vastille to retrieve my stolen journal.

"Now!"

We opened the doors in perfect synchronization. Ulysses thrust his blade into the cabin, but before he could deliver whatever clever one-liner he'd prepared, the carriage's lone occupant stole his thunder.

"Is this a hold up?" she squealed. "How positively quaint!"

She was a long, lean woman, taller than either Ulysses or myself. She wore a simple blue dress and an old pair of simple brown boots. A white bonnet sat loosely atop a tangled mop of thick black hair. She was caked from head to toe in a thin layer of dust and dirt, but the grime wasn't enough to hide her delicate Nefazo features.

"What the rut did she just call us?" Blue snarled.

She poked her head out around my shoulder to get a better look at him. "And a marii! With his own sword! That's adorable!"

Blue glared at her. "Ulysses, kick this peasant to the curb and let's get a move on."

Her features darkened and she pursed her lips. "You mean you're not going to ransom me for a lot of money?"

Blue looked at her as if she'd suddenly sprouted a second head. The idea of anyone paying any amount of money for the return of this loud, dirty farmer's daughter was so laughable that even the marii couldn't put it into words.

"We'll be taking your valuables, then," Ulysses said. "Give 'em up."

She presented him with her grimy palms. "All I've got are the clothes on my back and my charming personality."

"We'll take the clothes," the marii said. "You can keep the rest."

"Blue!" Ulysses scolded. "We will not leave this woman out in the wilderness to catch cold." He turned once more to the Nefazo peasant. "But we will be taking the carriage."

She shook her head. "If you wanted a ride, all you had to do was ask. Hop in."

"Ulysses, please tell me this woman smells like the wrong end of a seedy pub," Blue muttered. "I'm not sure I can deal with a universe that permits a sober individual to act this way."

She kind of smelled like manure, but I kept that fact to myself. "Blue, she kind of acts like you," I replied before I could catch my tongue.

A cackle erupted from deep in the first mate's gut. "As much as I'm enjoying this banter, I'm afraid we'll have to take the carriage rather than ride along with you," Ulysses explained. "It's merely a matter of good form. If the locals learn that dangerous highwaymen such as ourselves are riding along with anyone and everyone they highjack, well...our very way of life will be significantly threatened."

She fixed him with an intense stare. "Then I assume you have a means of getting into Vastille?"

"Yes," Blue responded. "Right through the front gate. Without you."

She wagged her finger at Ulysses. "Uh-uh-uh. Gates are locked up tight, and nobody gets in without a damn good reason. Since somebody offed the Emperor, L'Vaillee and his ilk have been seeing assassins in every corner."

"Pileaus is dead?" Ulysses and I asked at the same time. We glanced at each other quickly, each taking stock of the other's interest. The Empire was a long way away, and nothing traveled easily across the wild Shoro—not even information.

"Psssh," came Blue's response from the front. "And I'm a Thilan whore."

"Likely not a very popular one at that, I would imagine," the woman snapped back, "but if you don't believe me, just ask around after I've gotten you into Vastille."

Ulysses lowered his sword. "You've got one of these 'damn good reasons?'"

She smiled mischievously. "I do."

"Ulysses!" Blue shouted. "You can't possibly believe this talking clump of dirt!"

"Actually," I said tentatively, "Count L'Vaillee is famous for his paranoia. Locking down the city is exactly the kind of thing he would do if he had reason to suspect any sort of danger."

"Who told you to speak?" Blue asked. "You just stand there and be a good, quiet little piece of chowderhead calligraphy."

"He's lived under the count's rule, Blue," Ulysses said. "He may have a point." The first mate returned his attention to the peasant woman. "So how is it you intend to get into Vastille?"

"It's best for us both if I don't say—and even if I told you, you wouldn't believe me," she said. "Suffice it to say that the guards will not hesitate to open the gate at my approach."

"What kind of game are you playing" Blue called. "We're trying to rob you! Understand? You should be cursing our mothers, not insisting that we let you help us."

"He's right," Ulysses prompted. "It's all a bit suspicious."

"Perhaps," she said, "but I'm no fan of L'Vaillee, and I'm willing to bet that whatever business you have in Vastille will not be pleasant for the count or, at the very least, a few of his associates."

"How do you know that?" the first mate asked.

She giggled. "Next time Lagash sends you ashore, you might want to leave those weapons on the *Black Yonnix*."

Ulysses sheathed his blade. "We could, but it would ruin the mystique—and having been witness to many a battle in which my contemporaries proved their mettle, I've always felt that any man capable of taking one of these probably deserves to keep it. We humbly accept your invitation to accompany you to Vastille."

"Rut the world, we do not!" Blue shouted.

"Yes, we do."

"Ulysses, something funny's going on. I don't like this."

"Look...we'll able to see the gate with plenty of time to spare. If she's wrong or lying, we kill her and the driver and run away and try again. Deal?"

"No."

"Then you walk."

"Fine. Where do you want me?"

"You watch the driver, Vardallian and I will watch the woman."

Ulysses and I climbed into the carriage and took a seat on either side of the woman, shutting the doors behind us. Now the manure smell was almost overwhelming. The carriage rocked as Blue and the driver took their seats behind the team of horses. The marii played a quick score on his flute to get the horses moving again, and we were off.

It wasn't long before the first mate shattered his window with the hilt of his blade. "Sorry," he said, "but it smells like a barn in here."

"That's the smell of an honest day's work," the woman replied.

"Really? I wouldn't know."

"I've done a lot of honest work," I said. "None of it smelled like you."

A beaming smile on his face, Ulysses reached across the carriage and clapped his hand on my knee. "Vardallian, I'm really starting to enjoy your company. You're picking up this roguish thing right quick!"

The woman smiled at Ulysses. "Perhaps you should give honest work a try some time, so you might be better able to recognize and avoid it in the future."

He smiled back. "So does the mysterious woman whose carriage we attempted to steal have a name?"

"She does."

"And it would be?"

"Mine, until such time as I decide to give it to you."

"I shall be counting the seconds. Do you spend much time in Fromaille? I'm told the gardens are lovely."

Thus went my first carriage ride: cramped, uncomfortable, peppered with banter, and punctuated with a smell I never want to encounter again. It was slow going down that muddy road. Every stone we hit sent vibrations up through the wheels, into the hold, and right through my bones. I vastly preferred traveling by ship. Still do.

The jungle scenery rolled slowly by. I tried to keep watch through the little window in the carriage's door, but my attention kept returning to the woman beside me. If there was one thing I knew back then, it was peasants. I'd been one my whole life. That woman was no peasant. Underneath that simple attire and the layer of dirt was a well-fed, well-educated, well-spoken person who'd never lived like I had in Brennik's Reach. I could tell from Ulysses's line of questioning that he recognized it as well, but she deftly evaded his inquiries with barbs and jokes that kept her true identity at least partially veiled.

I'll admit, Your Highness, that I was a bit smitten. I'd met maybe three Nefazo women in my time. My neighbors had all been fair-skinned northerners with round, broad features. The woman's olive skin and dark hair made her all the more mysterious and exotic. I tried and mostly failed to ignore the weight of her thigh against mine in the cramped carriage.

The narrow road merged into a wider highway as we emerged from the jungle later that afternoon. Sun shone down on the weary travelers who'd plodded onward through the rain. Most traveled on foot, pushing carts or laden with heavy packs. Though Vastille teemed with wealth, the population supporting it clearly did not. These were undeniably my people—peasants. I'll never forget the jealousy on one older woman's face as our carriage trundled past.

"I can see the city," Blue called from the driver's bench. "It's still a dump."

I swung my door open and stood to crane my neck up and over the top of the carriage. The road on which we traveled led up a steep hill to a sharp bluff overlooking the ocean. The entirety of that bluff was overwhelmed by the Nefazo city of Vastille, most of which was hidden by the massive brick and mortar wall that surrounded it. A pair of massive iron doors protected the one obvious entrance. The only structures visible above the battlements were a pair of spiraling parapets right on the cliff edge, which were attached to an unseen keep—Count L'Vaillee's residence.

"A bit bigger than home, eh?" Ulysses said.

I nodded as I pulled myself back inside and shut the door. "I didn't know people could build things that huge."

The first mate chuckled. "Don't be too impressed. They build bigger."

"And better," the woman added. "The most impressive thing about Vastille is that it has yet to collapse under the weight of its own corruption."

"What do you mean?" I asked.

Blue answered. "She means that you're damn lucky you don't have a cent to your name, because if you did, the crooks that live here would find a way to talk you out of it within ten seconds of your arrival. The business of the Nefazo, however, is business—and if the local magistrate catches you with those empty pockets, out you go."

"These particular Nefazo, yes," she said. "Not all of us are greedy monsters."

"I've always heard good things about the previous count," I said. "He helped my family and neighbors found Brennik's Reach."

The woman turned and studied me with her dark, inquisitive eyes. I found myself falling headfirst into her gaze as she spoke. "Yes," she said warmly. "Count Jetain was much more... gracious ruler than Count Antoine."

"Vastille has always been a cut-throat town," Blue added. "The change in ownership meant a few things that used to hide in the shadows can now operate in the daylight. Also, your new best friend was right: the gate's locked up tight."

"How many guards?" Ulysses asked.

"Four on the ground, maybe half a dozen archers atop the wall."

"A good warm up, then, if it comes to that."

The marii snorted.

"The exercise would do you good, my friend."

"You just remember that the first throat you cut is the one sitting beside you."

This whole business had me a bit nervous. "And what do I do?"

"Hmm," Ulysses murmured, scratching his chin. "Hide, or run as fast as you can. Whichever seems best."

"Both seem dumb," the woman interjected. "I'll get us through the gate." She patted my knee reassuringly, a gesture which sent my heart leaping up into my throat.

Their lack of common dress and equipment made them look more like mercenaries than an organized military unit, but the guards were quick to surround the carriage when it pulled into their checkpoint in front of the gate. I could almost feel the archers taking aim from the battlements.

The leader approached the shattered window on Ulysses' side of the carriage. His suspicious eyes quickly took in the whole scene, and though I'm sure he wanted to ask a more specific question regarding how such a diverse group had come to his particular gate, he stuck to the script. "What's your business in Vastille?"

The woman removed a folded piece of crisp white parchment from a pocket by her thigh and handed it to the officer. "This should suffice."

He unfolded it, scanned it quickly, glanced suspiciously back into the carriage, and read it again. Obviously, he couldn't believe what was written on the parchment, and he was searching for any excuse to justify his doubts. Had I a weapon, my hand would've crept toward it. I wondered if my training with Ogrid had made me fast enough to outrun an arrow.

The woman, to her credit, fixed the guard with a steely stare the likes of which I'd seldom seen. If it was all an act, she did an excellent job of selling herself as annoyed without seeming desperate or attempting to push the issue. She had the look of someone who'd done this before, who'd suffered through the guards' disbelief and delays but always gotten through the checkpoint.

Ulysses gazed nonchalantly at a point beyond the officer. His soft smile was polite and content, making him seem willing to help the guard with any problem he might need addressed. After all, the man was only doing his job, and there was no reason to get snippy with him if he insisted on doing it correctly.

But none of that mattered, because the guard wasn't particularly interested in either of them. He was interested in the fidgety young man on the opposite side of the carriage who wasn't sure where to look or what to do with his hands.

"Boy," the guard said. "What is your party's business in Vastille?"

"Well, you see," Ulysses interjected. "We're—"

"I asked the boy."

I blurted out the first thing that popped into my mind, and luckily, it was something we could probably fake. "We're entertainers."

"Entertainers?"

"Yes," I stuttered. "We are but humble minstrels in search of unique tales to tell and new audiences to entertain."

Tehenessey Blue emphasized my response with a quick scale on his flute.

Luckily for me, one of the biggest days on the Nefazo calendar was right around the corner. "We're here for the S'espri Moiraube."

I could see the guard's suspicion melting away, but I hadn't won yet. "Who sent for you?" he asked.

Again, I blurted out the first thing that popped into my head. "The Lord Rocher." The name was like acid on my tongue.

He glanced at the parchment one more time, then he handed it back to the woman. "Enjoy your stay in Vastille." He whistled toward the battlements, and the two massive doors creaked apart.

"How did you know Rocher's signature and personal seal were on this letter?" the woman whispered as the carriage began to move.

I couldn't find the words to tell her that I hadn't known. There was only one obvious place I could think of where she could've acquired such a document, and that was from the Lord Rocher himself. It sickened me to think that she might somehow be in league with that pig. Had there been space, I would've shifted away from her.

"He can read minds," Ulysses said.

She fixed him with a doubtful glance.

"You think we keep him around for his good looks?"

I couldn't look at her, let alone add anything to the conversation. I wasn't sure whether I wanted to strike her or jump out of the carriage and run.

"Just how did you come into possession of such a document?" Blue asked from his perch beside the driver.

"I stole it."

That made me feel a little better, but I was still suspicious. I looked up at her for a further explanation.

"I needed a way to travel across L'Vaillee's holdings without interference. Rocher takes care of much of the Count's dirty work. His approval is more likely to get one through a suspicious situation than that of his master, whose signature would be the more obvious one to forge. We didn't get through that checkpoint because the guards believed the boy's story; we got through because that story was exactly the kind of thing someone would make up as a cover for one of Rocher's little tasks."

The gate closed behind us with a heavy *thunk*. Blue directed the driver to turn the corner onto a side street a few blocks further into Vastille. When the carriage stopped, Tehenessey Blue climbed down and stuck his face in the shattered window by Ulysses.

"Time to go."

Ulysses tipped his hat to the woman. "I thank you for the ride, madam, and for your assistance with the guards, but I fear this is where we part ways."

"Our farewell needn't be so soon," she responded. "I'm sure there are other ways we might assist each other."

"I don't doubt it, but we've an appointment to keep and much to do. Rest assured that we will be causing plenty of trouble for the good count, a task we must begin forthwith."

He opened his door and climbed out, and I did the same.

"Good luck then, noble pirates," she replied, her tone tinged with a note of disappointment. "Perhaps we'll meet again."

And then the carriage was off. I strolled over to Ulysses and Blue and joined them in watching it go.

"Are you sure we don't need her help?" I asked.

Ulysses shook his head. "No, that one's playing games we can only guess the rules of. Now come; Davanon's contact is waiting for us."

— CHAPTER ELEVEN —

I had always pictured Vastille as a vibrant, lively city, but my imagination didn't correspond to the reality I now faced. "Where is everyone?" I asked as we sauntered down the middle of the empty cobblestone street.

"Sitting on their fat asses in their seal skin chairs," Blue replied. "Snacking on fie liver pate and washing it down with the finest Uddani wine while their servants suck the fungus from between their lordly toes."

"I don't understand," I said.

Blue rolled his eyes. "The Nefazo who live here do not have to work. They do not have to clean, they do not have to cook, they do not have to wash their own hair. They have people to do all that for them. Vastille is not a city for people who have to work hard—except for the servants, of course."

"Jealous?" Ulysses prodded.

"A bit."

The city's architecture didn't echo Blue's description of the opulence of its inhabitants. What Grandfather and I had saved would've barely purchased a room for the evening in such a place. The buildings were all clean and straight and generally in very good condition, but they were all made of the same brown brick and red mortar, with brown clay shingles on the roofs, and they were all only two stories high. Some of them, however, enveloped whole city blocks.

"No residence is to be outwardly grander than the count's," Blue explained, "and L'Vaillee's citadel is to be the only structure visible from the outside of the wall."

"Was that the rule under the old count?"

He nodded. "It's been that way under as many counts as people can remember. Don't let their exteriors fool you, though: the interiors of these buildings are quite luxurious, and some of them extend four or five stories down into the earth."

The mirrored glass in all the windows kept me from peering inside to confirm the marii's description. "How do you know so much about this place?"

"Ha!" Ulysses cackled. "Our friend Blue here was once some rich old woman's pet!"

The marii stopped in his tracks and glared at the first mate angrily. "What have I told you about that?"

Ulysses's cocky grin spread into an ear-to-ear smile. "You told me that you spent four years living here as some senile old bat's little plaything."

"No. I told you that if you ever, ever brought that up again I'd do to you what I did to Lady Gershon's son."

Ulysses threw up his hands and feigned innocence. "My lips are sealed."

I was a bit confused. "Wait...you did what?"

"Same goes for you!" Blue shouted. "Especially for you! I am above defending my choices to some...peasant."

"He used to live in a tree," Ulysses explained. "It seemed like a good idea at the time."

"Shut it!"

"Fine, we'll stop. Let's get going before we draw too much attention to ourselves," Ulysses said. Blue stormed past us, intent on leading the way. When the coast seemed clear, the first mate leaned in close to me and whispered a further explanation. "She thought he was a dog. From what I hear, the whole affair was quite a show."

"Stop whispering behind my back!"

We took a left at the next intersection. Blue finally stopped another two streets down, in front of a small building that occupied a tiny corner of a block otherwise engulfed by another structure. Its footprint was maybe fifteen feet on each side. This was where we were to meet Nyomi, Davanon's contact. Little did I know she and Blue also had a history.

"Bit smaller than I expected," said Ulysses.

Blue shrugged. "She's happy here, even though she could call in a few favors and easily move into something bigger."

"You don't approve?" I asked.

"Not at all," he said, drawing out every word to emphasize his point.

The door behind him creaked slowly open. A young woman stepped into the street, short and thin as a rail, with thin pink lips and piercing green eyes framed by sharp cheekbones. Her hair tumbled to her waist in impossibly tight ringlets that started brown and became blond at the ends, a stark contrast to her pale skin. She wore a tight-fitting brown dress flecked with yellow paisleys, and her feet were bare.

"Tehenessey Blue." Her voice was soft as a whisper, yet it easily carried to my ears. "You remain as spoiled as the day I first saw you on the end of Lady Gershon's leash."

Ulysses and I couldn't help laughing. The woman's words left Blue utterly stunned and likely blushing somewhere under all that fur.

"Your friends, at least, have a healthy sense of humor," she said wryly. "Care to introduce us?"

"I am Ulysses," the first mate said with a deep bow. "And this is Kensey Vardallian." I nodded and smiled meekly. "And we thank you in advance for your hospitality and your assistance," the pirate added.

She raised one thin eyebrow. "I'm sure you do. My name is Nyomi. It would be best if we adjourn to the dining room, away from the prying eyes of my neighbors."

Blue's eyes lit up like he'd just been handed the keys to the local treasury. "Yes, let's. An excellent idea!"

Nyomi led the way inside with Blue nipping excitedly at her heels. Ulysses shrugged and followed. "No disrespect to Lori's cooking, but when one lives on a boat, one does not reject a free meal."

I closed the door behind me as I stepped into the small sitting room. Three of the four walls were covered floor to ceiling with bookshelves full of all manner of old, ragged looking texts. The only empty wall, the one to my right, was taken up almost entirely by a large bay window cloaked with thick navy curtains. Four candles lit the room from a chandelier suspended above a small round table and a pair of thickly cushioned chairs. The only item on the table was a rather large and ominous looking crystal ball. In front of me, the others were descending a narrow set of stairs.

"How's the fortune telling business?" Ulysses asked.

"Thriving," Nyomi replied. "How else could I afford such a palace?"

Perhaps she was being sarcastic, but I didn't detect that tone in her voice. I sure didn't think her house was anything special; it was small, it was cramped, and it was old. Truth be told, I was a bit disappointed.

"I was under the impression you were involved in some, ah, secretive business," Ulysses said.

"Good to know Davanon's mouth is still as big as his ego."

The stairs creaked as I descended through a beaded curtain to the dining room. The walls were a deep green above even greener wainscoting. The massive table dominated the space, seemingly grown from the hardwood floor on a thick, twisting stump. Thin brown rings spiraled outward from the center of the glistening mahogany tabletop. Four chairs lined in green cushions surrounded the table. Each corresponded to a large bowl of steaming stew, a thick spoon, and an empty wine flute.

"Seat yourselves wherever you please," Nyomi instructed. "I'll be back with the wine."

As our host descended the next flight of stairs, Blue rushed toward the table. His big black nose twitched with anticipation. "Fie liver in a sh'rung u'untu broth with basil and sweet potatoes—the type of delicacy only a mah'saiid could create."

I turned to Ulysses. "She's mah'saiid?"

The first mate nodded. "Aye, couldn't you tell? The hair, the eyes, the...bearing. Just like Davanon."

That gave me pause. I'd heard of the mah'saiid, who'd been exiled from the Dreaming Lands for losing their immortality in an accident, but like the marii and the shuen, my sheltered upbringing had kept me from ever meeting one in the flesh.

Somehow, I'd expected the differences between mah'saiid like Davanon and Nyomi, and lij like myself and Ulysses to be more pronounced. Our host seemed like just another person, air of mystery or not.

"How exactly does this get us into the palace?" I asked.

"Don't know yet," Ulysses replied. "Our ship's knowledgeable, well-connected engineer says his associate here can find us a means of entry. I'm inclined to believe him until I see otherwise."

Blue had already taken a seat. "Don't just stand there gawking! If you don't eat it while it's hot, it congeals! Show some class!"

Ulysses walked around the marii and claimed the chair on the opposite side of the table. "Friend Blue, you have more than enough class for the entire crew."

"A fact I am immediately reminded of every morning I wake up on that awful barge."

Nyomi returned just as I took the seat to Blue's right. She carried two long bottles made of deep blue glass that shimmered in the light cast by the candles in the wall sconces. One was open and almost empty, the other still corked.

"That Goddess-forsaken vessel is not a place in which any sane person should want to awaken," Nyomi said. She emptied the first bottle into glasses for Blue and Ulysses. The cork on the second bottle twisted a bit, then popped up and out and into her waiting hand.

I was impressed by her little trick, but Ulysses wasn't. He cut me off before I could express my surprise. "And just what, pray tell, do you find offensive about our ship? I do hope it's something a bit more relevant than Blue's hatred of its color scheme."

Nyomi took my glass and her own and began to pour from the new bottle. "It's tainted by the violence involved in its construction. The stench of such a blatant disregard for life lingers in its sails. Pileaus could not have christened your vessel more appropriately."

I had no clue what she was talking about. If Ulysses and Blue understood, they didn't show it.

"But it's bad form to insult the property of one's guests, whether the insult is warranted or not. Eat, and we'll discuss your means of entry into L'Vaillee's citadel."

The wine was extremely good and the soup even better. The broth was thick and warm, the meat and vegetables fresh and cooked just right—exactly the sort of meal one needs after a morning spent hiding in a rainy jungle and an afternoon crammed into a tiny carriage. The first mate's pet snake stuck his little head out through the cuff of the pirate's sleeve to sample the amazing aromas with his tongue. Blue ate quickly and finished off his serving before Ulysses and I were even halfway through our own. Nyomi disappeared down the stairs and returned with another bowl for him.

I wanted more than anything to ask about Pileaus, but I couldn't find the words. He'd always been a bogeyman of sorts for me, a terrible tyrant my grandfather used as both a crutch and a curse. He hated the man for driving him south and taking away his faith…and yet, there were moments of reminiscence where his tone would soften and he'd speak of the emperor as one would a long lost friend. Pileaus was my grandfather's hated enemy, but that hatred was tempered with an undercurrent of respect I wasn't mature enough to understand.

His bowl empty, Ulysses finally broke the ice. "We thank you for the fine meal and your hospitality. Before we get to the business at hand, there's the matter of a little rumor we'd like to verify—"

"Ugh, Ulysses!" Blue muttered, rolling his eyes. "Pileaus is not dead. Nothing short of an entire Omman regiment could kill that old bastard, and even then they'd have to chop him into more pieces than—"

"It's true," Nyomi said calmly. She daintily wiped her mouth with her napkin before continuing. "If my Brotherhood sources are to be believed, that's essentially what it took, but without the Omman regiment."

That was it, then. Apologies, Your Highness, but I was glad that my grandfather's greatest demon had finally fallen. Still, I felt a newfound pang of guilt that he hadn't lived to hear tell of it.

Ulysses shifted uncomfortably in his seat. I wondered if he were experiencing similar thoughts; he wasn't much older than me, and the elder pirates onboard the *Black Yonnix*, the Emperor's former flagship, surely must've told stories about Pileaus and the north. "Have you tried to get word to Davanon?" he asked.

"I haven't, and what I just told you was said against my better judgment. Without Pileaus, the north is an even bigger mess than it was with him pulling the strings. If Lagash rushes back up there out of some foolish attempt to restore his name, it'll be your heads on a platter."

Before Ulysses could protest, Tehenessey Blue interjected, "A discussion for another place and another time. At the moment, I'm most interested in how you're going to get us into L'Vaillee's palace."

Nyomi took a deep breath and straightened her dress. "It's simple, really. Count L'Vaillee is going to leave his front door wide open."

"And why would he want to do that?"

The pieces clicked together in my mind. "The S'espri Moiraube. It's two days away."

"There's that word again," Ulysses muttered. "I take it to be a party of some sort?"

"It's not just *a* party," Blue replied. "It's *the* party. The S'espri Moiraube is the most hedonistic, outrageous, disgusting date on the Nefazo social calendar—but I fail to see how this helps us."

"In years past, L'Vaillee has opened the doors of his palace to the inhabitants of Vastille, so that he might better show off his decadent home," Nyomi explained.

"In years past, L'Vaillee didn't lock the front gate because he thinks some crazy rutter is going around killing nobles," Blue spat.

Nyomi parted her lips in a small smile. "This is the part where I become useful. You see, all of L'Vaillee's paranoia stems from the suspected presence of one man."

"So we remove this man in a very public way and L'Vaillee opens the front gates," Ulysses said thoughtfully, stroking his chin. "Easy enough—so easy, in fact, that even the most bumbling of local garrisons, such as that at young Mr. Vardallian's Brennik's Reach, should be able to do the deed. No offense."

"This man is very good at concealing himself, and he's drafted others into his service," said Nyomi.

"A rutting bard," Blue cursed. "You're sending us after a rutting bard."

I'm sure I don't need to tell Your Highness that we weren't talking about your run-of-the-mill minstrel. The bards can do things with their magic that make Tehenessey Blue's songs look like parlor tricks. Nowadays, I hear they're quite useful against the Fae, but back then they were people to be avoided. Few ever know what their guild is up to, but in my experience, it's never anything good.

"Old sailors have been telling me not to piss off the guild since I learned how to walk," Ulysses said, stretching his arms out over his head. "You mess with one of 'em, you mess with all of 'em."

Nyomi ignored him. "Salg Hahn has taken up residence among Vastille's destitute. The homeless congregate in a section of the city a dozen blocks northeast of here called the Hollow. It's a place where the battlements create a large nook as they trace the cliffs along the ocean. The homeless are allowed to stay there because it's the one area in the city L'Vaillee can't catch a glimpse of through one of his windows. Out of sight, out of mind. Anyone caught outside of the Hollow after curfew—bard or not—will immediately be expelled from the city. Luckily, there've been rumors of hauntings in Vastille lately..."

Ulysses stifled a yawn and nodded thoughtfully. "Sounds like fun—and like it might work."

Scaring a bunch of poor people out of the only safe place they could sleep didn't sound like a nice thing to do, but I kept my mouth shut.

Across the table from me, Blue also yawned. "Ghosts are very good for business, aren't they?"

Nyomi smiled conspiratorially. "Rumors of the undead wandering the streets do tend to make people aware of their own mortality. It's the questions they have about that mortality that brings them to my doorstep."

I thought I heard someone snoring. To my left, Ulysses was fast asleep. Roderick crawled out of his sleeve to sit upon his lap and keep watch over the room.

Blue yawned again. "Nyomi, you're still a manipulative…"

And then he was out too.

The seer stood and turned to me. "Well then, I guess it's just the two of us. Dessert will be served on the patio. Follow me."

Nyomi stood and strolled down the stairs, flashing me a warm smile as she disappeared.

For a split second, I panicked. Without Ulysses and Blue I was alone and exposed. If Nyomi had evil intentions for me, I would have to face them on my own.

But reason soon overcame my fear. If she'd wanted to harm us, she would've spiked my wine too. She'd left me awake for a reason.

A few anxious, indecisive moments later, my curiosity about that reason propelled me to follow her.

— CHAPTER TWELVE —

I didn't remember seeing a patio attached to Nyomi's house. I supposed there could've been one hidden in the back, offering a grand view of the giant building enveloping the mah'saiid's home. In any case, further downstairs didn't seem to be the proper direction to go if one were looking to find a patio.

The next level down was a kitchen with a white tile floor. Cabinets lined the whitewashed walls, and to my right was a fireplace where a large iron pot of what I assumed to be the fie liver soup was still simmering. There was also a wine rack packed tight with expensive looking bottles of various shapes, sizes, and colors, and a large metal basin with a spigot for running water. I could hear Nyomi's footsteps heading farther and farther away, so although I wanted to explore, I didn't linger.

Next was a purple guest bedroom with two small beds heaped high with fluffy blankets opposite a large mirror. Bookshelves covered the far wall, lined with volumes that appeared to be much newer than those in the first floor sitting room. I continued down into the master bedroom. The white space was surprisingly spare; there was a large bed in the center, but the walls were bare save for a few small sconces, and there didn't appear to be another set of stairs. Nyomi had obviously continued downward. I wondered how far down into the earth her home went, how much it had cost to tunnel so far down—and how many of these Vastillian burrows had collapsed in on themselves.

"Dessert's going to melt!" Nyomi called, her voice echoing up the nearby stairwell.

I hesitated. This next set of stairs was different. Rather than descending in a straight shot, this one spiraled down around a central post. Each tread was a slightly different size and shape. Though it all appeared to be made of sturdy metal, I found its organic form odd and sort of off-putting. It almost looked like it had been grown in place. A cool breeze carried the salty scent of the ocean up through the into the master bedroom.

"Don't be afraid," Nyomi called. "The view is really quite spectacular."

I couldn't imagine what the view could be of. Did mah'saiid enjoy staring whimsically at walls of dirt and stone? I didn't understand. Every nerve in my body screamed at me to run back up the stairs and wait for Blue and Ulysses to wake up.

But as usual, my curiosity got the best of me.

I carefully made my way down the narrow, twisting staircase. A few of the smaller treads creaked or flexed under my weight. The floor below appeared to be sturdy brick. Nyomi sat in a black iron chair beside a little round table of the same material, delicately eating chocolate mousse from a small glass bowl. Thin iron rails enclosed the abrupt perimeter, the only barrier between the patio and the sky. She hadn't been lying about the view; we were suspended above the ocean to the north of Vastille, a good ten stories higher than the top floor of L'Vaillee's citadel. The city I'd previously been so impressed with looked so small.

I stopped halfway down the stairs, stunned. "What manner of sorcery is this?" I asked.

Nyomi smiled. "Just the proper charms and related incantations activated in the proper order. Not too difficult to achieve, though there is a good chance of blowing something up if you don't do it correctly." She indicated a second bowl of mousse and the other chair. "It's beginning to melt."

I took a seat and tried a spoonful. That mousse was even better than the soup. Though I had my worries and doubts about what my future with the crew of the *Black Yonnix* held, I was overjoyed that at the very least my adventures had brought me so many excellent meals.

"Now that you've seen my little hideout, there are two things I ask: don't fall off, and try not to go blabbing about it to all your friends. The good count would probably be a bit jealous. Even Tehennessey Blue hasn't been here."

I swirled a delicious chocolatey mouthful around my tongue. "How do you know Blue so well?"

"Business. He convinced Lady Gershon to come in for a reading once a week, and I taught him how to add a little something extra to that flute he plays. Things worked out well for the both of us...until Lady Gershon's son decided the family dog needed to be fixed so he wouldn't have to deal with any puppies. The boy was a bit dimwitted to begin with, but Blue played that flute so fast and so furiously that he broke something in the kid's mind. Now he walks around like some sort of zombie, mumbling gibberish and drooling all over himself. Blue took off before Lady Gershon could get the authorities. They say she doesn't know he did it, that she misses him obsessively, and that she wanders the streets at night looking for him. Kind of sad, but kind of cute."

My mousse was almost gone. "So how did he end up on the *Black Yonnix?*"

"He panicked and came to me. My, er...husband is a member of the crew."

Surprisingly, it didn't take me long to put two and two together. "Davanon?"

She nodded. "Unfortunately."

"But...if you don't like your husband, why did you send Blue to him? And why are you helping us now?"

"I never said I didn't like Davanon—or that I don't love him. I hate the things he's done. Some actions, no matter how well intentioned, just cannot be excused."

She changed the subject before I could press further. "Now that you've learned a little about me, it's only fair that you tell me a few things about yourself."

I found it hard to believe that such an interesting person would be curious about a simple peasant like me. "What would you like to know?"

She tapped her spoon against her tongue.

"For starters, show me the rune that bastard Thranax drew on your chest."

I almost choked on my last bite of mousse. I put the empty bowl and the spoon back down on the table. "How did you know about that?"

"How did I know that I'd need three bowls of soup?"

I felt stupid. "You're a fortune teller. You looked into the future."

She shook her head and laughed softly. "I can't tell someone's future unless I'm in their presence. And I refuse to look into my own destiny. I got a message from Davanon."

That made me feel even dumber, and I blushed. I pulled up the tunic the pirates had given me to hide the rune. Nyomi leaned across the table for a closer look.

"Thranax is a different breed," she explained as she traced the green curves with her fingertip. "They say he came from the north, that he's an outcast of some sort...but no one knows how such a one came to be in control of his own taishu. The shuen are decidedly unforgiving about such things. His people are fiercely loyal to him, and yet other taishus avoid him like he carries a plague, and none of them will say why. I suspect he's gotten himself into something he shouldn't have."

I cared a lot less about Thranax's fate than I did about my own. "Davanon thought I should be tossed overboard."

Nyomi giggled. "Good to see he hasn't changed."

"If you don't mind my asking, what was it that drove the two of you apart?"

She didn't visibly flinch or even look up at me, but something in her demeanor darkened. "Sail aboard the *Black Yonnix* long enough and you might find out." Her fingertip reached the end of the rune and she leaned back to her side of the table. "I have no idea what it means or what it does. It's not just one symbol; it's a mixture of obscure runes from the old world, many of which limit or cancel each other, and most of which have been forbidden. I suspect he's hidden the real charm somewhere in that mess of contradictions. A masterful job, really."

My heart sank a bit. Nyomi seemed so talented, so mysteriously intelligent. If she couldn't figure out what Thranax had done, who could?

"The old world?" I asked. I had a good sense of what her answer would be, but I had to know for sure.

She tapped a finger to her lips, apparently considering how much to say. "The Dreaming Lands."

Even back in those days, before the bastards had started laying waste to every settlement they could find, the Fae were considered taboo. A chill ran up my spine.

"Of course, there are resources I have yet to exhaust," she said conspiratorially. "If you'll allow me to use them."

"What would those be?"

"With your permission, I could peer into your future to see if I can catch that rune in action. I never peer into someone's possible destinies without their consent."

"Oh...why? Does it hurt?"

She chuckled softly. "Not in the slightest. It merely seems the polite thing to do. Your future is yours, and treating it otherwise would be quite the invasion of your privacy, don't you think?"

"I suppose so. If you think it will help, please do it," I replied. "But won't you have to go all the way back upstairs to get your crystal ball?"

This time she unleashed a sharp cackle that made me jump back in my chair. "Kensey Vardallian, you are just too cute," she said with a sincere smile. "It's a shame that won't get you very far in life. The crystal ball's just for show; my clientele finds my prognostications that much more believable when I utilize a prop or two. Now sit still, and Nyomi will take a look at your tomorrows."

Sitting still had always been an easy thing for me to do. I've never felt compelled to twitch or gaze disinterestedly around the room—but under Nyomi's intense scrutiny, I wanted to be anywhere but in that chair. There was something extremely unsettling about the way her sharp green eyes looked at me and through me and around me all at once, and all without blinking. The few seconds she spent examining me felt like a few hours.

"That's odd," she said.

"What do you see?" I asked.

She hesitated, apparently at a loss for words. "Nothing. I see...nothing. Where I should see bright rays of swirling possibilities, I see...absolutely nothing..."

I didn't have the slightest idea what any of that meant, but I didn't like it. "Is it something Thranax did?"

She seemed genuinely unsettled. "I...no, that's...that's not something someone should be able to do. You're sure you're not dead?"

"Pretty sure."

She tapped her lip again. I could see her mind spinning as she tried to get a grasp on the situation. I broke the silence a few moments later.

"Is there anything we can do about it?"

"There are a few others I can confer with, but that will take time. For now I suggest you join your companions in getting a bit of rest. You'll need your wits about you if you're to clear the vagrants out of the Hollow. You can use the guest bedroom."

I knew I wasn't going to get any more out of her; she genuinely had nothing else to give. I took one last look at the magnificent view, then I stood and headed for the stairs, a shuen-cursed man without a future.

— CHAPTER THIRTEEN —

The four hours of sleep I got on Nyomi's guest bed were the most restful I've ever had. I suspect there may have been a little something extra in the mousse, but I never asked.

Ulysses and Tehenessey Blue were already awake when Nyomi roused me from my peaceful slumber with promises of adventure. I joined them all at the dining room table. Nyomi poured me a mug of steaming coffee and Ulysses pushed a plate of scones my way.

"So how many people usually reside in this Hollow?" Ulysses asked.

"Most of the year, maybe fifteen to twenty," Nyomi explained. "Around the time of the S'espri Moiraube, that number becomes three or four dozen."

"I thought the gates had been locked down for the past few weeks," I said as I picked out a scone. They smelled of raspberry and cinnamon.

"That is of little consequence," she replied. "Most of the vagrants move in several months in advance of the holiday."

"When one is homeless, one learns quickly how to acquire a free meal," Blue added in between bites of scone.

"Yes," Ulysses said. "I imagine one would learn how to wag one's tail in an adorable manner quite quickly under such circumstances."

Blue shot him a look that would've shredded the sails on the *Black Yonnix*. "Spend a few years sleeping in a tree and we'll see how far you're willing to go change your station."

Nyomi extended her pale right arm over the table and flicked her wrist. A piece of yellowed, rolled up parchment appeared in her hand. "You'll need this." She handed it to the marii.

Blue unrolled the document and studied it for a few moments, his brow creased in confusion. I peered at it over his shoulder but couldn't make any sense of the jagged scribbles. "I've never seen such a melody," the marii said, his voice tinged with worry. "What exactly does it do?"

"The Hollow has seen its share of desperate men over the years," Nyomi said sadly. "Desperate men have been known to commit horrible crimes, and such acts leave an indelible mark upon the World Song."

Blue pursed his lips. "The notes are so low. No lij can hear this." His eyes continued to scour the parchment. "It doesn't look safe."

"Nothing that song summons can harm the living if you stay true to the melody," Nyomi explained. "Missing a note, however, would be a very bad thing."

That caught Blue's attention. "My playing is perfect," he growled.

"I know. There aren't many I would trust with that score."

Ulysses leaned back in his chair and took a quick swig of his coffee. "So all there is for me to do is watch our furry friend's back, then?"

Nyomi shook her head. "You and Vardallian go into the Hollow first and soften up the locals a bit. It's likely the bard won't be waiting out in the open. L'Vaillee's men have been through the Hollow three times, and they've yet to find him. You'll have to draw him out. Tell a few ghost stories to get everybody in the mood, and when Blue's song reaches its crescendo, be the first to announce that those stories are coming to life."

"Won't Blue's playing be enough?" Ulysses asked. "You spoke of that song as if it could drop the whole of Vastille into the ocean."

"Properly unleashed, it just might," she said, "but the version I've given our furry friend is a bit...restrained. We want to cause trouble in the Hollow, but we don't want to frighten the city into doing something rash, like canceling the Feast. Because of this restraint, some of the Hollow's hardier souls might require further persuasion."

"You do realize that this won't work on a bard," Blue continued. "He'll recognize what's happening and he'll act to counter it."

"And I'll carve his heart out of his chest," Ulysses said. "Problem solved."

"If you can't scare him out into the open where the guards can catch him, yes," Nyomi said. "Though you may find a bit of subtlety to be more effective than a blade."

"What do I do?" I asked sheepishly. Attacking the carriage outside of Fromaille had been exciting, but I hoped I'd get to do something even more thrilling in the Hollow.

"Sit here and keep Nyomi company," Blue said. "Maybe help her wash the dishes."

"Vardallian comes with us," Ulysses said. "I'll need someone to watch my back."

"A task I've proven to be very capable of completing," Blue responded. He sounded somewhat insulted.

"This is true, and I thank you for your past and future diligence, but your job tonight is to make that song do its thing. You're going to find a safe place to play, somewhere you can't be interrupted without a considerable amount of effort, and you're going to stay there. Kensey comes with me."

"Fine," Blue said, "but don't be surprised if he's the reason you get run through rather than the reason you don't."

"I'm terrible in a fight," I blurted out, suddenly worried that I'd be asked to accomplish more than I was capable of. "I tried to learn, but...I can't do it."

"See?" the marii said matter-of-factly, as if my admission settled the argument in his favor.

"You'll both live through the evening," Nyomi said. I wasn't sure whether the seer knew that for a fact or if she was just trying to placate the marii. Neither would've surprised me.

"Although I enjoy stimulating conversation with individuals as interesting and intelligent as yourselves, I suggest we embark posthaste on the day's adventure," Ulysses said.

"Not so fast," Nyomi interjected. "I have a few things for you before you depart—and you're not wandering the streets of Vastille again with those gaudy swords hanging out for everyone to see."

She disappeared down the staircase. Ulysses loosened his sheath from his belt and plunked his weapon on the table. He noticed my surprise.

"I have plenty more," he said with a smile. He pulled open one side of his big red coat to reveal a pair of dangerous looking long knives.

I realized then that this was the first time Nyomi had left the three of us alone—and awake—since our arrival. A quick discussion seemed in order. "Did you two know Nyomi drugged your food?" I asked softly.

"I rather expected she would," Blue replied as he deposited his own blade beside the first mate's. "Nyomi's quite famous for her secret ingredients."

Ulysses and I frowned at each other in confusion. "Then why did you let us eat it?" the first mate asked.

"Because if we hadn't, she would've found another less comfortable means of putting us out of commission," Blue explained haughtily, as if I should've already known the answer to my question. "That's something for which she's even more famous."

"What did she think of your new tattoo?" Ulysses asked.

I shrugged. "She doesn't know what it is, but she says it's old and complicated."

Blue snorted. "She's an expert on both topics, yes."

"Show our host some respect," Ulysses snapped. "She fed us a delicious meal, blessed us with refreshing slumber...and now she's going to arm us!"

I wondered what sort of weapons a mah'saiid kept on hand. Something magical, I was sure. Perhaps a flaming sword? A mace made of pure light? Or maybe a simple wooden staff that blessed the wielder with a few seconds of clairvoyance? Whatever it was, I knew it would be an upgrade on the pirates' cutlasses.

Nyomi reappeared carrying a long navy cloak trimmed in white and a pair of black boots. She put them on the table in front of me. "A few things to help you through your travels, and to make you appear less of a target."

"Thank you," I said. I hadn't expected such generosity.

"What about us?" Blue snorted.

"I've nothing that either of you scoundrels would appreciate," she replied with a smile.

Ulysses grunted, leaned back in his chair, and put his feet up on the table. "I don't know. I would very much appreciate a sword to replace the one you claim I can't carry into danger today."

"A sharp wit will do you more good this evening than a sharp blade," Nyomi said, "and I know you carry plenty of spares."

Both the boots and the cloak fit perfectly. Ulysses reached over and flipped the cloak's hood up over my head. "There. Now you look like a proper outlaw."

"An outlaw?" I said dumbly.

"Tonight, we're going to scare a group of vagrants out of the one place they won't get arrested for being vagrants. If necessary, we're going to kill a man. In two days, we're going to finagle our way into the private parts of the count's palace to steal a journal and anything else that happens to catch our fancy. Then we're going to escape back to our pirate ship," Blue said, like a father explaining life to his son. "Any one of those activities would earn the perpetrator a one-way trip to the gallows—and whereas you're participating in all of them, well, that doesn't exactly make you a good little Yuinite, now does it?"

The guilt I'd experienced prior about my affiliation with the pirates rose back to the surface. I wondered again what

Grandfather would think of my activities were he still alive. Mahlly's disapproving face appeared in my mind, and Ogrid's too. If I ever found my way back to Brennik's Reach, would my old friends accept me? It seemed unlikely, after that night in the town square. I banished my worries, convinced that I'd put myself on the wrong side of the law the very moment I'd decided to escort Tehenessey Blue into the settlement. And hadn't I been planning to murder Rocher long before then anyway? I'd been an outlaw for longer than I realized; hearing the word used to describe my person shouldn't have been such a shock.

Still, I have to admit: if I ever see Brennik's Reach again, I do hope Mahlly's happy I've returned. Not that I've much faith in such an outcome.

"No," I said. "That certainly doesn't make me a good Yuinite. I can live with that. Now let's get going so you've got time to catch plenty of beauty sleep before we go see the count."

"That's the spirit, lad!" Ulysses shouted. He stood and motioned for us to do the same. "I can almost feel all that treasure weighing down my pockets!"

Blue put his own blade on the table beside the first mate's. "Won't do you much good jingling around in your coat."

"Says you," Ulysses replied as he led the way up the stairs. "To beautiful princesses, that jingling is an irresistible siren's song leading to undeniable pleasure."

"Wouldn't a princess be rich already?" I asked as we stepped onto the next floor.

"This much is true," he admitted, "but in the upper classes of society to which I aspire, opposites do not attract, and romance is more a matter of the coffers than a matter of the heart. A bulging coin purse is as much a prerequisite for entry as piety for your Yuinite brethren."

We stepped out into the comfortable evening. A soft sea breeze wafted up and over the battlements, softening what otherwise might've been an oppressive night. The streets were dark and empty, save for the faint torchlight that spilled over from the sentries positioned atop the city wall.

"No unnecessary noise from here on out," Blue whispered. "The guards will toss us out for breaking curfew just as quickly as they're going to toss out everybody we're about to frighten out of the Hollow."

"So what do we do if we get caught?" I asked.

"We won't," Blue replied with a twitch of his big ears. "I'll hear them long before they hear us."

The marii led the way. Ulysses and I walked side-by-side a few steps behind. We traveled roughly in the direction of L'Vaillee's citadel, but we didn't take a direct route. Blue led us along a winding path that never took us too close to either the central street or the sentry-patrolled battlements. Occasionally we caught glimpses of torch light around the next bend, but never did I feel we were in any danger of being discovered. It was exhilarating nonetheless; I felt like one of the characters from the adventure tales I'd heard from the traveling minstrels who made Brennik's Reach a part of their annual itinerary.

It wasn't long before we finally came to the last block before L'Vaillee's palace. We were in the northwest corner of the city, across from a point where the round wall of the count's residence came within a foot of the square battlements. Faint light streamed through the entrance to the Hollow, but the surrounding area was pitch black.

"The guards don't come here unless there's trouble," Blue hissed. "L'Vaillee's oblivious, and what they don't see, they don't have to deal with."

"They're about to see it," Ulysses said, "and they're about to deal with it."

"Very dramatic, my friend, if a bit clichéd. I'll wish the two of you luck, for here is where we part ways."

"Where will you be?" I asked.

"That is something you do not need to know. If any of the vagrants notices you paying too much attention to any particular shadow, there will be trouble," Blue said. "Keep your eyes and ears focused on the Hollow's inhabitants, and don't let anyone put a knife in anyone's back."

"Unless I'm the one with the knife," Ulysses added. "You're to let me stab whomever I wish."

Blue shook his head and scampered back toward the heart of the city.

"Now I need you to be sociable, Kensey," Ulysses said. "The plan is to fit in, to be one of them. That means we're going to have to distort the truth. A lot. Can you fib in a friendly manner? If you can't, we'll have to pretend you're mute."

I realized that I was good at remaining quiet, but in this case, not speaking at all seemed like a worse cover than failing to speak deceptively. What if I should need to call for help, or shout to warn Ulysses that someone was coming up behind him? "I can try."

"Most of the time, that's more than good enough," Ulysses said with a wink. "Let's go."

Confident in Blue's assessment of the area, Ulysses strode right out of our cover without so much as glancing left or right and strolled straight through the thin gap that served as the entrance to the Hollow. I tried to look nonchalant like the first mate, but I probably just looked nervous. I pulled myself deep into my thick cloak, mentally if not physically. I knew I couldn't come off dashing and carefree like Ulysses, but I thought I might be able to pull off reserved and mysterious.

A horrible stench hit me as soon as I stepped into the gap: the pungent odor of unwashed bodies and human excrement mixed with the acridity of too many campfires in too small of an area. L'Vaillee might not have been able to see the vagrants in the Hollow, but I didn't understand how he couldn't smell them. I fought back the urge to gag and followed Ulysses further into the gloom.

The count's castle curved sharply away from the city wall just as quickly as it curved toward it. The Hollow spread out before us, a roughly elliptical area only slightly larger than the clearing around my childhood home. The majority of the area's inhabitants slept beside one of several small campfires spread around the perimeter. The dozen or so who remained awake had gathered around a larger bonfire in the center of the Hollow.

"Evening," Ulysses said with a smile. He briefly made eye contact with each of the men sitting around the fire. No one returned his greeting.

"Bit late to be sneaking into the Hollow," said a hard-looking man with a long, scraggly beard.

"We were supposed to be staying with my brother for the S'espri Moiraube," Ulysses explained. "His lovely wife, for reasons she shouted to the heavens but which need not be repeated amongst strangers, decided about an hour ago that she'd had enough of our company—which is just as well, as my companion and I had already devoured every scrap in their pantry worth eating."

A soft chuckle spread around the circle, though the man with the beard was unmoved. "If family was so quick to tire of you, it won't be long before we do the same."

A man emerged from the darkness to my left, seeming to congeal from the night. He was a tall, thick Mana'Olai, at least as large as Captain Lagash, if not larger. He took a seat at the head of the circle around the bonfire, on the side opposite the entrance to the Hollow, and positioned his long sitar across his thigh. He picked at its strings absent-mindedly, as if remembering every few seconds that he had a crowd to entertain. His soft eyes tracked Ulysses and I as we took a seat on the ground opposite him.

The bard strummed an ominous chord. The bonfire swayed along with the low note.

"Then I suppose we will have to earn our tolerance, if not our keep," Ulysses said. "We will begin with introductions. We are not beasts, after all, despite our current lack of a roof or anything civilized to sit upon. I am Dash Skipjack, and my mysterious compatriot here goes by the name Fillard Mize."

I was slightly disappointed that I didn't get to pick my own alias, but it was good to know that Ulysses, at least, had picked up on my detached attitude.

None of the men offered their names. The bard strummed another chord and this time the flames curled into a tight braid. "Who were you yesterday, and whom will you be tomorrow?" His speech was slow, his vowels slightly extended. "A name, Mr. Skipjack, is a gift easily given and easily taken back—especially by men in possession of several."

At first I thought he'd found us out, which meant there was going to be trouble. Then I realized the bard was alluding to the nature of most, if not all, of the men and women in the Hollow. We weren't in the company of individuals who particularly wanted to be known for who they really were.

"A good point, and one that seems to come from experience," Ulysses replied. "What say you, friend Fillard?"

I'd known he'd put me on the spot eventually, if only so none of the vagrants would get a chance. Unfortunately, the plan I'd been privy to included little more than going to the Hollow and scaring out the vagrants, and thus I wasn't quite sure where Ulysses wanted me to lead the conversation. I would realize later on that such was the point: the first mate had succeeded in making me so nervous that "fibbing in a friendly manner" was out of the question, and all I could do was speak from my heart. After a moment's thought, I scratched my chin. "This talk of names is a bit deep for my tastes. Such an evening is a time for tales, not philosophy."

The bard nodded. "Well put, Mr. Mize, well put."

I bowed my head, more to hide my smile than to acknowledge the bard. Pride swelled in my chest. I felt good about having played my part.

The first mate didn't miss a beat. "Yes, a story. Surely you've got one appropriate for the occasion, kind minstrel?"

"I tire of my tales, as I've heard them all a thousand times," the bard replied. A few slow notes on his sitar sent the tendrils of the flame braid pirouetting away from each other to crash back down into the coals. "The music, however, is something of the here and now, a thing to be created and experimented with rather than repeated again and again."

"Here, here!" said a man to my left. Several of the others nodded their agreement.

"Ah, but some stories never grow stale, as current events keep them alive," Ulysses said. "Such as the tragedy of Paton L'eure."

The bard shot him a skeptical look. "Never heard of the man."

"Paton's obscurity is part of his tragedy, I would say. 'Tis not a story spread far or wide, as many with wealth and influence have attempted to suppress it."

"Why's that?" asked a man to my left.

"In the wrong hands, it could threaten the very foundation of one of Nefazo's greatest heroes, Apros L'eure," Ulysses said softly. "The beggar who, in the course of one day, bargained himself a veritable kingdom? Surely you've all heard tell of his Feast and been privy to the feigned generosity of the Nefazo who celebrate his memory?"

"Ha!" the bard guffawed. "We've heard of it. And where would one such as you have come across such a tale?"

"I purchased a few drinks for an extremely inebriated old minstrel in Easlinder," Ulysses replied. "The man was dying, and he wanted to pass his greatest story on to someone worthy before he passed. A mixture of kindness and alcohol, I've found, tends to go a long way toward proving one's worth."

The bard plucked a few more strings, and the fiery braid bloomed into a flower with thick petals. "I believe your claims about as much as I believe I will one day be the captain of the *Black Yonnix*," he said. I hope I didn't stiffen too much at the name of our ship. "But you've a flair for the dramatic, and I find myself interested to see just how much garbage is about to spill from your lips. Tell your tale, and we'll listen for as long as we care to."

"Isn't that all any of us can hope for?" Ulysses leaned forward. The firelight cast odd shadows across his face as he spoke. "Apros L'eure, as you all well know, was a down-on-his-luck beggar who literally turned his fortunes around overnight, hence the reason for tomorrow's celebration. But the part of the story you don't know, the part that's been entrusted to me, concerns Apros' older brother, Paton.

"Paton, unlike his financially challenged sibling, was a success from the moment he left home. The man could've convinced Emperor Pileaus himself to pay a hundred gold coins for the lint he pulled from his pockets. Everything he bought he sold back at two or three times what he'd originally paid for it, and anything he couldn't immediately turn a profit on, he hoarded for the future until the price became right.

"You might wonder why anyone would dare do business with such a savvy merchant, a man guaranteed to give you bottom dollar for your wares only to turn around and sell them for an ungodly amount. But that's exactly why the other Nefazo continued to deal with him: his mastery of business transactions was considered an art form, and being fleeced by Paton was akin to taking a trip to the opera. Even one of the Monahrig, attracted by the challenge, tried and failed to out-bargain Paton. Everyone thought they could learn something from him, but no one could ever find a way to force Paton to lose money.

"Except, of course, Paton's younger brother. Apros would show up on Paton's diamond-crusted doorstep every few fortnights, dirty and drunk and occasionally bereft of clothing, and Paton would clean him and clothe him and feed him and supply him with more than enough goods and currency to start trading. Off Apros would go, with a smile on his face and a spring in his step, only to wind up flat broke again within a week. He once traded four priceless mah'saiid vases for a dying sow and a pot of coffee simply because he hadn't yet had breakfast. Another time he paid a small fortune for an ocean front palace in Lud's Teeth. Apros made a horrible Nefazo, but he didn't care. He had his fun, and his brother was always there to fill his pockets back to bursting so he could do it all again. Paton, for his part, enjoyed being so wealthy that he could support his brother's foolishness."

There was something about the way Ulysses spoke that I found utterly hypnotic. His audience was rapt, and some had reached over and roused a few sleepers. I'm convinced he could've been speaking complete gibberish and we all would've listened intently. Even the bard kept one half-interested eye on the first mate. I wish I could relay this tale as well as he did.

"All was well between the two for several years until, of course, a woman entered the picture. Upon completion of a deal that netted Paton fifteen habback, three carriages, a sterling silver tea set, and a bottle of his brother's favorite Uddani vintage in exchange for a dozen crates of ladies' hats that had been out of style for three years, the Nefazo on the other side of the deal threw in his daughter's hand as a bonus.

"But this wasn't just any Nefazo lady's hand. It was attached to the most beautiful woman in the land, a creature aptly named Rose, whose shimmering skin and pouty lips called potential suitors to her father's doorstep from lands far and near. The other merchant thought it would reflect well on him to marry his daughter off the Nefazo's best bargainer. Our hero, however, possessed a mind of the one-track variety, that track being business. Rose was a piece of merchandise, nothing more, and he took her back to his residence so he could keep her amongst the rest of his possessions, and then he immediately hit the road again.

"When he finally returned home a fortnight later, he found Rose in an outfit made from the best of the best of his collected wears. She'd wrapped herself in his finest silk and covered her ears and fingers in his most precious stones. One look was all it took Paton to realize that Rose was the ultimate manifestation of his wealth and thus the perfect means of displaying it. He began trading for things specifically to make her more beautiful, and when he went out on the town or to a fine party, she was never far from his arm."

Ulysses obviously had the whole Hollow distracted, and yet Blue seemingly hadn't begun to play. I wondered if he'd somehow gotten himself caught and was now staring at the outside of the city wall trying to devise a way back in. I fought back the urge to shift uneasily.

"But when Paton was out on business, he left Rose home alone. And that was how Apros found her, sad and alone and wearing an old rucksack, which, because it was part of Paton's collection, was actually very comfortable and quite flattering.

"'I care nothing for his things,' she explained through her tears. 'I used to. But all the riches in the world are nothing without a little attention, a little friendship. I make myself beautiful when I know he's coming home, but I put the luxuries away as soon as he leaves. They mean nothing to me. They disgust me...as does he.'"

"For the first time in his life, Apros found himself disappointed in Paton, in the brother he'd always thought had a perfect grip on the world. He saw then that Paton had been blinded by wealth, that he couldn't see the things that really mattered in life. Apros took Rose into his arms and they held each other for a long time, and then she gave herself to him, as Apros was a kind man, and her husband had refused to show her anything resembling the love she sought.

"The next morning, Apros' disappointment in his brother blossomed into righteous anger. Rose was as smart and as sweet as she was beautiful, and he could sense that her affection was genuine. She'd tried to love Paton, and he'd refused her; now she loved Apros, and he returned her sentiments. Alas, Apros knew that no matter how much they loved each other, they'd never be together for more than a few days at a time while Paton was out. She belonged to his brother.

"Paton arrived a few days later, oblivious to the new relationship growing between his wife and his brother. He gave Apros the usual fresh set of clothes and sack of loot and sent him on his way to waste it all yet again.

"Apros was headed for the pub and a sullen dive to the bottom of a keg when the Monarhig decided to make his presence known. Impossibly tall and impeccably dressed, the Fae prince melted out of the shadows and positioned himself squarely between Apros and the bar."

Ulysses deepened his voice for dramatic effect. "'It has come to my attention that the two of us might benefit from a...business arrangement,' the Monarhig explained. Time seemed to have stopped, and Apros was pretty sure none of the seemingly frozen people all around him could hear their conversation. 'I don't normally deal with mortals," the Fae prince spat, 'but in you, I see a capacity for a much deserved slice of irony.'

"'What do you mean?' Apros asked, for he was a simple man, and he was too much in awe of the creature before him to follow the twists and turns of the Fae's tongue.

"'Follow my instructions, and Rose can be yours.'

"Apros needed no further prodding. He blew through his brother's wares and money with impressive speed and returned to Paton's doorstep three days later. His brother was out on business...and while Rose slept, Apros took the opportunity to steal the Blade of D'laria, a one-of-a-kind dagger of ancient mah'saiid manufacture and the famous crown jewel of Paton's collection.

"Apros' first victim was the toughest. His initial slice didn't cut deep enough into the sleeping vagrant's neck, and he had to wrestle the man back to the cobblestones and cut him again. His next seven went as smoothly as these things can go, and he made sure to leave the murder weapon behind on his eighth. Even the daftest of deputies couldn't have misidentified that dagger. Whenever Paton attended a party, there were two things he flaunted: Rose, and the Blade of D'laria.

"Apros found his brother sleeping in a barn the next morning. 'The law's after me,' Paton said, 'but I didn't kill any of those men. Someone must've stolen my dagger.'

"'Calm down, brother,' Apros said. 'Have faith in the courts.'

"'It's not my absolution for which I worry. Tomorrow they're going to seize my property. We both know how famous the courts are for making such seized property disappear, even in the event the accused is found not guilty.'

"Apros scratched his chin thoughtfully. This was exactly the attitude he and the Monarhig had been counting on. 'But if your property wasn't yours anymore, the law would be unable to seize it.' He picked up a handful of the hay he'd been sleeping on. 'Paton L'eure, I offer you this in exchange for the entirety of your estate.'

"For a moment, and only a moment, Paton stared dumbfounded at his brother. Then his eyes lit up and he smiled proudly. 'Apros, my brother, you are cleverer than you let on. Deal accepted.'

"Paton wrote up a bill of sale right then and there. The two brothers signed it and shook hands. 'Take good care of my riches,' Paton said as he happily shoved the handful of hay into his pocket. 'I'll be back for them when I've cleared my name.'

"The next morning, Apros met the authorities on his brother's doorstep—now his doorstep—and presented them with the bill of sale. The men had no choice but to turn away, their dreams of ill-gotten gains shattered. Word spread quickly of the transaction, and people marveled at how quickly Apros' fortunes had changed. He'd merely been biding his time, they said, lulling his brother into a false sense of security and letting the wealth pile up before he swooped in and made the best purchase in all of recorded history. It mattered not that the deal had probably taken place under suspicious and unsavory circumstances. The details were nothing; the deal was everything.

"Apros and Rose couldn't have been happier. They spent their days and nights together, and Apros promised they would travel the continent—after one final piece of business.

"Through the Monarhig, Apros learned that his brother had beaten the false rap and was on his way to reclaim his property. Apros had no intention of returning any of it, and he knew he wouldn't stand a chance against his brother's bargaining. Luckily, the Monarhig had a plan for that as well.

"Just as the Fae had said, it wasn't difficult to convince the local vagrants that Paton had escaped on a technicality and thus they needed to take justice into their own hands. Apros called a feast at his residence for all the downtrodden people in town. Each and every one of them accepted the invitation.

"When Paton strode through the door, they descended upon him like a pack of ravenous wolves upon a fat habback. Apros and Rose watched from the next room. Neither shed a single tear, though Apros shivered a little at his brother's final scream. He felt no remorse for Paton, however; he only regretted having to drag the vagrants so deeply into the Monarhig's scheme. To make it up to them and assuage his conscience, he called them back to his house once every year to eat, drink, and be merry. The other Nefazo, looking to prove they were in the same league as the trader who'd finally swindled the great Paton, opened their own doors on the night Apros opened his, and the Feast of Apros L'eure was born."

Several moments passed before the crowd realized the story was over and reconnected with the world around them. Most of those gathered favored Ulysses with a smattering of applause. The pirate bowed his head in thanks. I never learned if any of it were true, or if the clever Ulysses had made it up right there on the spot. Neither would surprise me.

"Not a bad tale," the bard said, "though I fail to see how it concerns any current events."

Ulysses smiled menacingly. "Ah, but I'm sure by now you've heard the rumors going around town: the dead have risen, and they've come to Vastille."

"So?"

"So even in death, Paton is a bargainer second to none. The Feast may be Apros's, but the S'espri Moiraube, that night when morality turns a blind eye to the lust of the moment, is Paton's. Every year his spirit rises from his grave to attend—and every year, he convinces more and more of the dead to return with him."

A bone chilling breeze cut through the Hollow. Behind the bard's huge form, a ball of thin bluish mist began to coalesce into a humanoid form.

"Bah!" the Mana'Olai musician scoffed. "Nonsense meant to frighten children, nothing more."

I recognized an opportune moment to speak up. "Tell that to the shade behind you."

As the bard turned to look, the eerie specter raised a ragged, ghostly knife and charged forward. It ran right through the bard, right through the fire, and between Ulysses and myself to stab another spirit standing behind us. Similar specters had appeared throughout the Hollow, some attackers, some victims, but all locked in the throes of terrible violence.

"Paton has come!" someone shouted. "Run!"

The alarm spread quickly throughout the Hollow. The vagrants rushed away from the frightening scene, pushing and shoving their way toward the entrance. They tried to avoid the apparitions, but most of the time they stumbled right through them. I was caught up in the wave of unwashed bodies and forced away from the fire.

Just as Ulysses had expected, the bard wasn't fooled. He stroked his chin once in thought, and then his fingers began to fly up and down the strings of his sitar. I couldn't hear his song, but I could see its effects. The apparitions slowly became transparent, fading back into the World Song from which they came.

I was knocked to the ground by a large, wide-eyed woman screaming something about her dead husband looking for revenge. Unable to see Ulysses or the bard, I panicked and tried to leap back to my feet only to be knocked right back down by a heavy shoulder that collided with the back of my neck. I rolled to my left to avoid the pounding feet of the crowd and managed to pull myself into a sitting position against L'Vaillee's citadel. I'd lost track of both my friends and our enemy. My imagination warned me that the bard could burst forth from the departing herd at any moment, dripping with Ulysses's blood and ready to add my own to the mess. I grabbed a nearby rock and tried to make myself look small.

When next I had a clear look at the bard, a long knife was buried in the neck of the sitar, rendering the instrument useless. Ulysses flicked his wrist and a second blade soared through the night to find the bard's throat. The big man collapsed, and Ulysses strode over to the corpse to retrieve his weapons, wiping the blood off on the bard's clothing.

The first mate's actions hadn't gone unnoticed. A group of three stragglers were closing in on him from behind. I called out to Ulysses, but my voice was lost in the commotion. I hefted a nearby rock and hurled it at the trio. I missed by quite a few feet, but Ulysses had seen it coming and tracked its trajectory to my intended targets. He was a blur as he carved up the men with quick, efficient strokes.

The first mate turned from his gruesome handiwork and tipped his hat in my direction.

Moments later, when the last vagrant had left the Hollow, the apparitions finally faded. Tehennessey Blue vaulted down from his perch atop the city wall.

"What took you so long?" Ulysses asked.

"I wanted to hear the end of the story," the marii said. "Your telling was impeccable."

"Yeah," I added. "It seemed so real."

Ulysses returned his weapons to their sheaths inside his coat. "Whoever said it wasn't?"

"You mean—Paton and Apros—it's true?"

"That depends on how you look at it," he said mysteriously. "Now we'd best get back to Nyomi's while those vagrants have all the guards distracted. They're making so much noise out there, they're liable to wake the dead—"

A tremendous, booming voice cut off Ulysses, seeming to come from everywhere and nowhere at once. "Duine! Hark our warning dearly." It was as if the world itself were speaking to us. Remembering Nyomi's warning about the song, Ulysses and I fixed Tehenessey Blue with frightened stares.

Blue, for his part, looked white as a ghost. "That's not the World Song," he stuttered. "Look above and behind you."

I turned and aimed my gaze skyward. A huge cloud had moved to block Takata Shin, absorbing and reflecting the moon's eerie green light. It had taken the shape of a beautiful woman's face, a bit long and a bit angular, her eyes gaping holes to the stars beyond.

I hadn't known it then, but what I was looking at was a singular event that would change the Dying Lands forever.

"The Courts of Twilight consider the abduction of Nungisa, Lord of Nightmares, an act of war against the Dreaming Lands," the woman continued. "Return my brother and the man called Boruin, or your cities will be shattered, your fields will be made fallow, your mortal lives ended."

And then the cloud dissipated, and the three of us spun and bolted for Nyomi's.

CHAPTER FOURTEEN

My second stint on Nyomi's guest bed wasn't nearly as restful as my first. My dreams were haunted by that face in the clouds, by visions of death and destruction. I saw twisted, ethereal figures emerge from the forests and the seas, fire in their eyes and hatred in their hearts as their long fingers tore civilization to shreds. I saw the land itself turn against its inhabitants, fire bursting from the earth, mountains reaching out to crush armies, plants and animals overrunning villages and cities. Above it all, or perhaps woven into it, was another face; an old man, stoic and strong, with white hair and a square jaw.

Yes, Your Highness, I've since heard that many people dreamed of your father that evening. I don't dare guess his connection to the Fae plaguing our lands, although there are times I suspect the death of our greatest military leader emboldened their incursions.

I found Ulysses, Tehenessey Blue, and Nyomi waiting for me at the table the next morning. A deep malaise weighed upon the room. None of them looked as if they'd slept. I fell into a chair beside Ulysses, and Nyomi passed me a steaming cup of coffee that smelled vaguely of lavender.

"Drink it all," she said. "You'll need to be at your best tonight."

It tasted like an Omman's sweaty boot, but I didn't complain.

"We all had the same dream last night," Ulysses explained. "Death, destruction, people seemingly important to both."

"I swear to the World Song it wasn't me," Blue muttered, his head in his hands. "I missed a high L in one tricky stanza, but there's no way that was enough..."

Nyomi ran one comforting hand through the fur on the side of his cheek. "No, Blue, it wasn't you. That such an event occurred after your playing is merely an unhappy coincidence."

"The Fae," Ulysses said.

Nyomi nodded solemnly. "That face in the clouds last night was Obata, the Lady Dream, one of the Nai'Oigher who shape the forces of creation. Hence the visions that invaded our sleep."

"So that was all some poor sod's wanted poster?" Ulysses asked. "Remind me never to cross the Fae."

"Regardless, this Boruin is none of our concern. Best to stay as far away from Fae business as possible," Nyomi said.

"True, but Fae business may have just ruined our business," Ulysses said. "I suspect the good count, concerned for the general state of his neck as they say he is, will be keeping his palace locked up tight this evening."

No one offered a response. I took a long gulp from my cup of coffee. The previous night's mission had gone so well: we'd infiltrated the Hollow, dispatched the bard, and returned to Nyomi's without drawing attention to ourselves. And then all of our hard work was ruined by a mere coincidence, by a man I'd never met who'd angered a being I couldn't fathom. I decided then that if I ever met Boruin, I'd promptly hand him over to the Fae.

We spent most of the rest of the day in relative silence, each of us absorbed in our own endeavors. Nyomi busied herself with chores, dusting this and cleaning that. Half-finished melodies wafted upstairs from the guest bedroom where Tehenessey Blue practiced with his flute. Ulysses honed his various blades on Nyomi's kitchen whetstone, in between naps and a few rounds of shadow boxing.

I wasn't sure what to do with myself. I wandered to the top floor and perused Nyomi's bookshelves, eventually settling on a hefty old tome labeled *On the Fae and Our Dual Universe* in flowery script. I curled up in the comfortable chair in which Nyomi performed her fortune telling and tried to absorb as much as I could, thinking it warranted under the circumstances. Very little sank in; it could've been the archaic, long-winded, I'm-smarter-than-you language, or it could've been the surprisingly complex subject matter, but I soon found myself understanding only every other word. The Fae and their castes and their courts and the Aiemer with which they performed their magic, all products of some fantastic world attached to ours be a set of mysterious gates at the mercy of the heavens...even now that I've seen much of it firsthand, I'm not sure I fully believe it.

The first hints of the night's coming revelry began echoing from the streets at Diundawn, when the sun's warm light filtering through Nyomi's small windows was replaced by Diun's eerie silver glow. Children ran past, blowing screechy noisemakers and singing songs too mature for their young voices. A street cart rattled along behind them, its driver advertising all manner of sweets and liquor and mixtures of the two. Intrigued, I abandoned my frustrating reading and moved to the window.

"A shame we're here on business," Tehenessey Blue said as he joined me in peering out through the curtains. He sounded genuinely disappointed. "The S'espri was always my favorite day on the Nefazo social calendar. No pretending to enjoy the company of dirty beggars, like during the Foures de Apros L'eure. No silly competitions, like on the Dete de Avidade. Just pure, unadulterated adultery."

"And lots of easy marks made easier by drink and revelry and worse," Nyomi added as she emerged from the stairwell. She'd changed into a long, shimmering gown of wispy fabric patterned with silver fish scales, which made her appear even more ethereal and mysterious than usual.

"Indeed, the best part," Blue said with a wink. "Just as good for your business as ours, I would imagine."

Ulysses followed Nyomi up the stairs, smiling from ear to ear. "One couldn't ask for better atmosphere for a bit o' thieving. I've a good feeling about the evening, gents! A good feeling."

Blue sighed. "I doubt that'll open L'Vaillee's doors."

"We thank you again for your hospitality and your assistance, my lady," Ulysses said with a smile, "but I fear now is the time for farewells, as a good bye shouted hastily over one's shoulder while attempting to outrun the mob of angry guards our actions are sure to attract would do a great disservice to the kindness you've shown us."

Nyomi stepped between us and the exit. "No one goes to L'Vaillee's unarmed."

"Blue and I have plenty of hidden weaponry," Ulysses protested. "We'll take care of young Vardallian."

"Aye. If we give him something sharp, he's more likely to carve his own eye out than to actually fight off an attacker," Blue said.

I didn't protest. Given my failures with Ogrid, perhaps I really was better off without a blade.

"That's not the point," Nyomi insisted. "The three of you are supposed to be vagrants, and vagrants are always armed. If you try to bring Kensey into the citadel without a weapon, L'Vaillee and his men will be suspicious."

"You may have a point," Ulysses said, "and even if you don't, I suspect attempting to talk our way around it will take more time than we have. Point me to your armory, then, and I'll select a proper sidekick for young Master Vardallian."

"In the kitchen," she said. "In the cabinet below the silverware."

Ulysses bowed and disappeared down the stairs. I've always wondered if perhaps Nyomi somehow knew I was going to need a means of defending myself and just didn't say so. Perhaps she didn't want me to worry, a further protection against the judgment of L'Vaillee and his goons. Granted, the mah'saiid had been unable to read my future, but that didn't rule out the possibility that my destiny affected someone else's, and she'd deduced just exactly how I'd created that effect.

Blue turned to glare at me. "Whatever Ulysses gives you, keep the pointy end of it out of my general vicinity."

"I'd be less worried about Kensey and more worried about controlling your own acquisitive tendencies," Nyomi said. "Your pockets can only hold so much before they become suspicious."

"Ah, but my appetite knows no such bounds—and where there's a will, there's a way, so long as that will manages to avoid accident-prone peasants unfamiliar with the proper use of sharp implements."

Ulysses returned carrying a small dagger with a thick wooden hilt in a brown leather sheath. It was thoroughly unimpressive, and I'll admit I found the weapon a bit disappointing. "This is the weapon of a young beggar on the road for the first time."

"It'll do," Nyomi said.

I put the weapon in a pocket on the inside of my cloak. Its weight was slightly reassuring. It wasn't much, but it was something, even if all I had the confidence for was waving it in a threatening manner.

"May we depart now?" Blue asked haughtily.

"You may, and I wish you luck."

Blue nodded politely at Nyomi as he walked out the door. Ulysses stopped to kiss her hand and smile gallantly, then he followed the marii. I just stood there. I felt the need to say something meaningful, but nothing appropriate came to mind.

After a long moment, she smiled warmly. "I'm glad to see that you, at least, genuinely appreciate the things I've done. Before you go, I have one more thing to ask."

"Name it," I said without hesitation.

"No matter how far you travel, no matter what obstacles and hardships you face...please don't turn out like Ulysses or Tehenessey Blue."

With that she kissed me softly on the cheek and disappeared downstairs.

I lingered for a moment, staring at my boots as I pondered Nyomi's words. I decided she was right: looking up to the pirates and learning from them would see me through my journey, but actually becoming one of them would only take me several dozen steps backwards down the path my grand-father had helped fashion for my life. Looking back, it's a shame I wasn't able to follow Nyomi's advice. Life wouldn't let me, though I doubt she'd accept that excuse.

I stepped out of Nyomi's home and into the middle of an argument.

"I will not fetch the stick!" Blue snarled at Ulysses. He looked ready to tear the first mate limb from limb. Ulysses, despite the threat, appeared entirely too pleased with himself. A small branch lay on the cobblestones a little way down the street.

"Why not? It'll be just like the old days with Lady Gershon!"

"This is your last warning, Ulysses," the marii growled. "One more peep about Lady Gershon, and everyone will swear you and her son are twins."

Ulysses turned to me and winked. "I imagine our friend here made a most disagreeable pet. Now, let's go see if the good Count has any attractive young ladies in his family, shall we?"

"I thought we were here to get the journal," I said naïvely.

"Of course! But that doesn't mean we don't have time to enjoy the best that Vastille has to offer."

"Perhaps we should've stuck with the woman in the carriage, then," I said.

"If she was the best Vastille has to offer, I'll be sure to avoid a return trip."

The streets of Vastille, previously empty and oppressive, had come alive with sound and color. Vastillians mingled on every corner, sampling food and beverage from rickety stalls and parked carts, clapping and dancing along to one of the numerous minstrels and troubadours battling for control of the city's sound. Everyone was dressed in their finest, the men in dapper cloaks and elaborate tunics, the women in glittering gowns and ridiculous hats. Children roamed unchecked, darting here and there underfoot. Gossamer streamers stretched from building to building, creating a webbed canopy that shimmered blue and green in Diun's light. L'Vaillee's guards were everywhere, brutal, well-armed men who looked as uncomfortable with the controlled chaos as I felt.

"Quite the show, eh?" Blue asked as he snatched a coin purse from a drunk mumbling his way through a stuttering recitation of a Thilan poem. Finding it empty, he wrinkled his nose and tucked it into the back pocket of a little boy buying sweet bread from a vendor.

"I didn't think these tightwads had such revelry in them," Ulysses replied as he tipped his hat at a pair of women striding arm in arm toward a flutist on the corner.

"When one spends an entire year affectionately licking the count's behind, such energy tends to accumulate," Blue said, "and that's not taking into account all the nervous energy I'm sure last evening's warning has inspired. We should hurry to the square. L'Vaillee addresses Vastille every S'espri. That'll be our best chance to gauge the accessibility of his citadel."

Blue led the way through the ever-thickening crowd, a furry beacon in a sea of arms and legs. A few children gawked at pointed at the marii. Ulysses brought up the rear, stopping to chat up a woman or two, pausing to admire the performance of a musician or an acrobat. It was hard to stay focused on the task at hand, but the first mate didn't seem to be making much of an effort. I hoped he'd be able to focus more once we were inside the citadel.

"Did Nyomi tell either of you where the journal is?" I asked.

"Nope," Blue said dismissively.

"Same here," Ulysses added.

"So…how do we find it?"

The first mate shrugged. "We'll follow the general public into L'Vaillee's palace, mix and mingle as best we can, and remain vigilant for the fellow who stole it."

"That's not much of a plan."

Blue paused to sniff at a cart packed to bursting with pink and red candies. "We've succeeded with worse."

"And if it doesn't work?" I asked, annoyed. "We only get one night for this."

"Fear not, my dear Kensey, for we've a foolproof Plan B guaranteed to produce fantastic results!" Ulysses declared. He turned to me, doffed his hat, and bowed dramatically, favoring me with a lunatic grin as he straightened back up. "If we can't locate binding nor page of your beloved journal, well: we'll cause a scene and draw our quarry to us!"

I wished I'd never asked.

We reached the square just as L'Vaillee was about to begin his address. The semicircular area was really more of an amphitheater than a square; a dozen rows of whitewashed stone seats curved up and away from the square's round side like a giant set of stairs, opposite the impressive flat façade of L'Vaillee's marble citadel. The streamers were thicker here, six or seven entwined around each other and draped with bluestars and other flowers that only opened during Diuntyne, stretching from the rear wall of the amphitheater and over the gathered crowd to converge at a common point atop the count's keep. Each seat was filled by a rich Nefazo in his or her finest, most expensive clothing. All the latest fashions from the continent's cultural centers were represented in that square. Several of them looked pretty foolish.

The Count and his entourage stood just in front of the massive portcullis that led to the interior of his citadel. The statue in Brennik's Reach had been surprisingly accurate: L'Vaillee was a tall, striking man who obviously put a lot of effort into making himself look regal and wealthy. His jet-black hair and goatee were perfectly trimmed and styled. He wore a crimson and gold military uniform similar in cut to one worn by high-ranking Imperial officers that reinforced his propensity for strong-arming the opposition. A glittering scimitar hung from his belt beside his left hip.

L'Vaillee raised his sword, and all conversation in the square came to an abrupt halt. To my left, Ulysses snorted.

"It pleases me that the spirit of the S'espri has not been dampened by last night's strange events," L'Vaillee bellowed, every syllable sharp and precise and dripping with false bravado. "Neither that villain Boruin nor those riotous vagrants will darken our night of light!"

"And my purple habback speaks Uddani," Blue muttered. "What's his angle?"

"Allow me to introduce to you the evening's benefactor, Lord Selteir!" the count announced.

A tall, spindly man in a heavy white robe stepped forward from L'Vaillee's retinue. He had a strange bearing about him, as if he stood askew to the rest of the world. A shock of blue-black hair stood almost straight up atop his head, glowing faintly in Diun's glow. The crowd cheered, anxiously at first, then louder as L'Vaillee's guards glared at those assembled. Selteir returned their greeting with a wide, arrogant wave, looking for all the world like he would rather be anywhere else.

L'Vaillee added his own applause, then silenced the crowd with another showing of his sword. "Lord Selteir shall be joining us for the evening's festivities. I'm told he's quite the conversationalist. He's especially interested in any news regarding the evil Boruin."

Blue hissed angrily. "The rutter's already cut a deal with the damn Fae!"

I shivered. Maybe fear of the Fae is instinctual; even back then, before I'd had any interaction with the denizens of the Dreaming Lands, I somehow understood just how dangerous they could be.

Behind L'Vaillee, gears squealed as the massive portcullis began to rise. "Enjoy the S'espri, my citizens, and enjoy my home!"

The count and his retinue turned and headed for his citadel, and the crowd rose to join him. When I didn't stand, Ulysses grabbed my shoulder and gently pulled me to my feet.

"Worry not, lad," the first mate said with a smile I didn't quite believe. "I'm sure old Selteir cares not one whit about Lucifus Vardallian and his famous treasure."

— CHAPTER FIFTEEN —

The interior of the count's residence was the grandest living space I'd ever seen. We entered through a long, cavernous hall, swept along with the crowd of boisterous revelers. The floor was made of polished granite, the curving walls and ceiling of glimmering blue-black farlay brick found only in Nefazo, and only in three known quarries. Even the mortar holding the bricks together was expensive; it was a sharp white material flecked with glittering grains of some sort of gemstone. Artwork was arranged on the walls in a regular pattern, always with two paintings in between the gold sconces that lit the room. Every painting was the same size, and every painting was mounted in the same ornate mahogany frame. L'Vaillee's taste in art seemed to be limited to gruesome battle scenes.

The hall opened into a grand rotunda large enough to hold the entire population of Vastille. The room was four stories high, each story lined with a balcony overlooking the rotunda floor. Visitors flitted among tables piled high with food and drink, each manned by a squadron of waiters in white pants and tunics. A marii band on the stage at the far wall struck up a jaunty tune as we entered, beckoning guests to the raised dance floor at the center of the room. Above, the roof was a faceted piece of glass that transformed Diun's strange light into the various colors of the rainbow, casting each area of the room in a different color. L'Vaillee and his entourage disappeared into a private area concealed by violet curtains beside the stage.

We gathered beside a table stacked with more roasted turkeys than I'd seen in my entire life. Blue snatched a leg off the table, dipped it in a gravy boat, and took a big, violent bite.

"Mind your manners, friend Blue," Ulysses chided. His red coat glowed purple in the blue light.

"Tonight is a night of indulgence, Ulysses," the marii said in between mouthfuls. "You'll see much worse by the time this night is through."

"With any luck, it'll be attached to a long, slender pair of legs with a large inheritance and an eye for dashing rogues like ourselves," the first mate replied.

I hadn't seen Rocher or either of his goons anywhere, and I was growing impatient. "Sorry to ruin everybody's fun, but how do we find the journal? This room looks to be attached to at least a dozen others."

"Twenty-one, to be exact," Ulysses said primly. "Two of which are privies, and three of which lead to the kitchen. I've had worse chances than one-in-sixteen, but we'll not be blindly fumbling our way through L'Vaillee's palace."

"Then how exactly are we going to do this?"

Ulysses snatched the half-eaten turkey leg from Blue's hand and tossed it in the waste barrel beside the table. "First, we improve our odds a little bit."

We wound our way through the dancing, drinking, cavorting crowd, heading in the general direction of the stage and the marii band performing upon it. My imagination ran wild trying to determine what Ulysses had in mind. Maybe, with little more than a wink and jerk of his thumb, he'd instruct Tehenessey Blue to slip into the ranks of the band, using his flute to add a subtle harmony that would get anyone who knew about the journal talking. Maybe he recognized a member of L'Vaillee's entourage on the dance floor, and he was planning to steal his dance partner to make the man jealous and start a fight during which he could physically extract the information from the man. Maybe—

My heart skipped a beat when the first mate veered sharply to the right, making a beeline for the purple curtains that concealed L'Vaillee's private sitting area. Ulysses wasn't just trying to improve our odds; he was brazenly betting everything we had on a single hand. I pulled the hood of my cloak up over my head, trusting that an air of mystery would serve me as well here as it had in the Hollow. Really, I was just afraid that Rocher would be part of the count's retinue, and that he'd recognize me and ruin our plans.

Ulysses parted the curtain with a flourish and strode confidently inside, Blue and I hot on his heels. The air was thick and hazy with the smoke of some exotic drug, which felt like hot cinnamon in my throat. Lords and ladies of L'Vaillee's court lounged on luxurious pillows and cushions spread across the floor, sipping wine from oversized goblets and puffing daintily on long metal pipes. L'Vaillee himself sat on a gilded throne in the far corner, taking turns on a stocky silver pipe with a woman seated on a cushion beside him. She was long and lean, with jet-black hair arranged in a complex braid around a small red fez atop her head. Her gown was absolutely stunning, and didn't leave much to the imagination. The dress was cut at a sharp angle to reveal her left leg, and something in the fabric shimmered in the sunlight. Twisting leather bands traced her leg from the high-heeled shoes on her feet all the way up to her exposed thigh. A bright pair of brown eyes peered intelligently over the sterling silver fan she held to conceal the rest of her face.

"Is that—" I whispered.

Blue cut me off with a hiss. "If it is, I suspect we'll know soon enough."

I glanced to Ulysses for confirmation, but his eyes were locked on the woman. Something in the set of his jaw made me suspect that he felt a bit stupid.

None of the nobles seemed to notice or care about our presence, but a large, angry man wielding a heavy club stepped between Ulysses and L'Vaillee. "I'm sorry, sir, but this area is reserved for the count and his personal guests."

"Ah, but aren't we all personal guests of the good count this grand evening?" Ulysses asked, flashing his most charming smile.

The guard was not impressed. His only response was to tap his club in his open palm.

"To business, then," Ulysses replied, not missing a beat. "I bear news of that great villain, Boruin, and I'd like to share it with L'Vaillee and his friend Selteir."

I did my best to keep a straight face. What could Ulysses possibly know of Boruin? It was all an act, I was sure, and an exceptionally dangerous one at that. I worried that our success in the Hollow had made the first mate far too confident in his own bullshit. Surely Selteir would know if Ulysses was lying.

As if on cue, Selteir appeared beside the guard, hazy smoke swirling in his sudden wake. I was struck by the strange length of his fingers, by the high slope of his forehead, by his fiery eyes that took in the entire room and everyone in it all at once. He seemed to stand not inside the room but parallel to it, in such a way that he could affect it but that it could never touch him. One of his bare feet, toes too long like his fingers, tapped in some odd half-time to the music in the great hall. This was a creature from another world, a being like us in form only. He dismissed the guard with an awkward wave.

"Ah, there he is," Ulysses said with a big, fake smile. "I'm sure you've heard tell of the events in the Munier Valley—nasty business, that—but have you heard anything about Boruin's life prior to said event?"

Selteir shook his head, once to each side, slowly and deliberately and apparently warning the foolish mortal before him that wasting his time would be a big mistake.

And so Ulysses continued. "After we came south through the Shoro, we did a bit of business in Priyati 'round the time that terrible villain chopped and hacked and stabbed his way through town. Narrowly avoided that maniac's path myself, which gave me a great view of his final destination: the Underlund Trading Company."

At that, one of Selteir's wispy eyebrows rose slightly.

"Now, being a well-intentioned citizen firmly rooted on the proper side of the law, my virtuous mind couldn't possibly begin to imagine what that evil Boruin is thinking, but it stems to reason that if he's done business with Underlund once, he may be inclined to do business with them again…"

Before Ulysses had even finished his sentence, Selteir turned on his heel and glided out through a side door.

"How did you know all that?" I asked quietly.

"Nyomi provided me with a few choice tidbits garnered from her Brotherhood contacts. The rest, I made up," he whispered proudly.

Blue groaned. "And you wasted it all!" the marii hissed. "Typically, when negotiating one does not give away one's valuables until a fair trade of some sort has been agreed upon."

Ulysses glared at his friend. "I just successfully removed the biggest wild card in our little venture, and you're caught up on a lack of compensation? Friend Blue, I fear you've spent too much time among these Nefazo."

As the two argued, I watched the count over Ulysses's shoulder. The woman seated on the cushion beside L'Vaillee leaned close to his ear, the fan still concealing her face. Whatever she said convinced the count to stand and stride impatiently in our direction.

"The count!" I whispered as loudly as I dared.

Ulysses spun and crossed his hands behind his back, his widest, most gregarious smile immediately stretching from one ear to the other. "Ah, Count L'Vaillee. A pleasure to make your acquaintance this grand evening."

"I've not seen that bastard so interested in anything since his arrival," L'Vaillee said crisply. "I trust that the information you provided will be worth his time?"

"What is time to one who lives forever?" Ulysses replied. "But yes, my lord, I assure you that I would not trifle with your honored guest."

"Good. My companion overheard you telling Selteir that you came south through the Shoro."

As always, the first mate remained unruffled. "Yes, sir. Dangerous place." He punctuated that last bit with a sad shake of his head.

"And might you recall the approximate locations of these dangers?"

"More or less."

"It would please me greatly, then, for you to dine with my family and I this evening."

Ulysses nodded. "We accept your invitation."

The count returned the first mate's nod and snapped his fingers. As one, those gathered rose and strode quickly through a backdoor hidden behind a few wisps of purple curtain. The count's companion favored us with a wink over the edge of her fan as she passed, and Ulysses and L'Vaillee fell into step behind her.

"What was that about?" I asked Blue.

"The Nefazo have been trying to find an easy way through the Shoro since they first settled here," he explained. "L'Vaillee wants to add what we know to his maps."

"But why?"

"Why are you so full of questions?" he asked angrily. "Trading with the Mana'Olai and Easlinder is all well and good, but the Empire is where the money is—and to get to the Empire without the help of the shuen, you've got to go through the Shoro."

Blue and I followed the others through the door and into a long, opulent hallway. The floor and ceiling were polished black marble flecked with gold strands, the walls murals of great battles formed in gold leaf. Ulysses had wormed his way into the middle of the count's entourage, and he was laying it on thick. "...and that's when the biggest two-headed galula

I've ever seen sprang out of the brush," he declared. "I'd left my battleax back in camp, so I picked up the nearest pointy stick and prepared to do battle..." Our mysterious benefactor had linked her arm through his, her gaze peering over the fan in rapt attention as she savored his every exaggeration. Even a man as young and dumb as myself recognized the lust in her eyes. The rest of the group seemed to be buying it as well, save L'Vaillee himself, who gave no indication that he even realized anyone else was in the room.

The count stopped just before the double doors. "I must remind you that we have a guest chef this evening," he said pompously. "My niece, Nicolette."

L'Vaillee's lightly veiled threat was unmistakable. He probably wasn't expecting a response, but Ulysses gave him one anyway. "My lord, I'm sure a product of a bloodline as noble as yours will perform more than admirably." The count nodded dismissively and shoved the doors open.

The palace's dining room was even more cavernous than the front hall. It was twice as tall, twice as wide, and possibly twice as expensive. There was no threshold separating the rooms; the granite floor of the hall cut right into the reddish g'brickshaw wood floor before finally coming to a sharp point about a dozen steps later. The walls to my left and right were glistening white wainscoting, the far wall a massive stone hearth. Arched doors in each corner led to other areas of the citadel. An extravagant gold chandelier hung from a long silver chain above the magnificent table in the center of the room, which was piled high with steaming delicacies. The only other piece of decor was a huge portrait of L'Vaillee hanging above the fireplace, in which the count sported the same look of deep introspection—or perhaps constipation—as the statue in Brennik's Reach.

The group dispersed to take their seats, all of which already had a plate made. L'Vaillee led the three of us and the mysterious woman to the head of the table and motioned that we sit. We took three chairs side-by-side, with Ulysses closest to the count and Blue in the middle. Our plates were already made: Ouillane-style roast duck in a garlic and herb sauce with baby greens, roasted yams, and a tall glass of Thilan red.

Ulysses leaned across the table and smiled. "A pleasure to be dining with a woman of your beauty, miss...?"

"Marielle," she replied softly. It was then that she withdrew the fan, revealing a hooked nose and a large, hairy mole beside her slightly twisted lip. Tehenessey Blue gagged on a mouthful of wine, and I hid my smile behind my hand. This was definitely not the woman from the carriage. "Marielle Candreaux. And your name, kind sir?"

To his credit, the first mate only hesitated for a heartbeat before his instinctive charm kicked back in. "I am Dash Skipjack," he said, his winsome smile making a triumphant return, "and my compatriots are the dapper Fillard Mize and Slinnik, master of riddles."

Beside me, Blue gagged on his wine. His tail thumped against the side of my chair in irritation.

"It's nice to meet you, Mr. Skipjack." I swear to you, Your Highness, that the little hairs sprouting from that mole waved hello.

"Please," Ulysses stammered. "Call me Dash."

"You don't have to be so awkward," she cooed. "My husband allows me certain...indiscretions."

The first mate took a long, long swig of the Thilan red. Blue flashed me a nasty smile. He reveled in every moment of Ulysses' discomfort, and as I found it rather entertaining myself, I couldn't fault his amusement.

But my high spirits were quickly doused with darkness. A jowly, piggish face that I will never, ever forget appeared in the seat directly across the table from my own. I'd spent the months since my grandfather's murder wondering how I'd react if I encountered Rocher again. I'd always hoped I'd be brave enough to act on my anger, and despite the knot in my gut and the lump in my throat, my shaking hand slipped slowly into my cloak and took hold of the dagger Nyomi had insisted I carry. Memories of Ogrid's lessons bubbled up through my mind's eye. I knew how to fell the rutting pig, if only I could make my body cooperate, but something stayed my blade. I would tell myself later that I didn't act right then and there because I realized the situation it would create, because attacking Rocher would destroy any chance of recovering my ancestor's journal and possibly endanger the lives of Ulysses and Tehenessey Blue.

The truth was I was just a scared kid.

A boy about my age took a seat between Rocher and Marielle. He was the spitting image of the count with the same dark hair and his military-style outfit, though he seemed a bit shy and a little soft around the edges. He nodded at us awkwardly, as if he hoped we didn't see him, and then he dove into the food on his plate.

L'Vaillee grunted and fixed Marielle with a leer.

"May I introduce the good count's heir, Rensalier L'Vailllee, and his tutor, the Lord Phillippe Rocher," she said.

Neither of them acknowledged the introduction. If Rocher had replied with a greeting, I would've burst into tears. The fact that he didn't seem to notice me was a huge relief. He'd probably wronged so many people that he couldn't keep them straight anymore.

The meal was a polite, mostly silent affair, the raucous noise of the rest of the party kept at bay by the thick walls. The only consistent conversation took place between Ulysses and the count. The first mate, it seemed, could instantly become an expert on any topic of his choice, provided his audience was less than an authority on whichever subject he chose. The count's lust to learn about the Shoro was such that he ate up each and every lie Ulysses fed him. At one point, he even summoned an assistant to bring his maps of the region. The first mate made several corrections to the maps, muttering to himself and cursing whoever was responsible for such inaccuracies as he alternately worked and shoveled food into his mouth. Marielle interjected occasionally to remind the two of her presence, but the men ignored her.

When L'Vaillee's plate was clean, others, myself included, were still working. The count didn't care; he unleashed a massive yawn and rose from his chair. "Dessert, I believe, will be much better after a nap. We'll return to the grand hall in an hour." He turned to Ulysses, completely ignoring Blue and myself. "You're welcome to explore my home, as is custom. I'm sure you can imagine what will happen if anything turns up missing."

"Of course, m'lord," the pirate replied with a slight bow, "but before you retire, it appears the chef has come to inquire about the quality of her work."

All eyes followed Ulysses's gaze to the far corner of the room, to the woman who'd helped us into Vastille. In her long blue gown and her glittering diamond jewelry, she outshone every other woman in the room, as well as every woman I'd ever met—and she did so in a plain, classic style that was a sharp contrast to the flashy attire of L'Vaillee's other guests.

"How did I do?" Nicolette asked.

The count moved to speak, but Ulysses cut him off with a round of thunderous applause that quickly spread to the rest of the table. Nicolette blushed as she curtseyed, then she strode quickly to L'Vaillee and gave him a peck on the cheek.

"Did you enjoy the meal, uncle?" she asked.

"It was excellent, my dear," he said. He gave her arm an awkward squeeze, trying and failing to appear affectionate. "I'm sure dessert will be even better. If you'll pardon me, I'm feeling a bit peaked."

She nodded. "Rest well."

The count left the dining room, and the rest of those gathered followed suit. A line of well-wishers formed to shower Nicolette with compliments. Marielle leaned across the table and smiled at Ulysses.

"Would you care to adjourn to my suite?" she asked as seductively as she could manage. "The view is quite...spectacular."

"Sorry," Ulysses replied uncomfortably. "Got a wife and son back north."

"News travels through the Shoro so unreliably," she cooed, tracing her fingernail along the back of his hand.

"Err...well, you see..." he trailed off. "What I mean is..."

"Oh, just cut to the chase," Blue snapped. "A group of savages took him captive in the Shoro. They required certain body parts to perform a heathen ritual. Fillard and I finally managed to rescue him a few days later, but not before the bastards got what they needed. Dash Jr.'s going to be very, very disappointed when his father tells him he won't be getting a baby brother or sister any time soon."

I tried to feign sad compassion, but Blue's story and the corresponding looks on the faces of Ulysses and Marielle were too much. A soft laugh burst through my lips. Marielle scowled at me, then at Blue and Ulysses, and then she stomped away.

"That is what one gets when one asks Tehenessey Blue to fetch the stick," the marii said with a triumphant tip of his wine glass.

The first mate slumped down in his chair. "I can't decide whether to thank you or toss you out the nearest window," he said thoughtfully. "Well done."

We sat back and watched Nicolette work her way through her throng of admirers. Hands were shaken, curtseys dispensed, and beloved cheeks chastely pecked. Her smile somehow kept getting brighter with each interaction. My tiny peasant brain struggled to process that the elegant woman so graciously interacting with these foolishly rich Nefazo was the same creature as the filthy farmhand we'd met on the road to Vastille. Yes, there had been plenty of signs that the woman wasn't exactly what she seemed, but seeing her in action like that—I was confused, and honestly quite smitten.

Still, a terrified little voice in the back of my skull wondered if we shouldn't linger. "Is it safe to wait around like this?" I whispered to Ulysses.

"Has anything we've attempted in the last three days truly been safe?" he replied rhetorically. "Her opportunity to out us and summon her uncle's heavies to roughly toss us from the premises has come and gone. Let's see what she wants."

The first mate's eyes lingered on Nicolette as he spoke. A pang of jealousy twisted my gut. I slouched down in my chair and studied the swirling gold embroidery on the white linens.

Her duties complete, Nicolette turned to us and strode confidently to the table. "I expected you three to make an appearance," she said with a sparkling smile. "I'm so glad you came!"

Faced with the beautiful Nicolette, Ulysses was once again on top of his game. "We wouldn't have missed it for the world," he said. "That meal was truly exquisite."

"I'm glad you enjoyed it, but I'm quite sure you didn't go through all that trouble in the Hollow just for a free meal."

"What makes you think we would ever risk sullying our good names in such a place?" Ulysses asked.

"Because you're known carriage thieves, and more importantly, because your friend here is blushing like a school girl in a bath house." My already warm cheeks felt like they were about to explode.

"He has a medical condition," Ulysses deadpanned.

"Sure he does. So tell me...how can I help you annoy my bastard uncle?"

Ulysses scratched his chin thoughtfully, obviously considering how much to tell her. "We're literature connoisseurs, and it's come to our attention that the good count has recently come into possession of a very rare volume we'd like to add to our collection."

"It's a small book," I added. "Bound in leather, very old."

She playfully mimicked the first mate's chin scratching. "Hmm...a vague description, but it sounds familiar..."

My heart leapt. "You know of it?"

"I believe I do. It never leaves Rensalier's side."

— CHAPTER SIXTEEN —

Nicolette brought us to her suite in the top floor of the palace's northeastern tower. Matching her pace as she wound through the crowd of revelers in the grand hall—and then again as she all but ran up the spiraling staircase—left the three of us gasping for breath.

"Don't be fooled," she explained from her perch at the edge of a plush sofa. She'd kicked off her shoes at the bottom of the stairwell and remained barefoot. "I was not granted such a grand space as a measure of hospitality. This location of this suite makes it as much a prison as the dungeons beneath the keep, just with fewer bars and chains."

"If this is prison, lock me up and throw away the key," Tehenessey Blue said. He'd been exploring Nicolette's rooms, occasionally stopping to examine the contents of a drawer or a cabinet. Though I never actually caught him stealing anything, I was sure his pockets weren't empty. Nicolette didn't seem to mind.

"Still, it must be a welcome change from the farm," Ulysses mused from across the room. He'd identified a bare space on the wall against which he could lean roguishly, his arms crossed. "Just what was the count's niece doing in such a place?"

She sighed. "Sneaking away from home to embrace my rebellious youth. Count Jetain—my grandfather—used to abscond from Vastille to work with his subjects regularly. He said it helped him understand them. I believe he was correct."

I leaned forward in the gilded chair I'd chosen to sit upon. "Did he ever visit Brennik's Reach?"

The curls gathered atop Nicolette's head bounced when she nodded. "The Yuinite community there was one of his pet projects. That's why Uncle Antoine's tax collectors have been hitting it so hard." She glared at the floor. "My uncle is an animal."

"It's always a shame to see a family divided," Ulysses said, "especially one of such fine breeding." In the corner, Blue looked up from a dresser drawer just long enough to roll his eyes.

"Uncle Antoine is a liar and a cheat, and he's a barbarous oaf to boot."

"He seemed like a good enough sort, inviting us for dinner and all," the first mate prodded, "but if he attempts an expedition to any of the marks I made on his map of the Shoro, it would be wise not to join him."

Nicolette flashed her beautiful smile. "Perhaps I'll encourage him, then. Here's my story, for which I have no physical proof: Count Antoine is not my grandfather's rightful heir. Jetain told me on his deathbed that that my father was to be named the lord of Vastille. I believe that Antoine stole Jetain's last will and testament before it could be executed and then had my parents put to death on false charges of conspiracy against the Nefazo

Council. I have been his ward ever since. It is only through my own sheer cunning—and a not insignificant amount of luck— that he has not yet succeeded in marrying me off to some slob in exchange for something he wants. In the meantime, I search his palace for evidence of my uncle's misdeeds and occasionally run off to participate in the lives of the Count's subjects, as my grandfather once did. Got it?"

Blue closed one dresser drawer in disgust and moved on to another. "It is unlikely L'Vaillee kept anything that might prove his guilt. Seems you have an easy enough time getting in and out without detection. Why not just leave?"

She shook her head. "The bastard would find me. My uncle is relentless. Not to mention that doing so would mean I'll never find what I need to have the man ruined."

"Kill him, then," Ulysses said nonchalantly, as if the task were as easy as fetching a drink from the local pub.

"I'm no murderer. I would prefer to see Uncle Antoine face the council."

"What do you need us for, then?" Blue asked as he stuck his nose in a closet, sniffed, then shut the door without further examination.

"As I've mentioned, anyone looking to make my uncle's life slightly less comfortable is someone I'm interested in working with," Nicolette replied. "And I imagine being owed a favor by the crew of the *Black Yonnix* could be useful to me someday, should the option to flee becomes a necessity."

She turned to me. Her dark eyes weighed heavy on my shoulders. "The journal...what's so important about it?"

"It's a family heirloom," Ulysses said dismissively. "Valuable, but nothing special. His beloved's parents are insisting upon it in exchange for their daughter's hand in marriage."

Nicolette ignored him. She wanted an answer from the only person in the room she knew wouldn't lie to her.

"My last name is Vardallian," I said slowly. "The coded language in that journal leads to Lucifus's legendary treasure. Rocher stole it from me while collecting taxes in Brennik's Reach—and he killed my grandfather that same day."

The Nefazo's eyes softened. "I am sorry for your loss, Vardallian. I will do what I can to see your property returned. My grandfather would've done nothing less."

I wasn't sure how I felt about that. On the one hand, the thought of Nicolette L'Vaillee helping me with anything buoyed my spirits and set my dumb adolescent heart aflutter. On the other hand, I had no idea if she could be trusted. That sort of promise could've been a trap.

Surprisingly, the others kept their usually busy mouths shut and allowed me to process her offer and respond. "I appreciate that," I managed. Ulysses met my eye and offered a subtle nod of encouragement. "Tell us about Rensalier," I said more confidently.

Nicolette pushed herself off the bed and took a few steps into the center of the room, her hands clasped loosely behind her back. "There's more Jetain in the boy than there is Antoine, but not by a large margin. He's intelligent and well-spoken, but moody and reserved."

"Like Vardallian here, but without those first two positive qualities," Blue interjected as he dropped onto the sofa beside me.

She ignored him. "I've done my best with Rensalier, but he's become covetous and selfish like his tutor and his uncle. He is obsessed with that journal. He believes it to be something special. I never imagined he'd be correct."

"Nevertheless, that is Mr. Vardallian's property and we will be leaving with it," Ulysses said firmly. "How do we part L'Vaillee's spawn from his favorite tome?"

Nicolette pursed her lips and looked up at the ceiling. "He's under constant guard, but I can arrange an introduction. Typically, he watches the S'espri from one of the balconies overlooking the grand hall. The tougher problem to solve, I believe, involves making a clean escape."

"I'll settle for a successful one," Blue replied. "It's unlikely we'll manage to avoid notice, or at the very least suspicion."

"Could you put the hall to sleep, like you did in Brennik's Reach?" I asked, impressed with the intelligence of my own idea.

"Of course I could, but it's unlikely they'd stay that way, what with so many people coming in and out of the palace," the marii said. My ego deflated.

Ulysses pushed himself off the wall and took a few steps toward the sofa. "We need something more disruptive. Friend Blue, last night's performance in the Hollow comes to mind."

"I left the sheet music behind at Nyomi's," he said. "Attempting such a powerful melody from memory would be amazingly stupid."

"Or amazingly courageous," Ulysses prodded. "Surely a musician of your skill could make it work."

"Oh, I can make it work, it just may not work the way we expect."

"Good enough. It's chaos we'll need, not precision. Listen up, friends: I know how we can complete our little caper."

— CHAPTER SEVENTEEN —

I can't say I felt particularly confident in the first mate's plan. The idea, as I understood it, was to create as many layers of messy distraction as possible, so that L'Vaillee's household staff wouldn't notice a lone peasant escaping with a freshly pilfered journal, regardless of Rensalier's protests or commands. Acquiring that journal in the first place would be my responsibility. I was the only one capable of identifying it, and the others were better at drawing attention to themselves anyway.

Before we departed Nicolette's suite, Ulysses sternly reminded all of us that we were to continue with our respective roles regardless of what else might be happening. Deviation from the plan would get us nowhere, and likely ruin our one and only chance to recover the journal. We'd each need to trust that the others would accomplish their tasks. I had no reason to doubt any of them.

We separated on our way back down the stairwell. Ulysses and Tehenessey Blue continued their descent to the first floor and the grand hall. Nicolette and I peeled off at the second floor in search of Rensalier. The prospect of working together with the alluring Nefazo, even for a short time, buoyed my spirits. I wanted to impress her almost as much as I wanted to reacquire my stolen property.

I gasped when Nicolette suddenly grabbed the front of my tunic and dragged me into an alcove lit by a gaudy sconce. There was not much space between us. She smelled amazing— like lilacs—and the weight of her knuckle against my chest felt like a blade preparing to pierce my heart. Yes, Your Highness, I'll spare you and continue.

"Do you trust them?" she asked. Her dark eyes flickered magically in the candlelight.

It took my addled mind a few moments to decipher her question. "Ulysses and Blue?" I asked dumbly. She nodded, insistent. "To be honest, I haven't much thought about it."

"Do it quickly," she said, lifting her chin toward mine. The subtle lilt of her Nefazo accent was music to my ears. "You seem like a good enough sort. What happens after you've recovered this journal for them? If there's an even a small possibility this ends with a knife in your back, it would be smarter to flee. I can help you. They won't leave you alone like this again."

I tried not to get lost in her eyes—sorry, Your Highness—but in an odd way it helped me think. Cavorting through Vastille had been one of the most enjoyable times of my life, and I'd begun to consider Ulysses and Blue my friends, which I realized was a very dangerous assumption. Did our growing bond work both ways, or had I simply been blinded by the thrill of adventure? I couldn't be sure. These were hardened criminals who'd kidnapped me from my home and murdered at least one of my neighbors.

My answer came quickly. "For now, I trust them because they need me. The journal does them no good without someone who can read it." In hindsight, I do wish I'd paid this realization more heed.

Nicolette raised a slender eyebrow. "Astute observation. And what's in all this for you?"

"Ever been to Brennik's Reach?" I asked. Her smile lit up the alcove. "My decision to fall in with a bunch of pirates is not that different from your excursions out of the palace."

"My activities carry a significantly lower risk of incarceration or execution, but yes, I see your point." She released me, unfortunately. "Rensalier will be on one the balconies on this floor. There will be two guards, and Rocher will not be far away. Are you ready?"

The little knife Nyomi had given me suddenly felt heavy against my hip. "I'm ready," I replied with what I hoped was a confident nod. My hands trembled under my cloak.

A few dozen paces further and the corridor intersected the grand hall. Nicolette and I proceeded slowly, walking side-by-side and chatting cordially about life in Brennik's Reach. Her interest in the peasantry was well known, she'd claimed, and so the idea was that no one would find our meandering discussion even remotely suspicious. Nicolette exchanged polite nods with the other guests we passed, but I kept my gaze on either the floor or my companion. We heard the revelry below long before we saw it, a constant hum of discussion and laughter that almost drowned out the marii band's perky tune.

The first several balconies we passed were packed to the gills with people. When we finally found one we believed to be empty, we discovered instead that it was already occupied by a drunken couple locked in a messy embrace against the wall. Nicolette shooed them away with a grunt and a glare.

"Nobility has its uses," she mused as we stepped toward the railing.

Tendrils of narcotic smoke rose around us, spicing the dull odor that comes when too many drunken people expend too much energy in too tight an enclosure. I leaned over the railing and searched the crowd, which had swelled even larger since our arrival. My attention lingered for a moment on a trio of young men racing to finish their steins of beer to the amusement of a pair of women in matching gowns, and then upon a large man executing perfect backflips on the dance floor. I found Blue in his assigned position beside the band where he could similarly scan the room.

Nicolette tugged my sleeve. "There," she said, pointing toward a balcony at the far end of the great hall. "That's Rensalier."

Squinting, I could just see the boy seated alone upon another balcony, somehow focused on a book amidst all that noise and chaos. He seemed like such an easy target. Rocher was nowhere to be found. I couldn't decide whether to be relieved or disappointed.

A burst of bright red crossing the dance floor drew my attention back downward. "There's Ulysses," I said. The first mate pirouetted around a dancing couple, intercepted and dipped a twirling woman in a billowing green dress, and then passed her into the arms of a gentleman in a feathered hat waiting for a partner at the edge of the dance floor.

"That man is far too charming for his own good," Nicolette said as Ulysses disappeared behind the curtains concealing Count L'Vaillee's lounge.

I shifted uncomfortably. "Luckily he's on our side," I said.

Nicolette snorted. "Hopefully his ego is too."

The first mate reappeared moments later as Marielle dragged him back out through the curtains and toward the dance floor. Count L'Vaillee tolerated his new wife's dalliances because he didn't like her that much, Nicolette had explained, but only to a point. The count himself emerged a moment later, right on cue. He watched, arms crossed, as Marielle and Ulysses cleared a spot in the middle of the packed dance floor and began to twirl.

I looked to the marii. Blue drew his flute from his vest, twirled it once across his fingers, and pressed the instrument to his lips. "That's our signal," I said.

We zipped off the balcony and back into the corridor, moving more quickly this time but still conversing idly about my background in Brennik's Reach. She appeared genuinely interested as I told her all about my medical work with Grandfather, and of our simple home, and that we'd been saving up what we could from our meager income so I could one day attend university in Mana'Olai. I wished we could've spoken that way for hours.

We soon passed throngs of partiers searching for available balcony space from which to watch the roguish young man who dared dance with the Count's wife. "The fool must have a death wish," one man in a violet tunic trimmed with white lace said to his date, who appeared to be dressed as a peacock. "L'Vaillee will run him through himself!" My own experience with the first mate's swordsmanship suggested otherwise. I hoped it wouldn't come to a duel; his role was supposed to simply draw the Count out into the open.

As we rounded the corner, Nicolette asked me a question that made me trip over my own feet. "Is there anyone back in

Brennik's Reach you've missed during your travels, or anyone you're looking forward to seeing when you return?"

My mind flicked to Mahlly, but I couldn't say her name. "I'm sure my neighbors will greet me warmly, but there's no one in particular." From the sharp tilt of her head, I could tell Nicolette knew I'd lied.

A single guard waited outside our target balcony, dressed in light green finery and wearing a long sword on his hip. The man stiffened at Nicolette's approach. "Evening, my lady," he said with tight military diction.

She nodded in greeting. "At ease, corporal. We've come to pay Rensalier a visit. Mr. Mize here is a travelling scholar specializing in obscure texts. I suspect he and the young master would have much to discuss."

The guard eyed me suspiciously. I certainly didn't look scholarly. "Of course, my lady," he finally said.

Nicolette patted his arm and smiled affectionately. "Why don't you go find a pint or a slice of pie? It is the S'espri, after all. I will protect the sanctity of our lord's bloodline for a moment while you enjoy the much-deserved fruits of your labor."

The guard hesitated again, and then visibly relaxed. "Yes, my lady," he said with a relieved smile. The man all but ran down the corridor. Nicolette smiled and led me forward.

Rensalier was still reading. He'd covered the entire balcony in parchment pages covered with notes scrawled in uneven handwriting. The tome in his lap was definitely Lucifus's journal—I'd know those scratchy, runic symbols and those yellowed pages anywhere. We stopped at the edge of his work. He didn't seem to notice our arrival, or more perhaps he simply didn't care to acknowledge it.

"Cousin Rensalier," Nicolette said primly, "may I present to you Fillard Mize?"

I bowed. The young noble didn't look up. "We met at dinner."

"Yes, but you didn't have the opportunity to converse. Mr. Mize here is a scholar specializing in obscure texts."

"Good for him," he replied dismissively. "I'm busy, as I'm sure you can both see."

I wanted to jerk the journal from his hands and toss him over the balcony, but instead I squatted down and examined his notes. Most were attempts to map Lucifus's coded symbols to letters or phonetic sounds. All of them were incorrect.

"Please depart immediately," he muttered. "I am on the verge of a breakthrough you couldn't possibly comprehend."

I leaned a little closer so I could read the characters in the journal. It seemed that despite his difficulty deciphering Lucifus's language, he'd correctly surmised that the appropriate way to read the journal was to start at the middle pages and work his way outward, alternating between pages of lower and greater number.

"...and in the springtime, when the orchids bloom and the yellow thresh sing for their mates, Diun lights orange the grove of the forgotten..."

Rensalier froze, and then his face snapped my way. Curiosity twinkled in his eyes. He looked so much like his father. "You can read this?"

I nodded. "It's a tricky old dialect, but yes, I can read it."

"How?"

A collective gasp pierced the revelry. The band suddenly stopped playing. I could've heard a pin drop in the ensuing silence.

"How dare you kiss my wife?" the count's voice bellowed from below, echoing back and forth off the great hall's architecture. "I demand satisfaction by combat, Mr. Skipjack, and I demand it immediately!"

There came another collective gasp, this one accompanied by a low murmur as the count's challenge was discussed. Rensalier raised his eyebrows, shut the journal, and stood up to get a better view at the railing. Nicolette and I joined him, walking right through his notes. L'Vaillee's niece twisted the back of my tunic in her fingers. I could almost hear the breath lodged in her throat.

This was not the way things were supposed to go. The dance floor had emptied, leaving Ulysses and Marielle alone in an embrace that appeared much more than friendly. I spotted Blue in the corner, playing the inaudible notes on his flute furiously, but his song's magic had yet to manifest. I worried that he truly couldn't play it from memory, or that perhaps somehow no one had ever lost their life in a horrific manner within those walls—which had seemed an impossibility not long ago.

Ulysses released Marielle and she fell to the floor. "I must sincerely apologize, my lord, for such inappropriate behavior was not within my intentions. Your wife, I must make clear, decided to kiss me, and I feared that rejecting her advances would not end well for yours truly." He raised his hands in a gesture of submission. "I will make my way from your property posthaste, my lord, and you shall never see me again."

"Lock the doors so this dog cannot escape," L'Vaillee commanded as he stomped toward Ulysses. Guards hurried off in several directions to do just that. "We settle this now, coward!"

Nicolette grunted in frustration. We'd planned to exit right through the front door. Without that option, we'd need to take a much more treacherous route out of the palace. I was not looking forward to jumping out the window of Nicolette's suite and hoping the ocean would be kind enough to break our fall.

I risked a glance down at the journal. Rensalier held it loosely at his side. Could I jerk it from his hand, rush down the corridor, and somehow make it out before the doors were locked? I doubted it. My knife begged for consideration. Did I have the stomach to slit Rensalier's throat? And if I murdered her kin in cold blood, would Nicolette continue to aid us? Indecision left me frozen.

A page delivered a pair of matching short swords to L'Vaillee, then darted back into the masses. The count hefted each blade, chose one, and tossed the other to Ulysses. The first mate deftly caught it by the haft and spun on his heel into a ready stance I recognized from Ogrid's lessons. "I'm told it's bad luck to spill noble blood at the Sespri," Ulysses called out, "but if I must curse myself to protect my honor, so be it!"

"Oh no," Nicolette muttered, twisting my shirt even harder.

"Father will skewer this fool like a roast over the fire," Rensalier said. His voice dripped with unmistakable blood lust.

I heard a group of men below us hastily placing bets on the two competitors. Very few of them backed Ulysses.

Tension settled in over the great hall like some sort of fog as the count and the pirate sized each other up for what felt like eons. I swear Nicolette, Rensalier and I stopped breathing. My eyes went so wide that they started to hurt.

And then their blades crashed together with a thunderous clang. The two men spun and struck and parried in twin blurs of motion to which my sad storytelling skills couldn't possibly do justice. L'Vaillee was the aggressor, pressing in close. When he went high, Ulysses parried, turned, ducked, and went low—but the count was waiting with an answer. Metal collided repeatedly against metal as the two spiraled around each other on that dance floor. The crowd hooted and hollered, clearly enthused at this addition to their S'espri. Beside me, Rensalier bobbed and weaved in a poor imitation of his father's movements.

L'Vaillee pirouetted away from Ulysses and the two men stopped to consider each other again, breathing heavily. The Vastillians went wild, but the count quieted them with a wave of his hand.

"You fight like a northerner, yet I don't detect an accent," L'Vaillee said in between breaths. "I would know from where you hail, swordsman."

Ulysses chuckled. "Would you believe me if I claimed to be the first mate of the *Black Yonnix*?"

The crowd, and L'Vaillee laughed. "Not for one moment," the count replied. "With no homeland to which to send it, I suppose I shall have to cast your corpse into the sea!"

He pounced. Ulysses rolled away, unwilling to engage. Stalling for time wasn't his safest option, but perhaps he could keep the count busy just long enough.

A murmur from above called my attention to a balcony a floor up from our own. I looked that way just in time to see the semi-corporeal spirit of a young woman shove the ghost of a wiry old man over the railing. A woman beneath us screamed.

L'Vaille pounced again. Ulysses parried and swept out his foot. The count hopped up over the pirate's boot and swung the pommel of his weapon down toward the first mate's head. Ulysses caught the count's wrist with his free hand, but

L'Vaillee used that leverage to spin himself away from the pirate's blade. Something small and green flicked out of the pirate's gaping sleeve and splattered to the floor. The count hopped lunged sideways to avoid a right cross and crunched down on Roderick the snake with a satisfied grunt.

Ulysses took a step back, shaking his head. "Oh, that just won't do. Now it's personal!"

He lunged forward. L'Vaillee parried his blade with a spiraling stroke, side-stepped, and drove his fist into Ulysses's kidney. The pirate dropped to his knees, then let himself fall all the way to the floor to avoid a slash that would've separated his head from his body. Nicolette gasped and grabbed my wrist.

The first mate feigned a roll and instead lashed out again with his foot, catching L'Vaillee in the calf. Ulysses rolled backwards over his shoulder and brought his weapon downward in what would've been a killing blow. The lightning-quick count somehow caught it on his own blade, punched Ulysses in the gut, and then stabbed outward to scrape the first mate's left flank. Ulysses stumbled away, clutching his side with his free hand. Blood spattered down onto the floor from underneath his torn coat.

My heart sank. I'd seen that sort of wound before; it wasn't the sort of thing someone could push through easily. I looked down at the journal again, considering my options.

By the dance floor, a woman screamed. Cries of terror burst out from the gathered throng. Some turned and ran toward the now locked exit.

"Look!" Nicolette said, her voice quivering.

A shimmering spirit had appeared right behind Ulysses. Count L'Vaillee stood frozen in shock, his mouth agape, as the shade strode straight through the first mate as if through empty space. It was an old man, dressed well in a uniform similar to the count's own. There was a physical resemblance, too, especially in the nose and forehead.

"Grandfather," Nicolette whispered. "That's the shade of Count Jetain."

I saw a chance to help, so I took it. "That's the shade of Count Jetain!" I screamed as loud as I could.

The crowd's shrieks echoed my own. More of them rushed toward the door. I heard the guards trying to deflect them, to convince them to head back into the great hall. Angry voices demanded that the doors be opened once more. Eventually, I knew, the masses would win that discussion. In the corner, Blue played furiously.

On the dance floor, Ulysses slowly backed away. Count Jetain raised one spectral arm, pointed right at his son, and shook his head.

I grabbed Nicolette's wrist with my right hand, gave it a squeeze, and then jerked the journal free with my left. Before Rensalier could protest, I turned and dragged Nicolette toward the corridor.

Lord Rocher blocked our way, tapping a heavy mace against his shoulder, an evil smile curling his lips.

— CHAPTER EIGHTEEN —

I thought I recognized you at dinner," Rocher snarled, spittle flying from his plump lips. "Thuroth Vardallian's grandson, isn't it? I see neither a wedding band nor a uniform, *boy*, so I'll assume you didn't follow my orders."

I recoiled in horror. The object of my vengeance had made himself known at the worst possible time. I wasn't ready to face him. Not like that, with Nicolette watching and the pirates trusting that I could escape with the journal.

He took a step forward, backing us against the railing. Rensalier stepped aside, his eyes wide. I released Nicolette's hand and quickly drew the knife from within my cloak.

"Cute," Rocher said with a chuckle and another tap of his mace against his shoulder, "but I know you Yuinite scum are all pacifists. You'll not scare me with a butter knife."

"You will let us go," Nicolette said sternly. "Vardallian is under my protection."

Rocher spat in her face. "I will do no such thing, and I remind you that you have no power in this palace. I've already sent word of your betrayal to the good count. I suspect that ocean view of which you've become so fond will soon be replaced by something much darker. Now step aside, girl, I've a skull to crack in the name of Count L'Vaillee."

I cringed back, awaiting the blow. To my utmost shock, Rensalier reached out a hand and stayed Rocher's attack. "No, sir. In the name of Count L'Vaillee, my father, I command you to spare this one."

I blinked in confusion. Had Nicolette been right? Was the spawn of the vile Count L'Vaillee more like his grandfather than his father? Surely the look of concern on the young man's face was proof enough of that.

And then Rensalier sucker punched me. The little worm got me right in the gut and drove the wind clean out of my lungs. I bent over and staggered, gasping for breath. I turned toward Nicolette and she took hold of my shoulders to steady me. "He can read the journal," Rensalier said to Rocher. "You said he's a Vardallian, right? Think what Lucifus's treasure would do for the Count's coffers." He smiled at me with a menace I've rarely encountered. Rensalier L'Vaillee didn't see me as a living, breathing lij; in that moment, I understood that I would merely be a thing to be used and then discarded. "He'll do us more good in the dungeons, where he can spill all his family's secrets. You have promised to teach me the most painful way to remove a man's fingers."

The tax collector's smile spread ear-to-ear. "Yes, I suppose that will do indeed. Tough kid, too. That blow should've dropped him. He'll be a lot of fun to play with."

I'd had enough. I had to do something. Instinct took over. Ogrid's voice echoed in my skull, as if the old Omman was whispering in my ear.

Perhaps being tough and persistent as a mule will be enough. For now, if you find yourself in a fight, run. If you can't run, fight dirty. There's no honor to be found at the bottom of an early grave.

My breath finally caught. I grabbed Nicolette's hips for leverage and kicked out backward at Rensalier's gut. Pain shot up my leg as my boot collided with his hip. He staggered sideways against the railing, shouting as he toppled over the slender iron. Rocher, his eyes wide, reached out for his student. Rensalier caught the man's sleeve and pulled the big tax collector over with him.

They landed with a sickening splat.

For a moment, neither Nicolette nor I moved. She stared agape at the spot where her cousin had just stood. A tear ran down her cheek. I wanted to say something, but my tongue wouldn't move. I fully expected her to shove me over the balcony after the two men I might have just murdered.

She shook her head, dragging herself back to reality. "Oh, grandfather," she muttered.

Grandfather, I thought, echoing Nicolette's own entreaties to her deceased loved one. *Mother. Father. Mahlly.* Though that last name on my list was not among the dead, I knew that for all intents and purposes she may as well have been, because what I'd just done would certainly make me dead to her.

Then Nicolette did the most surprising thing: she reached out and squeezed my hand. "I believe I'm going to need that favor I suggested the crew of the *Black Yonnix* will owe me."

I sheathed my blade and stuck the journal into a pocket of my cloak. "You'll have it. I swear to you."

Voices roared as the doors of the great hall were finally opened. Sensing our opportunity, we took off down the corridor, fleeing our crimes hand-in-hand, unsure of what worse things we'd be forced to do in the future.

— EPILOGUE —

We met Ulysses and Tehenessey Blue at the designated spot, across the street from Nyomi's, and then fled Vastille without incident," Vardallian said. "More shades had appeared in and around the palace, it turns out, and even L'Vaillee's most faithful men had no interest in locking themselves into a city haunted with marauding spirits.

"I managed to patch up Ulysses's wound with a strip of Nicolette's gown and a poultice made of local ingredients. Apo met us a few days later at the designated pickup point. No one protested when I insisted that Nicolette come with us."

The prisoner shrugged, unsure of where to go next. "That's how I got my family's journal back, Your Highness. Can't say I'm proud of it."

The Black Queen studied Vardallian for a few moments, then stood. At her full height, Losa was the most intimidating person—man or woman—that he had ever seen, Captain Lagash included. "What of Rensalier and Rocher?"

Vardallian tried to collapse inward on himself, making himself small. "Rensalier survived and joined his father's pursuit of the *Black Yonnix*. Rocher did not. We learned from a traveler that the big man's girth broke Rensalier's fall, although he's walked with a limp since."

Losa strode right up to Vardallian, finally stopping so close to him that their bodies almost touched. The captive shivered, certain that the Empress would tear his guts out with her own hands now that she had the information she'd asked for.

The Black Queen smiled at him. The gesture was awkward, as if it were a motion her face was not used to making, but it was not without warmth. "I believe you, Kensey Vardallian."

The prisoner didn't dare display the relief warming his veins. "Thank you, Your Highness. Thank you."

"Come. We will relocate to a more comfortable part of this damn palace, and my staff will do their best to make up for your harsh treatment and the hands of my military."

"Thank you, Your Highness."

"In return...you will tell me more. I must know the true story of the final voyage of the *Black Yonnix*. Once I have it, I will offer you one further boon: one more chance for vengeance, this time against Ulysses Lagash and all those who betrayed you after you found your ancestor's vault.

"We need Lucifus's ship, Vardallian. I fear it is the only thing that can help us stop the Fae."

— ABOUT THE AUTHOR —

Frustrated with the generic, paint-by-numbers state of modern fantasy writing, Scott Colby is working hard to give the genre the kick in the pants it so desperately needs. Shouldn't stories about people and creatures with the power to magically change the world around them be creative, funny, and kind of weird? Scott thinks so.

A BOOK OF KNOWLEDGE:
PILEAUS

— WELCOME TO PILEAUS —

The emperor is dead. What's left of the once proud Pilean Empire is under siege from threats both internal and external. Ommany, Thila, Ud, and the pirates of Brailee's Steps have all set their sights on the empire's land and resources. It is a time of war and strife, but also of discovery and opportunity. The race to control the north has brought with it major steps forward in science, technology, and sorcery, all of which are also contributing to the chaos in their own unique ways.

Meanwhile, there's a whole wide world out there many northerners have forgotten about. A race of aquatic zealots plunders the seas and coasts. Far to the south, a small cluster of younger, more progressive nations becomes more powerful every day. Dark secrets and ancient ruins await discovery in the center of the continent. More and more musicians learn to weave amazing magic with their songs. Immortal demigods in a wondrous parallel dimension endlessly debate the fate of these chaotic mortals—and occasionally intervene. Life on the Pilean continent grows more interesting by the hour.

The scene is set. The world is ripe for the rise of terrible villains and the crusading heroes who will appear in response. Which will you be?

YUINISM

The state religion of Pileaus, the Yuinite faith is a monotheistic practice centered on worship of the god Yuin. The religion began almost eight hundred years ago as a small cult based on the philosophy and powers of a single man in Thila. This man, now only known as the "Oprin," received his divine calling at the age of twelve in a mystical incident while tending a flock of sheep. It is said that his father left him tending their flocks high in the mountains of Lud's Teeth in order to return home for supplies. When the father returned, he found an elderly man unconscious beneath a tree. After much questioning and discussion, the father realized that the old man was in fact his son. They spent seventy days and nights on the mountain, now known as Yuin's Throne, speaking of the events that had befallen the boy.

Both father and son set about preaching the glories of Yuin and anointing any who would listen to their words. Approximately twenty-five years later, when the Oprin knew he was soon to pass on, he identified a twelve-year-old child to take his place. He returned to the head of the western branch of the Tybur with the child, the same place where he received his calling, to anoint the boy as his successor. The Oprin left the boy beneath the same tree he had been found under years before. Night fell, the new dawn came, and when the Oprin returned, the boy had become a middle-aged man. The pattern was set.

The Yuinite religion is founded on the idea that one day, Yuin will come and collect the faithful and take them to a heavenly afterlife. In order to attain this grand gift, certain requirements must be met, and only the just will achieve the ecstasy promised by the Oprin. The Yuinites shun magic and anything remotely claiming power outside the influence and sanction of Yuin.

The priesthood is a patriarchal order that gains its membership from the faithful. Among the truly devout, if a family's first-born child is a son, he is sent to the order as a tithe to Yuin. Families whose first-born is a daughter or who do not have children are required to tithe from their material wealth. Members of the priesthood are commanded to spread the laws of Yuin to the rest of the world and ensure the purity of the people at all costs. They keep a secular and spiritual record of their lives and spend their days serving and teaching the people around them. The Yuinites have gathered a number of the teachings of the Oprin into a collected volume called the "Maunin."

THE SHUEN
The Waveriders

Self-proclaimed lords of the sea, the shuen are an aquatic race of religious zealots that controls the oceans surrounding Pileaus. Their religion dictates that the sea is sacred above all else and the unclean landlocked races (known to the shuen as the Riku Chou) must not be allowed to foul it. Those who trespass into shuen territory are dealt with swiftly and decisively. The shuen eschew setting foot on land at all costs lest they also become tainted.

Tall, lithe, muscular mammals, Aiemer streams flowing out into the ocean twisted the shuen's porpoise-like ancestors into their current bipedal form. Their faces are elongated and they do not have a nose, possessing instead a type of blowhole similar to that of a porpoise or whale on the tops of their heads.

They have three fingers and a thumb and long, webbed toes. Many lij view the shuen's large, opaque eyes and piercing gazes as disconcerting or even frightening. Due to the size and length of their oddly jointed feet, they tend to walk on their balls of their feet rather than flat-footed. This gives them an almost graceful, bobbing gait. The shuen are air-breathers and cannot live continuously underwater. They wear the skins of the animals that their laws allow them to hunt (sharks, mammals, marine reptiles, etc.) and decorate their costumes with obvious water motifs. Their clothing is also embellished with dangling shells, carved bone and ivory beads, and coral trim.

The mah'saiid long ago made a concerted effort to aid the shuen in their cultural progress, but the shuen quickly rejected this aid in a violent encounter, preferring to form their own identity. Despite this break, the mah'saiid are the only race the shuen respect and fear.

TAISHU

The shuen make their homes in coral cities atop the backs of marine leviathans. These floating communities, called taishu, are marvels of organic engineering, complete with running water, careful sanitation, and enough weaponry to easily destroy any Riku Chou vessels. Each comfortably supports a community of between five and fifty thousand, although the largest, taishu Tian Yi, is rumored to support some three hundred thousand souls.

Over centuries, scholars believe, the shuen developed a symbiotic relationship with the leviathans, building entire ecosystems along the backs of these creatures and building their cities from living rock and coral. The leviathans are filter feeders that gain nourishment from anything that flows into their tremendous mouths. The taishu functions as its own ecosystem that typically provides enough food its shuen dwellers. Some even feature mangroves at the waterline or palm trees shortly beyond the water's edge. Although the taishu share similar biological structures, each city has a unique symbiotic relationship with its leviathan.

Each city is governed by an Osei Xio (the Voice of the Sea), a religious and political leader who interprets the signs and portents of the ocean and its various spirits. The Osei Xio's rule is absolute law.

THE MARII
Children of Song

The marii are short, fox-like humanoids often mistaken for Fae, weidt, or other more magical creatures. Their bodies are covered in dense, neutrally colored fur and their long fingers sport retractable claws useful for climbing or defense. A thick tuft of lighter or darker fur sprouts from the tops of their heads in a way similar to the hair atop a lij's skull. Although most are born with bushy tails, several secluded communities have begun producing offspring with thin, prehensile tails. Despite their small stature, the marii sport a wiry strength much like an orangutan or chimpanzee. They are also incredibly agile and harbor no fear of heights, although many feel unsettled in large open spaces. Their musical abilities are unmatched.

The marii tell a number of legends to explain their creation. Some believe they were brought to life by the World Song and that their duty is to act as living notes for the rest of the world. Others believe they were brought to this world by the Hamabi Ushou (the Dancing Gods) in order to bring life and beauty to the dreary lives of the rest of creation. In truth, the marii were first encountered by a band of exploring mah'saiid who came across a large Aiemer lake in the Shoro about 3,900 years ago that had slowly mutated the local fauna into a bipedal race. The mah'saiid saw the intelligent but rudimentary tribal society already growing among the early marii and decided to nurture the fledgling race. Over the course of seven decades, the marii advanced to a point that the mah'saiid finally felt comfortable leaving the tribes and returning to their explorations. Some of the marii accompanied them, but the majority remained in the area until the society grew too large to support itself. The marii leaders then followed the examples of the mah'saiid and went in search of new homes, scattering themselves across the face of the planet in the process.

A friendly, peaceful species, the marii strive to live in harmony with nature via their reverence for the World Song. On more than one occasion they have opened their doors to the lij and other races in order to share their wisdom. They, like the mah'saiid, have learned harsh lessons from this practice, but the marii have not retreated from the world as their mah'saiid patrons have.

The marii often braid naturally carved beads, feathers, shells, and precious stones into their manes. They also are fond of reflective metals and shiny stones, regardless of their inherent value. Clothes tend to be simple leather smocks or kilts. They generally do not wear footwear except in extremely cold winters.

THE WORLD SONG

Music is central to marii society, a racial gift they discovered in trying to mimic the language of the mah'saiid. The marii are the inspiration for the bardic tradition amongst the lij, but they do not often settle in urban places. They will, however, travel to the cities of the lij to trade.

The marii religion revolves around the World Song. This music is sacred to them, and their lives revolve around the natural rhythms of the universe. Most marii see no need for technological advancements that would distort the World Song's sound. Instead, they focus on reshaping existing natural elements rather than changing them into something new. Their creations are interpretations of the song that each individual marii hears.

Most marii refuse to live in or near urban lij areas because of the distortions that artificial and unnatural creations introduce into the World Song. Some, however, have managed to acclimate themselves to city life by accepting a chaotic new rhythm they've come to call the Song of the Masses. These marii are typically looked down upon or treated as eccentric by their forest-dwelling cousins.

Even their written and spoken language is musical. Buru is an adaptation of the ancient mah'saiid language with a distinctly sing-song bent. Timing and pitch are just as important as the sounds identified by Buru letters. Time signatures and measures within the language's sentence structure set the pace at which pieces are read. The other races have great difficulty speaking Buru.

Major marii celebrations occur on the summer and winter solstices when day or night is the longest. On each of these days, all the marii join together in a chorus, and through their magic they literally bind themselves together in a single unified song. This singing often causes the Iraemun to stir in their sleep, and the Surtys keep a very close eye on their charges on these days. As the marii grow in number, their stirrings have become more noticeable, causing strange things to happen in both the Dreaming and the Dying Lands.

A DANGEROUS WILDERNESS

Most of Pileaus remains wild and untamed. Terrible creatures prowl the forests, plains, skies, and seas. For many seeking their fortunes, however, braving the danger is more than worth it. Mysterious ruins left behind by a long-vanished civilization of great power and learning are hidden in the darkest corners of the continent, promising untold wealth to those brave enough to reach them.

TWO REALMS, ONE WORLD

Magic gates spread across the continent connect the Pileaus to a parallel realm known as the Dreaming Lands. Here, a caste-based society of immortal Fae commune with and shape the forces of reality itself. Their realm is a twisted, wondrous landscape where the rules of traditional physics no longer apply.

A PERVASIVE MAGICAL ELEMENT

At the heart of the Fae's debate is the Aiemer, an invisible element that flows into the Dying Lands from the Dreaming. The Aiemer is a source of great magical power available to mortal sorcerers and bards, but it's also an unstable substance with the power to change anything it touches. In places where it pools, evolution works at amazing speeds, twisting and changing all living things it touches. In the worst cases, it spawns massive storms that cause all sorts of illogical effects. The Aiemer is unpredictable, dangerous—and undeniably useful.

THREE PHASES OF DAY

The planet of Baeg Tobar is part of a very complex system of celestial bodies. Its most prominent moon, Diun, bathes the land in silvery light that creates a period of extended twilight between day and night. Diuntyne is an ethereal, magical time during which all manner of specially adapted flora and fauna become active. It's a time for ritual and celebration, but also for the working of dangerous magics.

—◖●◗—

DID YOU KNOW THERE IS ANOTHER NOVEL
SET IN THE WORLD OF PILEAUS?

BE SURE TO PICK UP *THE UNMADE MAN* IF YOU'D LIKE
TO ADVENTURE INTO THE WORLD OF PILEAUS AGAIN!

READ ON FOR A SNEAK PEAK OF THE FIRST TWO
CHAPTERS OF *THE UNMADE MAN*, BY D.T. GOODEN.

—◖●◗—

THE WAITING BOY

The boy felt the man descend from the ridgeline like his own hand held out into a numbing cold and now returning as a stranger to the warmth of his pocket. He was glad. The Fae had searched long for them both, reaching out with eyes and whispers from their home in the Dreaming Lands. Now the boy would journey home, if this new man could bear the weight of the burden he'd come to carry.

The boy listened to his grandfather's last breath as the man and his three riders broke through the jungle's edge. He held his mouth shut and watched them ride into the field. When they were halfway across the thin valley the child inhaled again, no longer fearing that his grandfather's last dead breath would be sucked into his own body. In life the old man would never have done the boy harm; he was a protector. In death, the boy knew, spirits tend to do odd things.

He laid his small hand on the dead man's chest, feeling the heat slip from the corpse. He felt his grandfather's magic fade too. The ties snapped like a broken spider's web. The strands began to sever and would soon wipe clean what life he knew in this hidden glade.

The riders came to a halt before the porch. This is where his life would now go. His grandfather was gone, and he'd taken the protection of the valley with him. The boy thought little of that, noticing only the runes tracing down the arm of the man standing before him. There was much power there. A keen few would see them: those that still knew the smell of old magics, those that heard the hum of coarse power even trapped in script. Why did the man risk laying that secret bare for those watchful few? The boy gazed at the others in the group. There was much strength here, almost as much as there was weakness. He rubbed his palm against his grandfather's chest, one last goodbye and a measure of what little time they had left for introductions.

Boruin ran his hand through his short gray hair, deciding what to make of the scene. The smell of the dust rising up where his boots stirred the earth was too sharp. His scabbard smacked against his leg louder than it should have. He could feel it all changing. The jungle around them was coarse as rock salt rubbed into a wound; this place was smooth and fine, but it was cracking. The dead man's magic had polished down this deep valley. He had held the land in check, held his valley in a chosen image. Now he was gone, and this place was on its way out.

Boruin could feel Pile's eyes pricing the items on the porch, peering through the open door into the gloom. He didn't have to see the young man's hands to know they were already twitching, ready to take his share. They had all been relic hunters in their own way and time, but it was engrained in Pile, part of the young man's fabric.

Wraethe kept Pile in check with her imposing presence alone. She stayed wrapped in her shadowy cloak, her raven hair and pale skin hidden from the sun. Only her blue eyes appeared under that dark hood as she dreamed of the day and waited for night. She could wake now, if needed, and come forward into the world, but rarely did those eyes rise into the bright sunlight without riding on a wave of rage.

Toaaho showed no sign of eagerness, no pleasure at finding the boy. Perhaps the mask of tattoos laid across his face kept his emotion hidden as well. The broad strokes covering his sun-darkened skin seemed overdone as just decoration, but they kept the Mana'Olai hidden from more than just his emotions.

Boruin stepped forward, and the boy took his hand off the dead man's chest. He did not shy away, did not run and hide from the four strangers. The old man watched the boy's eyes dart across his left arm and it made him nervous. His tattoos were not visible to all—to very few, in fact—and for a child to see them meant something. The boy was not what he expected, much like this whole contract. Every time he swore off that damn Nefazo merchant, the next job was doubly strange.

The boy reached out to touch the black runes, and Boruin almost stepped back. He took the small hand and dropped to his knees before the boy.

"Do you know me?"

The boy shrugged.

"You know why I'm here, or who sent me?"

The boy nodded yes. He stood up and walked to the horse as if he had expected a ride. The stirrup hung shoulder high. Though the steed stamped about him, the boy did not flinch. He placed his small hand on the horse's flank and it quieted.

"Do you have anything to take, anything you need? You won't be coming back," Boruin said. The boy pointed south, where the jungle closed in to swallow the valley at its needle point. A brown cloud had stirred up—dust, probably. The wind had begun to descend out of the hills. Wind didn't suck the thick grass down into the ground, though.

"Time to leave," Toaaho said in his quiet, ever undisturbed voice.

Pile spat in anger and the wind blew it back on his jungle-stained pants. "What about all this? You promised us some treasure! I didn't hack through the Fae-cursed jungle to leave empty handed." He sidestepped his horse closer to the porch, and Wraethe's black shift rustled in response. His eyes darted toward the shrouded woman. "Come on, Boruin. I'll be quick. Anything will do. It'll just go to waste."

"I see wooden bowls and a dead man, Pile. Search for more if you want," Boruin said, placing the boy on the horse and vaulting up behind him.

"The time is almost past," Toaaho said, turning his horse to the north.

Boruin followed and shouted over his shoulder against the rising rush of the wind. "Half the valley is gone. Take what you can if you wish to join it!" Pile looked back and saw the valley behind him was now a whirlwind of destruction. The air sucked down out of the hills, pulling the soil toward the pocket storm. Pile's mouth snapped shut as a heavy gust made his horse stumble backward toward the swirling mass.

"Have it your way!" the young man shouted as he spurred his horse into a gallop after them.

Pile hurried his mount forward and soon led the galloping riders through the field. The grass lay flat before their horses' hooves. They all leaned close to their mounts, save for Wraethe, who seemed to flow as part of the gale.

The moisture drained from the dirt and great cracks split through the soil. Boruin glanced back and watched as the storm engulfed the small cottage. The old man's body rose into the air, or maybe it was the ground collapsing beneath. It hung still and then pulled apart as if made of dust.

Boruin drove his horse on harder as they crashed back into the thick jungle. The horses did not slow and their riders did not try to rein them in. They plowed along a shallow stream and stayed low, ducking under the trees. The wind continued to blow down off the ridgeline, whipping the tangled branches and vines across their skin.

"Up! Up!" yelled Boruin as he felt the first tremor. The horses staggered as the earth began to shift, and the riders turned up the slope. Toaaho led them, switching back and forth up the steep walls of the valley.

Pile swung free from his saddle, leaning off the side of his horse as a boulder burst from the underbrush. It passed behind his mount's head and flew down into the valley.

"I'm going to pass you if you don't flog that beast!" Pile yelled at Toaaho. He dug his spurs in and his horse tore forward. Wraethe followed after, and Boruin pushed his steed onward, cursing from the rear.

The horses halted as a great tremor shattered half the valley. The bedrock snapped with a loud groan and the shelf sagged beneath them. A cleft in the hillside, virgin gray of exposed stone, ran upward from their feet. Toaaho did not hesitate to gallop up this strange track. The others followed. Boruin could smell the sharp spice of sparks as iron horseshoes clattered against the tilting rock. The trail canted steeper as they rushed on. The valley was dropping away and soon there would be nothing but air under their feet.

As the gray stone began to crumble, Boruin felt a wet mist blow from beneath them. The top of the ridgeline was right there, and he stopped cursing the gods to offer one quick prayer. Perhaps it did them good; perhaps the crash of water and splinter of stone drowned it out. Regardless, Toaaho reached the top just as the stone began to slide. Boruin saw Wraethe's horse slip, so he rammed it forward with his own. It was enough to drive them both up off the tipping stone and onto the stable ground of the jungle above.

Pile leapt, wide-eyed, from his horse. "Yuin's whores, what a ride!"

Toaaho turned to watch as a great geyser of water shot out from below. The sliding walls of the valley had uncovered a deep river, and the wash now vaulted into space and tumbled into a bottomless cavern. The valley was gone, swallowed by the earth. The dead man could have received no deeper grave.

The horses pranced about, their blood still churning in excitement. Pile dropped to his knees, panting. He searched through all the hidden pockets of his red vest. On finding a charm, idol, or trinket he kissed each in turn as thanks and then tucked it away again. Toaaho soothed his horse, whispering quietly into its flickering ears.

Boruin wiped the sweat from his neck as he watched Wraethe's horse back into the shadows of the nearest tree.

In the full light of the sun Wraethe seemed weak, and to an extent she was. She sat still in her shadows, never seeming to move in the light. Still all of them feared her, even in day. Boruin would deny that, but in day and certainly at Diuntyne, he was as wary as any. Wraethe was like the trained war cat; fierce, loyal, and just wild enough to never take your eyes off of completely. Her nature was more cruel than kind. And at Syan, at full night... she could be pure nightmare.

The boy alone turned his back on the valley. He sniffed at the air, his tongue licking out as if he were catching a scent the way a northern boy would catch a snowflake. When he had smelled enough, he turned to catch Pile's attention.

"Father of Yuin!" Pile yelled when the boy placed his hand on the back of the man's neck. "Don't sneak up on me like that, boy! I'm a trained killer and I almost did you in!" The boy did not flinch at the barrage, but held out a strand of beads and tied rocks. "What's this for?" The child shook it, as if enticing a baby.

"Treasure," Toaaho answered, his face motionless.

"Kind of worthless."

"Only kind you'll get today," Toaaho replied, his eyes sparkling.

Boruin pulled himself to his feet, laughing. "He's right, Trained Killer. Better hold on to your share."

He left Pile to grumble at their teasing and stepped to the edge of the valley wall. The rock had shorn clean off, and a new granite cliff followed the waterfall down into the deep gloom. Boruin wondered if he could have seen the bottom even with the sun directly overhead. He looked up, checking its position, but it was lost above the thick jungle canopy.

Boruin turned his gaze to Wraethe. Only her eyes were visible behind the veil of shadow. They watched him back, dark as Diuntyne's setting. They would brighten nearer sunset when she would come forward. She was mostly asleep and that meant it was still afternoon. Wraethe would follow and she would flee, but she would remember little of the day except as fading dream. This was her slumbering hour, her weakest hour when he watched out for her. At night she returned the favor.

"It may not be wise to linger here longer," Toaaho said, stepping beside Boruin.

The older man nodded. "There is more magic to that man than the valley. I felt it, too."

"I would guess more protection," Toaaho replied. "Something ranging that let us pass before."

"Why did it drop? Why so much magic here? Do you think he was Fae?" Boruin asked. Toaaho shrugged and did not answer. "Well, Belok better have more of an idea than you. I knew I should have sent him to peddle his contract elsewhere when he offered so much gold."

There was nothing but brush in the deep jungle, but Pile found some way to lead them on. Smart-mouthed, selfish, shallow, and short, Pile was more annoyance than good companionship, but he had his uses. Boruin kept him around mostly because he could swallow a joke. They tried at least once a day to get him riled, but Pile could take it as well as he could dish it out.

Pile could also find a trail, even if there wasn't one, and he could see far. Despite the brush, despite the sun hidden behind the thick leaves, Pile could see what was coming.

So, when the dead man's guardian found them, Pile had long seen it on its way, and they were as ready as they could be for a twelve-foot construct of mud, rock, and wood—the life of the jungle—twisted into new form by strange magic, sentient and seeking them out.

Boruin was not worried about Wraethe. She would wake if she felt the need, but the boy was going to be a complication. They hunkered down, waiting while the monster sniffed them out. The boy stepped lightly around Boruin, looking up at the trees, waving at colorful birds. The old man took his hand and hid him behind a thick tree root. Soon the child was back on his feet, undisturbed, unafraid, and unaware of the rising tension.

Toaaho disappeared into the brush, his movements slow and perfect. Years in slavery had not dissolved his training, and he'd had plenty of time to develop his skill since Boruin had purchased his writ. Pile watched the creature come and tapped his fingers across his axe blade. It echoed out a light ring, a tinny reverberation that sounded eager to be put to work.

Boruin licked the fingertips of his right hand and considered a small prayer. Maybe his last had delivered them out of the valley, but he decided against another. No reason to make a habit of it.

His fingers grazed the tattoos on his left forearm. He tried to forget about the creature, forget about the boy prancing in circles around him. The old man flicked his fingers over the dark runes, spinning them like a street shark's gambling wheel. He felt the pull on his flesh as the line began to move.

The runes curled over his shoulder and down his bicep. They turned under his arm and over his wrist, climbing back up his forearm. The line crossed his shoulders and dropped down his back. They twisted around his chest and down across his hips, a long line of black characters that made no sense to him at all—at least very rarely. Boruin dragged his fingers across a choice few as they spun across his wrist, pulling them out of line and into his palm where they settled like fallen leaves. He had created spells before, finding the right arrangement, or right match, or right sub-category, something right—but it was rare. Working combinations came to him in odd moments of inspiration, and he was hoping for one now.

The guardian was bigger than he had first figured. The hard rock spikes shoved into its shoulder blades and forearms did not mark it as a peaceful creature. Its body was clay, with part of the forest shoved into the wet mass to give it more strength. Heavy limbs jutted out of its thighs and vines bound its chest into a dense and solid torso. Briars wound about its lower legs, placed there on purpose or mindlessly collected as it roamed about the forest.

Boruin had selected four runes when the boy sat down beside him. The child watched the symbols flip by and examined the ones on the skin of his hand. The old man was sliding the fifth into his palm when the boy stopped him, motioning that it should be returned and the search should continue. Boruin would have ignored anyone else, but that the boy could even see them was odd. He slid the rune back onto his wrist and moved the line along. The boy's pointed finger followed a sharp-cornered rune down from Boruin's shoulder, snaking around his arm, to his wrist. Boruin pulled it onto his palm, though he did not recognize it, and the boy clapped silently.

The old man stood behind Pile and tightened his left hand under a growing burn. He felt the runes heating up in his hand; he felt their combination mixing. He wasn't sure how effective it would be, but he knew it would create something. There was a feeling about a rune combination, a power that radiated when they matched. At times they matched too well and Boruin let them run back up his arm for fear of their strength. This time they felt just right. As the creature stepped out of the brush and turned to look at him, Boruin flung the runes out of his hand.

The magic sliced through the air and hit the clay monster with a wet smack. The flesh of its body rippled back as the spell hit, forming a crater on its upper thigh. Blood red flowers erupted from the hole. They sprouted out of the clay and ran across the beast's dark, muddy skin. The monster froze, watching the old man with his arm still outstretched. The matched gaze held until the flowers opened and all burst at once, gold pollen showering out from the wide blooms. They shone like stars where they crossed the thin shafts of sunlight piercing the canopy.

"The rutting Mother!" Boruin cursed. The boy clapped out loud and squealed in glee. Pile laughed through the horrified look on his face. Toaaho dropped out of the trees and drove his dagger into the creature's back.

The monster roared and twisted, flinging the Mana'Olai off its hump. It tore at the flowers, dragging them out by their roots. It did not clear them all before dashing forward at Boruin. Pile met it halfway, swinging his axe up into its kneecap. The blade hit with a dull thud, and Pile dragged it out covered in mud. The creature came on, undeterred by the blow.

Boruin pulled his sword from the scabbard on his back. "Go!" he shouted at the boy. The child dashed off behind a tree, peeking around the other side as if in play. The guardian swung, the rock barbs severing the branches and scoring tree bark as its heavy fists came down.

Dancing aside, Boruin flicked the tip of his sword up under the beast's arm and into its armpit, through where its vital organs should have been. The blade came back out of the monster's body with nothing but clay streaking the well-oiled metal.

Toaaho drove his blade into its back again, trying to sever the beast's spine, if it had one. The dagger opened a great gash, but no blood welled out.

The three fought fast, circling, turning the beast like a bull on festival day. They fought and tired and the creature raged on.

Pile stumbled back, trying to catch his breath. "Köpeka's bloody sons, Boruin! You got more than flowers for us?"

"Now would be the time," Toaaho agreed, dropping below a thundering punch that felled the tree behind him.

Boruin glanced back down at his runes. The growing gloom left little to see. The thing was big but not slow. They were tiring, and in the dark there would be little chance of blindly outrunning it.

The light was still low and tinged orange with sunset, but Boruin knew that day was gone and Diuntyne was upon them as a flash of black swept out of the jungle.

With shadows trailing behind her, Wraethe vaulted up the creature's body, climbing the protruding rocks and shattered branches. Thick clay fingers dropped severed to the jungle floor as the creature's hand tried to close about her. She rose fast and graceful up its body to perch on the golem's crown, like a crow on a gargoyle. The creature groaned as Boruin saw her white hand wipe the creased clay smooth across its brow.

The monster's knees shook and buckled. Pile dove out of the way as the mountain of clay came down. Wraethe stepped free from the softening creature. Her body shivered and her hands clenched. She leaned her head back, lungs sucking in the moist air as if she were drinking in the night to wash down the taste of battle. Boruin and the others held still until her breathing steadied. They knew better than to rush her out of a fury.

Fighting always gave rise to her blood, and it was unwise to approach her even after the heat of it had passed.

In the darkness her face glowed like the great moon, her skin pale. She drew back her black hood, swinging the cloak over her shoulders, and seemed to step fully out of shadow. Wraethe tugged a red bloom from the dead clay and rubbed the mud from her hands with the petals.

Her eyes flashed like sisters of the moons and she turned to Boruin. "Your work?"

"Mine and the boy's," he said.

"The boy helped?" she asked. "When almost no one can see them, the boy helped?" Wraethe frowned. "I've warned you about fooling with what you don't understand."

"Yes. You have."

"But we did find him, then," she said, turning to the child. "I dreamt we had." The boy stepped out from behind his tree and came forward. He bent to grab a fallen red petal and took her hand in his. The red leaf wiped the last smear of mud off her wrist, leaving her skin as pale cream.

Wraethe smiled and smoothed back his wild hair. "You are a good boy, aren't you?" The boy nodded. "Learn no lessons from these three and we will get along brilliantly," she continued. The boy widened his grin until it outshone her pale shimmer.

"How did you beat it?" Pile ventured to ask.

Toaaho answered for her. "The sigil. She saw the sign on its head that bound the material animate."

Wraethe nodded. "Some details stand out in my day dreams better than others. The sigil on the beam of the porch shone like a dying star."

Pile shook his head in exasperation at Toaaho. "Why didn't you do that if you saw it?"

"Didn't see what it was," Toaaho said calmly.

"What's done is done," said Boruin. "Now we know what to watch for. If there are others, hopefully they will be the same."

"Are they ever?" Wraethe asked.

"Never," he replied.

UNDER THE SHADE
OF A TRAVELING TREE

Boruin tossed the bones of his dinner into the fire and looked in disbelief at his companion. "An Aiemer flow?"

"That's right," answered Wraethe.

"You're saying that the man, after he was dead, somehow drew upon a fable to destroy his valley?" Boruin said.

"No. That is impossible," said Wraethe.

Boruin raised his hands in exasperation. "Exactly!" He opened his mouth to continue, then stopped, confused. "Then what are you saying?"

Pile pulled a stick from the fire and held it above their cooking stone. "She's saying the valley was torn apart by the Aiemer after the old fellow died." He dashed the ember against the rocks and let the rising sparks of the dead coal serve as example.

"When you know more about any subject than I do, I'll ask your opinion," Boruin said, giving Pile a sidelong sneer.

Pile saw an opening, and his teeth shone in the firelight. "Like who your mother is?"

"Or where you were born?" Wraethe added. Her rare smile matched Pile's in its eagerness.

"Like why every time we drink, you slip into some northern sailor's accent?" asked Pile.

"And why, for as long as you and I have traveled together, neither of us remember where we started or anything before," said Wraethe, her right eyebrow cocked.

Boruin knew that look. He didn't remember any more of his past than she of hers, and now was not the time to get back into that saga. They had the best of him, and it was either time to storm off or to give in. Boruin leaned back against the high tree root and sighed.

"Fine, so what do you know about the Aiemer?" he asked.

Pile played stubborn, his lips twitching to turn up into one of his wide, lop-sided grins. "Nothing."

"Pile, what do you want to enlighten us about?" Wraethe asked.

Pile held back his smile at her firm tone. "You know, your good moods are too short lived," he replied, waving off her sour look. "I know a few things from back when I worked the old mah'saiid ruins with Graemer. He could translate the old glyphs and he told me some of what he'd read," said Pile.

"Like what?" Boruin asked.

Pile poked around in the fire, uncomfortable as Boruin and Wraethe turned their full attention to him. "Here's how I understand it. The Aiemer comes from the second realm of Baeg Tobar. Though the two realms of this world are split, the Dying and the Dreaming, the Aiemer can move freely between both. In the Dreaming Lands, the Aiemer saturates the land like it's a sponge. It is part of everything and everything exists because of it. Maybe some of that is bedtime tale, maybe not."

"All things in the Dreaming Lands originate in the Aiemer?" asked Boruin.

Pile leaned forward as if giving his mind a push before it stalled out. "No, and don't stop me; I'll lose my train of thought. In our mortal realm—the Duine Lands, as the mah'saiid called them—the Aiemer is untouchable; unseen, unsmelled, untasted, unheard. That's really the main thing. I mean, it still influences things, but mostly it is very subtle, and we don't see it. Here, Aiemer moves of its own accord, like tides in an unseen sea. Where it does slow and pool, it saturates the ground and changes it. Maybe in the image of the Dreaming Lands. I don't know."

"That's the children's story part," said Boruin.

"Fingle and the Floating Mountain of Emeralds," offered Wraethe.

"Imber's Ocean of Glass," added Boruin.

Pile waved his finger in agreement, but kept his attention in the fire as if the flames were spelling out his tale. "There is little that affects the Aiemer, and even less that can harness it. Graemer thought though that the Aiemer was where all magic rises from. The sorcerers, the priests, the bards—they all draw from the same source. It seemed to him that the Aiemer must touch everything, and those that make magic use the Aiemer that has touched and settled in their bodies as fuel. We Duine, then, are limited in power, as we can only draw from the Aiemer inside us. It's not like the fables that tell of the Fae's direct control of the Aiemer turning mountains into emeralds." His glazed eyes rose from the fire, and the return of his smile told them he'd reached the end of his speech.

"But again, the guy in the valley was dead. There is no controlling anything after you've gone under," said Boruin.

"Right!" Pile agreed. "The Aiemer didn't destroy the valley after his death. The Aiemer *was* the valley. He held it in place, controlling it until he was gone. That's the problem, and that's big." There was no trace of humor left on his face.

"Give me your idea of big," Boruin said.

"That kind of power could have brought down the whole nation of Nefazo, turned them all into goats and their shit into gold. But instead it was providing a safe place for a mute, near-mindless kid," said Pile, digging around in the coals of the fire. He held up the glowing brand and pointed it at Boruin. "What is with this kid?"

Boruin stood up from the dirt and looked around. "Where is he?"

Wraethe pointed off into the darkness to some hidden spot in the murky gloom. "Keeping watch with Toaaho."

"Well, he can keep him. That boy has been nothing but trouble. I'm going to sleep," Boruin said.

"He does make a nice bouquet of flowers," Pile offered, regaining his humor. Boruin ignored this and lay down with his back to the fire. They would begin moving again in six hours, and he needed to sleep. He was sure it wouldn't happen, but he could lie still and think. Pile was right about the boy; there was more to him than there should be.

Boruin wondered why Belok had offered them this job. The man had a habit of profiting well on a contract, and Boruin wondered who was behind this one. He turned the events of the day over in his head. Pile was right about the Aiemer and the valley—he had to be. Boruin knew of no magical crafts that would bring down that valley. Certainly no mortal ones.

The boy was special.

Belok had passed the job off as a retrieval and escort, but it was more than that. Though his mind kept churning, Boruin slipped away into the darker field of sleep. He slept lightly, still bothered by Pile's reminder that the details of his own life were more of a mystery than any of this mess.

Every night as Diuntyne arrived, silver Diun breached the horizon like a titanic ship entering the open sea of dark sky. The stars were smothered under the polished light of the moon's swirling gas surface. It lost little of its size as it arced above the land. To hold one's fist up against it was to see it well around like liquid spilling over the brim.

In the jungle west of Nefazo, Diun seemed to illuminate Wraethe no matter what shadow she led the horses through. After their dinner and mid-night sleep the woman glowed even in the moon's absence, when Diun dropped behind the horizon and Syan, the moonless, star-filled cycle of the day was upon them. Boruin watched her skin dimly shimmer in this jungle darkness where the starlight refused to enter. It was almost as if she gathered the cool light of the moon about her as armor against the blackest night. Even her coal-black hair shone, dark blue flashes reflecting out of the loose coils.

Pile ambled before Boruin and Toaaho followed behind, but in the darkness, he only made them out by the sound of their horses' hooves on the trail. They all followed the woman, because at night her vision was as bright as her skin.

"It's Diun, I'd wager," Pile had once ventured. "She shares its eye as her own. If the great orb beholds it, I'd lay coin that it's known to Wraethe. It's unnatural."

Boruin did not dispute it. Wraethe's uncanny nocturnal senses had often kept their hands out of the irons and their feet off the branding plates. It wasn't natural. The lij had spread wide across this massive continent and there were all sorts of people different from another, but Wraethe compared to none Boruin had met. The alternative—that she could be from the Dreaming Lands—was not something that he liked to think of.

Boruin heard the boy sigh and felt him lean back against his chest. As mixed as his feelings were toward the boy, Boruin held him tighter. The kid slept, his hands wrapped in the mane of Boruin's horse, his heels bouncing against Boruin's thighs as they rode. They continued through the night, stopping only once as Pile dozed and slipped from his horse. He woke, cursing the fall, and climbed back into the saddle to sleep until dawn.

Wraethe stepped down from her horse at the first sign of twilight. A faint blue line, heavy like a welling tear, rose from the edge of the horizon. It would be another few hours before the sun would break that same edge, its light washing out to burn off the thick mists. Its bright wink would soon tease the great flowers, dangling as ornate tapestries from the tall trees, into opening again and paying homage to its brilliance.

Pile stretched, hands on his hips and leaning as far back as he could without tipping over. "Time for a rest?"

"Could use one, huh?" Boruin asked. "Snoring take a lot out of you?" Pile raised his thumb and clucked through the side of his mouth in his sarcastic "you got it boss" fashion. Boruin let him be and stretched his own tired limbs.

Toaaho tethered their horses and set to breaking out his equipment. First, he'd rub oil into his leather scabbards and harnesses, then he'd check his knives for rust and sharpen them. Black tiger stripes of whetstone grit stained his leather pants where he constantly wiped the blades clean. It was a morning duty that the Mana'Olai attended to better than a Yuinite priest to his prayers. He didn't even budge as the boy, weaving half-asleep toward him, curled up behind him to share the heat of his broad back.

Pile had his own routine when they ended a ride. He'd check that damn red vest for tears, pockets and all, and sew it back into shape. Only Yuin knew who he was trying to stay presentable for. All Boruin knew was that faded, blood red fabric wasn't the best camouflage in the jungle. Just as routine as his sewing, Pile's head would soon be nodding, and they'd find him asleep between stitches with a shirt or pants in hand. He'd finish that jacket first, though; he was enamored with the damn thing.

"We've made good time," Boruin said as he felt Wraethe walk up behind him. She joined him in peering back along their route. They had followed a ridgeline up to this small peak, perched like a watchtower over the next valley. There they would wait for dawn.

"The other guardians?" he asked.

She pulled her cloak around her shoulders as if she could already feel the touch of the sun. "I saw nothing of them, though a large cat tracked us for an hour."

"That would have been nice to know," Boruin responded.

"Toaaho handled it when it got too close," Wraethe replied. Boruin grunted his acceptance. It didn't surprise him that he had heard nothing.

The sky brightened, and the wind teased the fog pooled in the valley below. It swirled and rose as if the ridge were a sleeping giant, slowly pulling its white comforter over its shoulders.

A great tree in the center of their small hill had grown wide, its branches hanging over the crown like a wool cap stretched too big. Wraethe followed Boruin to its massive trunk and they sat facing the brightening horizon. They discussed the coming day, where they were, and where to go. It was a pre-morning ritual as much as the other's.

The changing of the guard came at dawn as Wraethe retreated into sleep, her sharp senses blinded by the hot light. They watched in silence until the first edge of the sun broke over the jungle.

"Keep an eye on that boy, Boruin."

"I will."

"He's different, and I like him," she added, her voice lighter, sounding tired.

"I know you do. You've always had a soft spot for the odd ones," Boruin replied, but Wraethe was already asleep. He watched as her hands pulled the black hood over her head. Her blue eyes receded into the darkness from where they would gaze outward without seeing.

"HUMBRUEWUM," a rumbling sound like grinding rock shook the hilltop. Boruin rolled out from under the tree, standing on guard and searching for the source of the sound. No other creature stood on the hill; Boruin and his companions were joined atop it only by the bright sun. He dashed around the other side of the tree as the sound rumbled out again into the morning air.

Pile circled the tree, peering down into the morning mists curled about the base of the hill. "Another guardian! Sounds bigger, too." His axe swung back and forth beside him. It was a nervous twitch Boruin had seen before. He wondered how long it would be before Pile swung the weapon a little too close to his thigh and shaved off a strip of meat.

Toaaho gazed out from under the tree's wide branches. The old oak had long lorded over the hilltop, smothering the rest of the undergrowth with shade and giving a far view on all sides. "No guardian. There's nothing moving at all."

"Maybe it's not a guardian, but moving or not, something is here," Boruin replied. He turned back to the tree and ran his hand along its bark. The rumbling had quieted to a deep chanting. It moved in a strange, melodic murmuring, reminding him of a contented house cat and its purring sigh. Boruin could barely hear it, but the vibration tickled his fingertips through the bark.

"It's below us," he said, dropping to his knees to press his hand to the ground. The whole hill reverberated with the chanting. It rumbled through the rock and up into the leaves above. The hill began to heave; little tremors bounced them on their feet as if the ground was trying to break free. Boruin turned to see the boy standing on its tiptoes, his ear pressed against a knothole in the tree.

The child's face was crunched up tight, his lips pursed as if deciding whether he liked a particular spiced meat or not. He decided he did not and stepped back with his arms crossed, his face a mix of contempt and impatience.

Like he's the adult, and whatever this may be is being childish, Boruin thought.

Toaaho stepped up beside the child and placed his ear over the hole. He motioned to Boruin, but Pile rushed up to put his ear there first. Boruin pulled him back and listened.

From deep somewhere in the roots the voice rose as a mix of echoes bouncing around inside the hollow trunk. "Boombruem wholiday. Fineriy, fine certainly fair morning to hill."

"Fae, if I've ever known 'em," Pile said.

"Oh, that's your expert opinion?" Boruin replied. "Then it must be."

"It is," Toaaho added.

Boruin grabbed the boy up around the waist. "I know, damn it. Let's get out of here." They turned, but there was no leaving. Their horses were gone, their small campfire distant and the ridge slipping out from under them. Boruin's head snapped around to find Wraethe, but she was still leaned up against the trunk, rolling lightly with the motion of the hill. The boy wriggled out of his grasp. Never good with ships, Boruin sat quickly, cursing his wavering feet and his turning stomach. Though he knew this was no boat, his body had yet to arrive at the same conclusion.

"Yuin, hear my prayers," Pile said, his hand tracing the god's sigil in the air as his mother had taught him long ago. Toaaho moved back to the knothole, his ear listening while his eyes watched the moving landscape. Boruin just sat, nauseous, watching the land slide by as the hill moved off the ridge and into the valley. The boy had taken to the front of the tree to watch the jungle break before them.

Pile sat by the boy to watch and shouted back in amazement. "This is not normal, Boruin! Not normal at all!"

"Great Mother, damn the Fae," Boruin whispered as the hill turned to ride up a shallow crest and roll down into a neighboring valley. He watched the dense jungle part before them. It slid around their hill and then came back together as smooth as if there had been no great mound of rock plowing through. The hill and the tree meandered about and then headed south, back over the ground they had spent all night covering. Boruin took a deep breath to calm his rolling stomach and climbed next to Toaaho.

"Listen," the Mana'Olai said. Boruin pressed his ear next to the hole and heard the voice again. It thrummed and piped and hummed and gurgled, a mix of noises that betrayed only childish play.

"It's definitely Fae. Doesn't sound too civilized, and the wild ones are usually the most troublesome," said Boruin. "Any ideas?"

Toaaho shook his head. Wraethe was still leaning against the tree trunk, though now on the opposite side of the sun. She would be no help.

Well, when in doubt for the right idea, try what's probably wrong, Boruin thought to himself. He placed his mouth over the knothole and hollered as loud as he could. "BY THE MOTHER, HILLS AREN'T SUPPOSED TO MOVE!"

"No?" bubbled up the answer through ground. "I'm moving quite nicely."

Boruin grabbed tight to the knothole as the hill rolled down a steep trench and back up the other side. "You're not a hill, though."

The burbling echoes bounced up from the deep roots. "I look like a hill."

"And I look like a lij," Boruin retorted.

"You're not a lij?" the voice asked. "You look like a lij."

Boruin's chest rose as he summoned as much commanding impatience as he could. "I'm not a lij! I'm your uncle, and I demand to know what you are doing out here milling about with this hill!"

"Do Fae have uncles?" Pile whispered.

"Careful," Toaaho cautioned.

The hill ground to a halt in the middle of a wide stream. Fish flopped downriver as the water began to back up on the other side of the mound. The boy pointed upward, and they all turned to stare as the branches above wove into a new shape. After a few moments a face began to appear out of the layers of leaves and limbs. Boruin leaned to one side and the face disappeared; he stood straight again and the face reappeared. It was like teasing your eye into seeing shapes in the clouds, except this shape moved as the voice boiled up through the ground around them.

"Which uncle are you: of the dew or the mid-month morning mist? For no uncle of mine ever dressed so lij-like," the voice said, now deep, stern, and doubtful.

"Of the tides of Diun's dawn, and I have my reasons for being shaped as such. It is not for you to question," Boruin answered, trying to stare down the illusion of a face above him.

The eyes, blue from the sky behind them, squinted back in consideration. "Curiosity is our vice of choice," the hill said.

"And its consequences our bane," Boruin responded in turn, the words snapping into place. The phrase was new to his lips, and Boruin could not remember where it came from. It rose from that place still lost in his mind, but he pushed wondering away for after this bluff.

"Humbreuwum... fine, Uncle Lij, what do you wish of me on my day of play?"

"Just to give you a gift, is all. You have caused all this... bruhuum-brum for nothing," Boruin chided.

Pile leaned close and whispered to Toaaho. "What is he talking about?" The Mana'Olai shrugged. The tree began to shiver in anticipation, the leaves flipping about as if a storm gust had blown down upon them. Burbling rumbles shook the ground around their feet. Boruin grabbed Pile's hand and slipped the silver charm bracelet off the young man's arm before he could even look down to see it disappearing.

Boruin broke off one of the silver discs, caught a sunbeam on its polished surface, and let the light flash up toward the makeshift face. The leaves forming the lips pulled back in an eager grin as the reflection danced about.

"Oh, ew, ew, a present not past, but all not part," the hill said childishly. Boruin agreed and slipped both the disc and the rest of the bracelet down into the knothole.

Pile jumped to the trunk, his arm down the hole to the shoulder. "Those are my charms!"

"Snap it shut," Boruin ordered.

"But I've been collecting them for years!" he replied, turning to Toaaho. There was no sympathy behind the mask of tattoos.

"You find the gift to your liking?" Boruin asked the Fae in the hill.

"Flitty pretty little meetel metal," the voice burbled. "I do, I do. For two or three I'll beg and plea," the hill answered.

"A gift's a gift and a favor owed is a favor owed," Boruin said.

"Aye, and a trick is a trick," the hill said. Boruin crossed his arms and sucked up his chest as if to holler. "But the rights have been met, and I've accepted your bauble and grant your favor," it continued.

"It's not so bad," Boruin said. "Continue your day of play, but let us ride along. I hear there is great hilling to be done in the northwestern jungles. If you know the Mountain of Three Hands, take us there," he ordered.

The hill roared in laughter as if it had gotten the best of its uncle. "I do and will, and yes, it's no great favor you've asked." The branches rustled and the face disappeared as the hill turned back north. The river rushed back into its stream, covering the flapping fish none too late. The hill moved up a steep ridgeline, and Boruin's stomach lurched again.

"How did you know it would buy into all that nonsense?" Pile asked softly.

Boruin sat and tucked his legs under an exposed root as the hill tipped down the other side of the small mountain. "You know a little about the Aiemer, and I know a little about the Fae. Now tie me down."

"You owe me for my charms," Pile said.

"You cheated a half-drunk whore out of those at Tragle's Tavern. I watched it happen," Boruin said, and Pile cursed under his breath.

As the hill pushed up steeper hills, Toaaho lashed down Wraethe as well. "Do you think it will really take us into Nefazo?" Toaaho asked.

"That'll be a relief. I forgot how much I hate this jungle," Pile said.

Boruin spat and held his stomach. "Be happy while you're here. We've got some answers to beat out of Belok, and that, my friends, will take a con from Apros L'eure himself."

"Or just Wraethe's godawful stare," said Pile.